LOVE STORIES
ARE TOO VIOLENT FOR ME

WILL VIHARO

LOVE STORIES ARE TOO VIOLENT FOR ME

The Definitive Edition of the First Vic Valentine Novel

GUTTER BOOKS

www.gutterbooks.com

Love Stories Are Too Violent For Me: The Definitive
Edition

Copyright © 1993/2013 by Will Viharo

Cover art by Matt Brown. Christian Slater image used
with permission.

Cover design by Matthew Louis/Outland Grafix

The original text has been slightly revised and modified
from its initial publication by the author for this definitive
edition.

ISBN: 978-1-939751-10-2

Visit www.gutterbooks.com for other titles and
submission guidelines.

Printed in the USA

Acknowledgements

The author would like to thank the following for their support:

My editor, Joe Clifford, for boldly reaching out to me, taking the intuitive chance, and expertly fine tuning the text; I am humbled and honored.

Matt Brown for this definitive edition's fantastic cover artwork; I am forever grateful and stunned.

Christian Slater for keeping the faith and showing me so much respect.

And last but not least, my beautiful, talented wife, Monica Cortes Viharo, and our two wonderful cats. Without their love, I'd be nothing.

Onward Christian Slater

Introduction

I FIRST WROTE THIS novel on an old school portable typewriter, *rat-a-tat-tat* style, in the tiny kitchen of my lonesome little Berkeley studio back in the spring of 1993. I was thirty years old. At that point it was my eighth full-length book—and I was still unpublished, at least as a novelist. However, this was during my two-year courtship by famous New York editor Judith Regan, already a rising celebrity in her own right. An author I'd interviewed, Wally Lamb (*She's Come Undone*), had sent her one of my manuscripts, *Chumpy Walnut*, my very first effort, completed at age nineteen (I've been on my own and writing steadily since age sixteen, raised mostly in South Jersey by a stepmother with whom I did not get along). *Chumpy* is a Runyonesque fable about a guy only a foot tall, featuring my own crude, Thurber-ish illustrations, which I finally self-published in 2010. I still remember the night I came home from my job as a delivery driver for the ACCMA Blood Bank and heard Regan's astonishing message on my answering machine. She was taken with my literary "voice" and "promised" to publish "something" by me. This was like Elvis getting the call from Col. Tom Parker. After over a decade of dejection, I was more than ready for my ship to finally come in.

Creatively motivated by this improbable prospect, I almost immediately began work on a modern film noir-ish piece of fiction inspired by some of my pathetic experiences at my workplace, the hospital blood-delivery gig being the latest in an epic series of odd jobs I took to support myself while following that seemingly impossible literary dream. The title, *Love Stories Are Too Violent for Me*, popped up accidentally (or at least incidentally) during a phone conversation with my father, now-retired actor/filmmaker/artist Robert Viharo, wherein I was lamenting my latest, largely self-imposed amorous atrocity. Like my protagonist, Vic Valentine, I was constantly pursuing unattainable women. Then again, given my critical lack of self-esteem, vehicular mobility, formal education, social skills, and disposable income for dating, they *all* seemed pretty much unattainable at the time. (I actually *did* "The Date That Never Was," with similar results—you'll see.) I think Pop was suggesting I watch a certain film of a romantic nature he enjoyed, and I automatically retorted, "I don't think so. Love stories are too violent for me." And he laughed and said, "*That's* the title of your next novel!"

Suffice to say, Judith Regan did *not* come through for me, despite her initial enthusiasm. Cutting to the chase, she unceremoniously dumped me by farming out my stuff to an assistant, who obviously had no idea who the hell I was, after requesting I write a memoir (!), which I completed and submitted, an epistolary autobiography called Graffiti in the Rubber Room: Writing for My Sanity, composed of imaginary letters to people in my life, including my own fictional characters, like Chumpy Walnut, along with various relatives and love interests. Several were addressed to my late mother, a virtual stranger to me named Charlotte Glenn, formerly Miss Houston 1960 and an aspiring actress until she went to New York City with my father, circa 1962, and got knocked up with yours truly, biologically coinciding with the onset of her schizophrenia, which eventually proved fatal, after enduring the most tragic life I've ever witnessed, at least second hand. She is the inspiration for Vic's own mother, though the similarities are vague outside of the mental illness. As always, this book was cheapjack self-therapy. But with Judith Regan egging me on, I was determined to appeal directly to the mainstream tastes of the general public by concocting an easily promoted and digested *product*. I was always a fan of crime fiction, and had just completed a straight-up pulp piece called *Down a Dark Alley* that was also sitting idly on Regan's desk, so I decided to meld genres and create something both uniquely personal but also commercially viable. Apparently, it wasn't enough. As widely reported in the mass media, Regan left behind Simon & Schuster (*and* me) to start her own imprint at Harper Collins, then went on to her own glory, publishing the likes of Howard Stern and hosting her own TV show, until she decided to publish O.J. Simpson's "confession," which ended her career as a publisher. (I'm still going as a writer.)

By the time of this heartbreaking, soul-shattering, disillusioning disappointment, I had already written four successive sequels to *Love Stories—Fate Is My Pimp*; *Romance Takes a Rain Check*; *I Lost My Heart in Hollywood*; and *Diary of a Dick*, in addition to the "commissioned" memoir, working late into the night after returning from my depressing blood bank shifts, determined to take full advantage of this once-in-a-lifetime opportunity. But just as it was pulling into port, my ship suddenly backed up and left without me, leaving me stranded on the dock, staring sadly at the barren horizon. Until *now*, that is.

Around 1994, a pair of old friends, who will go unnamed here for personal reasons, approached me with an offer to publish *Love Stories* under their brand new venture, Wild Card Press. They procured fantastic cover art by professional graphic designer Tim Racer, and promised to eventually publish the entire series. This would be their first book. As it turned out, it was also their last.

Soon after the book was published in December 1995, these enterprising entrepreneurs decided to quickly move on to what would become their signature achievement: the Parkway Speakeasy Theater, an extremely popular Oakland institution and Bay Area-wide destination due to its unique format as a community-oriented movie theater offering eclectic programming, funky sofas and comfy seating, a wide-ranging menu including beer and wine, and many other attractions that secured its place as an iconic local legend. Unfortunately, due to various factors, both internal and external, Speakeasy Theaters (including the Parkway's new sister theater in El Cerrito) abruptly folded in 2009, taking Wild Card Press and my alternate career down with it.

Love Stories was now officially out of print, though to be honest, the couple pretty much abandoned their small press after the Parkway took off, never publishing the sequels or any other book for that matter, and I was left to promote the book myself—but with a public platform they provided.

During a particularly tough time in my life, circa 1997, following the breakup of my first so-called marriage, the Parkway owners offered me employment at the theater, first as a ticket taker and editor of their monthly newsletter, then eventually as full-time programmer/publicist. It was the Speakeasy CEO's suggestion that I host and produce my own weekly midnight movie show, with the idea that if I became a locally known "personality," it would generate interest in our book. I caught that ball, ran it down the field, and scored, inventing a lounge lizard doppelgänger I dubbed "Will the Thrill" (my nickname back at the blood bank), initially calling the gig "The Midnight Lounge." Though it never translated to literary success, my tenure as host/programmer/producer of the long-running cult movie cabaret Thrillville, its eventual moniker, ironically turned out to be my ticket to localized fame, if not fortune. It ran in various forms and time slots for the duration of the Parkway Speakeasy Theater's operation (1997-2009), as well as subsequent independently booked road shows around the Bay and beyond before—and after—it closed.

I met my beautiful wife and best friend, actress/educator Monica Cortes, at my midnight screening of *Jailhouse Rock* on May 31, 1997. She showed me her Elvis/Navajo tattoo on her upper right hip. *Wow*. Since I was now divorced from my first "lovely assistant," I was selecting comely female audience members to spin the big wheel on stage and help me give out prizes, auditioning new lovely assistants—as well as potential wives. I didn't have the guts to ask Monica out that night, but I happened to run into her again at an Elvis birthday party I was hosting at the Ivy Room in Albany, CA, on January 8, 1998. The rest is history. Monica—AKA "The Tiki Goddess"—got *both* gigs, and we were married on May 31, 2001, at Frank Sinatra's old joint, the Cal-Neva Lodge in North Lake Tahoe, with our friend Robert Ensler presiding over the ceremony as "Dean Martin," and a mariachi band performing Sinatra and Elvis tunes. My lifelong loneliness—the major impetus for this and most of my novels—had come to an end. But there are always other forms of artistic inspiration—healthier ones, too.

Something else magical and momentous with lingering impact and life-altering ramifications also happened in 2001, months before our marriage: Wild Card Press received a letter from representatives of renowned film actor Christian Slater, who had decided to option the book for a film! I received a check from his lawyer annually for the next eleven years, even after Wild Card Press went out of business, until 2012, when Christian contacted me directly, offering to bring me out to his adopted hometown of Miami to work on his adaptation, which was extremely faithful to the source material.

Christian finally told me how he had come upon the book, seemingly against all probable odds: he had randomly picked it up while browsing the shelves at Dutton's Books in Brentwood, Los Angeles, which was managed by my father's wife, who had made a point of stocking a few copies of *Love Stories*. Christian explained how he instantly related to the tormented voice of the main character and his unfortunate yet oddly heroic experiences, which still stuns me. Dig: shortly after finishing *Love Stories* in 1993, I saw the late Tony Scott's cult classic *True Romance*, which turned out to be one of Christian's signature roles, and I thought it had been made *just for me*. The references all resonated with my own sensibilities and tastes, and Christian's character, Clarence Worley, is like an idealized version of me (as well as fellow former video store clerk/female foot fetishist, screenwriter Quentin Tarantino). Ironically, that's exactly how Christian responded to my obscure, similarly titled novel, he told me. Needless to say, we hit it off right away after finally meeting in person ("a true bromance," as my wife called it). Christian wanted to relocate the action from the Bay Area and Los Angeles to South Florida, so he graciously flew me out, first class, and put me up in a Miami Beach luxury hotel, as we went about location scouting. He took me deep sea fishing off the coast of Miami, where we smoked Cuban cigars and caught (then threw back) a rare Cuban night shark, and later we rode the actual African Queen down an estuary in Key Largo. (How Bogey can you get?) When I returned home, burning with vindication, I immediately overwrote his script, transferring the settings with ease, since Miami's Art Deco and midcentury modern architecture suited Vic's retro world even more accurately than the Victorian environs of San Francisco. It was like a spiritual and virtual rebirth for the book—and me, as a professional author.

Our updated script and storyboards (by this edition's amazingly talented cover artist, Matt Brown) are currently in circulation as of this writing. Forget Judith Regan. This was, and is, the million-to-one shot I had been waiting for all my life. My ship is back on the horizon and steaming towards port.

Now to briefly back track and then come full circle:

I kept my Thrillville gig going for a while in a downsized version called "Forbidden Thrills," a monthly movie night at Forbidden Island Tiki Lounge in Alameda, CA, where I worked as a bouncer for several years after the Parkway closed, and where I met Scott Fulks, who later commissioned me to write our sci-fi epic *It Came From Hangar 18* after reading several of my self-published pulp novels (including the four Vic Valentine sequels, as well as *Chumpy Walnut, Down a Dark Alley, Lavender Blonde,* and my "bizarro" novella, *Freaks That Carry Your Luggage Up to the Room*). Moreover, Forbidden Island now features the official "Vic Valentine" cocktail, created by ace bartender Susan Eggett—and thanks to proprietor Michael Thanos for putting it on the menu! Currently I program (but do not host) a franchised film series dubbed "Thrillville Theater" at The New Parkway in Uptown Oakland, miraculously reopened by a whole new crew. As far as I'm concerned, "Thrillville" nowadays is the online pimp headquarters for my own pulp fiction, not just other peoples' B movies.

When I suddenly lost my career as a film programmer, I returned to my first true love, writing, completing and self-publishing a very dark, surrealistic pulp novel I'd started then abandoned once the Parkway opened, called *A Mermaid Drowns in the Midnight Lounge,* now informed by my experiences during my twelve-year hiatus from fiction. Four years later, up-and-coming pulp author and established Gutter Books editor Joe Clifford contacted me via Facebook. We'd already been in steady communication since accidentally discovering we shared the same literary idols (Holden Caulfield, Philip Marlowe, and Batman), and he had been following progress on the *Love Stories* movie. As soon as I posted a status report publicly announcing I was planning to reprint *Love Stories* myself, Joe immediately pounced on the opportunity, offering me a contract without even having read the out-of-print book, since used copies were going for hundreds of dollars on Amazon. But he *had* read and immensely enjoyed

Mermaid, and Christian's film option had validated its value as a literary property, so it was a somewhat informed decision, but still an educated dice roll. And now, here we are.

This book is a time capsule of a particularly colorful period in modern hipster history, within which several earlier eras resonate and echo due to Vic's (and "Will the Thrill's") nostalgic obsessions. As a freelance journalist on these particular subjects, my knowledge of classic cult cinema, lounge music, and particularly the local burlesque/surf/swing scenes increased rapidly during my tenure as "Will the Thrill." Hence, I've made some rather stylistically significant if substance-wise superficial adjustments to the text, mostly cosmetic, but all strategic in terms of overall mood, which for me is an essential ingredient to any piece of literature, art, film, or music. The characters and storyline remain almost entirely intact, but I've inserted a little extra exposition here and there, fleshed out some characterization and a number of retroactively informed pop cultural references, which artfully authenticate the context.

Also, benefitted by two decades worth of maturity, while preparing and retyping the text for republication (since I didn't have access to the original Wild Card files), I was much more cognizant of Vic's (relatively innocuous) sexism and misguided misogyny than I had been that first time. His bitter, generalized observations about the opposite sex all came from a place of intense loneliness, for both character and author. So while I haven't gone back and politically corrected or rationalized any of these sometimes cringe-inducing comments, I have made Vic (and those around him, particularly his confidant, Doc) slightly more aware of their innate wrongness. Don't confuse this for an apology, though. These characters are slaves and victims of their own flawed human natures, as are we all. That, in my view, is what makes them so relatable.

As I write this, I've just turned fifty years old, having celebrated with dinner in Seattle's Space Needle, which for me represents a beacon from my own future. The film is deep in the development stage, with promising prospects. The republication of *Love Stories Are Too Violent* marks both a personal and professional milestone. Finally, it is something in which I can take great pride, given its professional presentation and distribution. This is more of a re-introduction than an introduction. This time, though, our collective efforts got it just right.

So to sum up in cinematic parlance, this is basically my "Director's Cut." Dig.

Will "the Thrill" Viharo
Alameda, CA
Spring 2013
www.thrillville.net/fiction

LOVE STORIES
ARE TOO VIOLENT FOR ME

1

Heart Full of Rain

San Francisco, 1994

PEOPLE TELL ME I live in the past. We all live in the past, I tell
them. We just don't know it yet.

My name is Vic Valentine. Half Italian, half Irish. Vic is
sometimes short for Victor, sometimes for Victim. It all depends
on when you ask. I'm a P.I. specializing in surveillance of errant
spouses and sweethearts. My office is in the Richmond District of
San Francisco, right above a combination bar and video store called
The Drive-Inn. I have a long line of credit there, and the proprietor,
a forty-something black guy named Doc Schlock for business
purposes, is an old pal of mine. We both share a penchant for old
monster and detective movies, particularly the cheesy ones, and
many of the customers who frequent the place are more drawn to
the conversations over hooch than to the film selection. There's a
big screen TV behind the bar like in any other neighborhood pub,
except this one never plays sports, only cheap thrills. A lot of loner
types sit at the mahogany bar, surrounded by strange video images
and memorabilia from seventy-odd years of cult cinema, and pour
their hearts out to Doc, who listens and laughs and nods sympa-
thetically. I often listen as well to their tales of heartbreak and
loneliness and dejection, until it gets to be too much for me, and I

3

turn a deaf ear on them and focus on the blood and guts and sex on the TV screen, trying to block out the mayhem and dismemberment of the human soul beside me. I have a weak heart. I admit it. Tell anyone and I'll kill you. It's foggy a lot out in the Richmond, as any native will tell you. I like it that way. I find the mist soothing, and at night I enjoy being snug in my apartment, which doubles as my office, engulfed in marine melancholia. The isolation gets to me, however, especially now, after everything that happened. I dream about it all the time. The memory won't fade in the sun like mist.

I still don't understand it. Maybe it will make sense to you. But I doubt it. It's a story with no clear-cut beginning or end.

I told Doc all about it. It unfolded day by day for him, like a soap opera. Well, *almost* day by day. There were a few detours that took me out of town on some senseless sojourns, and I lost touch with him briefly. But I always returned to The Drive-Inn to fill him in, and he always appreciated it. He doesn't get it, though, and he's a wise man.

It's nice to have someone to talk to, who listens, even if it isn't the person you really want to talk to, who refuses to listen to you. Doc is my surrogate confidant. He fills that capacity for a lot of people around town. He has no Ph.D. in psychology, just a well-rounded understanding of human nature that probably comes from growing up poor and black in Oakland. Rejection comes in many forms, but has virtually the same effect on anyone it touches, whether it be racial discrimination or romantic tragedy. Any way it comes at you, it leaves you broken and feeling alone in a world that doesn't want you.

Doc's love life is still a mystery to me. He never talks about it. Maybe he lives vicariously through his patrons, or his videos, though he doesn't stock traditional love stories. He hates that saccharin crap. I don't blame him.

It was about six months ago at the beginning of the rainy season that I met the first catalyst in this story, a Major League baseball player named Tommy Dodge, believe it or not, but I've changed his name slightly to protect the guilty, in case you've heard of him. Though I found out later he was something of a local celebrity, being a left fielder for the Giants, I'd never heard of him myself. Not directly, anyway. He was a tall, dark, handsome guy, the kind I hate immediately since you know his only real romantic problems probably stem from over-exertion. When I met him he was somewhat on the skids, having been bounced from the Majors temporarily back to the minors, though still Triple A. I didn't know at the time since my interest in sports is limited to bowling, but there's Single A, Double A, and Triple A, depending on your talent. Tommy Dodge's problem was that while he was AAA in the minors, he was AA off the field. He'd always had a drinking problem, but that only got worse after his wife, whose name he told me was Rose, disappeared one day with only a cryptic note in her wake. He wanted me to find her. That's where this story begins, a story I wish had never happened, in some ways. In other ways, it was inevitable, a collision course with a fate both cruel and seductive, an investment that you made a long time ago and had written off as a complete loss but which comes back to haunt you, torment you, and cause you to regret the best days of your life.

If life is a learning experience, I want to drop out. I can't afford the tuition anymore.

I was watching an ultra-violent Hong Kong gangster flick called *Hard-Boiled* on the big screen TV when Tommy Dodge walked in and sat beside me. It was the off-season and he lived nearby. I didn't know this right away. Like I said, I didn't recognize him as anything but a big, good-looking athletic type who probably just had to stand still and women would be clinging to him like beautiful barnacles. I hated him at first sight and tried to ignore him, but his bulk and bad mood began to grate on me. We just sat next to one another while Chow Yun Fat wasted a warehouse full of Uzi-toting badasses. It was a while before I noticed the guy was sobbing.

Personally, gunfights never break me up. Watching guys blow each others' limbs and heads off doesn't faze me. But tie me up and force me to watch *Romeo and Juliet*, the one with Olivia Hussey, and I'll choke on my own vomit.

Doc took notice of the weeping giant, who kept ordering shots of tequila with beer chasers. It seemed after a while Doc could've recycled the guy's tears as booze. He kept tossing back the stuff like it was fuel for his leaking eyeballs. He looked like hell, actually—unshaven, mussy hair, and bloodshot eyes, though on a guy like him this kind of appearance made him look appealingly vulnerable to most women. If it were me, I'd look like a pathetic slob. It's all a matter of showcase and perspective. I find women only like vulnerability in a man they haven't conquered yet. As it turned out, Tommy Dodge *had* been conquered by the only woman he wanted. He could have parlayed this into a smorgasbord of meaningless sex, but for some reason he didn't want to take advantage of it. Otherwise, why would he be sitting here on a rainy day in December instead of lying entwined with a model beside a fireplace in Marin? The Drive-Inn was for losers, after all, and Tommy Dodge didn't look like a loser. He just *acted* like one. Despite myself, I became interested and I went with it. Maybe I smelled a job. Of course, I got a lot more than that, as it turned out, so maybe I sensed my own destiny and couldn't help getting sucked into the vortex. I was a victim of conspiring circumstances. In any case, I spoke up, and the rest just happened on its own.

"I don't mean to sound insensitive," I said rather snidely, "but you're drowning out the dialogue."

"It's Chinese," he shot back without looking at me, obviously resenting my intrusion.

"With subtitles," Doc said, raising his eyebrows in bemusement.

"Except for the screaming," I said. "That's a universal lingo."

The big guy didn't seem interested in pursuing this conversation as it started, so I re-routed it, largely out of curiosity, and largely out of boredom. "The Doc is a great guy to talk to about personal problems," I said.

The big guy looked at me. "What're you, his fuckin' press agent?"

"Sorta, yeah," I said, trying to act nonplussed when in fact he was intimidating as hell even while overcome with grief. "Doc, talk him off the ledge?"

"Hey, I just walked in to get out of the rain," the big guy said. "I'm looking for the guy upstairs, the detective guy, not a goddamn shrink. All right?" He finished his third beer and pulled out his wallet. "I don't need *this*."

"Whoa, whoa, easy does it, guy, just settle down," Doc said. "Don't go away mad. My friend here *is* the guy upstairs."

"Only I'm downstairs," I said. "I'm the dick you're looking for."

Tommy Dodge looked at me for a beat, as if sizing up a blind date that seriously disappointed him. Then he said, "Oh," and sat back down, putting his wallet away. "I'm Tommy Dodge," he said, extending his hand for a shake. "I'm, uh . . . I've been drinking since, well, for a few days and nights, actually. I like to drink. But it makes me rude. I apologize."

I shrugged. "Don't sweat it. I'm Vic Valentine."

"Yeah, you said. That a fake name?"

"No. How about yours?"

"No, why?"

"Just thought I'd ask. Have another round on me, and relax."

"Coffee time," Doc said, pouring a steaming cup of java for both Tommy and me. "On the house. You guys talk shop all you want. My man Vic here is hardly ever in the office. It's a wonder he gets any business at all."

"Tell the truth, I was having second thoughts," Tommy Dodge said. "About hiring a detective, I mean. I probably wouldn't have come back. It's weird you were sittin' here, and I just came in and found you. If you hadn't spoken up, I woulda walked right out and never saw you again probably. Rose believes in that kinda stuff. Karma. You heard of that?"

"It's in my face all the time," I said. "Who's Rose?"

"My wife. Here." He pulled his wallet back out and showed me a picture. Actually, it was an old photo that had been torn up and taped back together. I could make him out easily enough, but the woman with him, ostensibly Rose, was hard to discern. She was obviously quite a looker—sultry, slender, radiantly brunette. Something vaguely disturbed me about her visage, but I couldn't decide what and let it go, at least for the time being. I remember a danger siren going off in my head, a flutter in my heart and a feeling in my stomach like someone had plugged me and I was slowly bleeding to death, but I get this sensation several times a day, so I was used to it. This time I should've paid more attention to it.

"She's . . . very attractive, near as I can tell," I said, mesmerized momentarily by the photo.

Tommy pulled it out of my hand and looked at it. "I got better pictures of her. At home. I live close by and I was just walkin' around the neighborhood. I saw the sign in your window up there, and I thought, what the hell?" He put the photo back in his wallet. He wasn't crying now but his face exhibited a calm sadness that almost made me feel sorry for him. It was the look of defeat. I'd seen it too often in life. Particularly in the mirror. "Rose sure loved old movies," he said softly. "I didn't know too much about that stuff. She was into artsy stuff. Sometimes I wonder what the fuck she ever saw in a guy like me."

I let that pass. "I'm picking up on an accent. You from back east?"

He nodded. "Pittsburgh. I used to play for the Pirates, but I got traded."

"How long ago was that?"

"Hmm . . . six years. You never heard of me?"

"I'm not a sports fan. Pirates are baseball, right?"

He laughed, then caught himself. "Sorry. Yeah. I play for the Giants now. Well, I *did*. I'm back on the farm until I get myself together."

"You keep referring to Rose in the past tense," I said. "Is she . . . gone?"

"Hey, you're pretty good," he said.

"No, I mean gone, as in, y'know . . . *dead*?"

He looked at me curiously. "Why would I hire you to find her if she was dead?"

"I don't know, the way you're all broken up, I thought maybe you got framed for her murder and wanted me to find the guy who set you up. Somethin' like that."

He shook his head, laughing softly. "Boy, this is *just* like one of those old movies Rose used to watch on cable. Those old black and white things. They always bored the shit out of me, but I pretended I was into 'em so we could cuddle up and watch 'em late at night."

"Sounds nice," I said, looking into my empty beer glass. Doc took the cue and refilled it for me. He had turned down the sound of the video. Doc also didn't want to miss anything. This was getting good, although I still had that tingling sensation of dread coursing through my veins like poison. I took a swig of my beer and hoped I'd piss it all out later.

"So, you want me to find Rose, huh?" I said after a few silent moments.

"I dunno," he said into his shot glass. He was practically licking the bottom with his massive tongue. And he wondered what she saw in him. It's funny how a guy like him wouldn't know women better than that. Maybe he did when he was sober. And maybe Rose would be waiting for him back in his digs since she missed that big ol' tongue of his too much. Women only like their independence when all the men around them are bums. But then I was beginning to wonder about this Tommy Dodge—maybe the big guy *was* a bum, after all.

"You don't know if you want me to find her or you don't know if you ever want to see her again?"

"Oh, I'll die if I never see her again," he said patly. "I'll fuckin' *die.*"

"In that case maybe I should help you out, best as I can. This is what I do, after all."

"I'm, uh, kinda broke," he said quietly. "The minors are quite a comedown, salary-wise. I got a little saved from last season, I mean before I got sent down, but . . . I wanted to save it for a trip to Hawaii."

"What's in Hawaii? I mean besides Don Ho and Jack Lord?"

"That's where I went with Rose on our honeymoon. I want to take her there again, try to get things back to how they were before . . ." He faded away.

"Before what?"

"Before she fuckin' *vanished* on me. I mean like into thin fuckin' air."

"When's the last time you heard from her?"

"I got a letter she left the day she skipped out, and a postcard about a month ago."

"Where was the postcard from?"

"*Here.* Frisco. It drove me nuts to think she was so close. She loves it here. But then she grew up around here, so I doubt she'd leave the area, anyway."

"Where'd she grow up, exactly?" I asked.

"Up north a bit," he said. "Vallejo. Her old man was in the Army."

"You mean the Navy."

"Whatever."

"She's into the arts but she grew up in a military household?"

"Yeah. Go figure. But she was a lotta fun, y'know? Really down to earth, like the girls back home. You from back east?"

"New York," I said. "Been a long time, though."

"You sound like it," he said. "Why'd you come out here?"

"It's a long, sad story," I said. Something about this was beginning to seriously disturb me, and I had trouble listening to him now.

"Aren't they all," he said.

"All what?"

"Long, sad stories."

I sighed. "Seems that way. So Rose is from Vallejo, huh?"

"Yup."

"You try getting in touch with her folks there?"

"Naw. They moved away a long time ago after her old man retired. I don't know where. Florida, I think. I don't think they liked me very much."

"Why not? You're the all-American hero. Ballplayer and all."

He looked at me closely to see if I was being sarcastic. Fortunately he was either too drunk or too dumb to pick up on it. "Yeah. Well, they *used* to like me, until I married their daughter. I don't think they ever trusted me. I think they wanted Rose to be a nurse and marry a doctor or somethin'. Fuckin' suburbia. You know how it is."

"Not really. I grew up in the city." Brooklyn. Close enough.

"I grew up in a town outside Pittsburgh, really. I know the score. Small towns are the same all over. Full of scared, stupid people."

"Doesn't sound like Rose was either."

He nodded. "No. Rose was different. She was down to earth, like I said, only really, really smart. She had a brain, y'know?"

"Maybe she still does," I said. There's that past tense again.

"It's not her brain I miss, though," he said seriously.

"Oh? So what do you miss about her?"

"Her heart. She had—*has*—a really good heart. It just got cold sometimes. Like it's covered with ice. All of a sudden she'd go from being the sweetest, funniest, funnest girl I ever met to an ice-cold bitch from hell. I couldn't keep up with her."

"Just moody. Or that time of month."

He shot me a deadly look that collapsed quickly. "Naw. These weren't like moods, like regular people get. I mean it was like she had two personalities. She kinda spooked me sometimes."

"You think she might be . . ." I was trying to be delicate about this. "You know, schizo?"

His eyes flashed angrily, and I grew tense. "You mean like *loony?*"

"Well, not exactly loony." I swallowed hard. "Just confused. Unbalanced a little. Emotionally. Not mentally, necessarily. Just mixed up a bit, beyond her control."

He let out a long, boozy sigh. "I dunno. Maybe. I mean I saw bits and pieces of this before we were married, but it was after we got married that she really started acting strange. But I figured, she's an artist, she isn't like regular people."

"So that's the distinction, then."

"Huh?"

"I was just wondering why you had disassociated her from the rest of us mortals."

"Are you bein' wise with me? I mean, I really can't tell."

"Tell you the truth, neither can I sometimes."

"Well, *don't* be. I'm not in the mood for a wiseass."

"I'll keep that in mind," I said warily. "So Rose was, is, an artist. What kind?"

"Whaddya mean, what kind?"

"I mean what type of art did she do?"

"Oh. All kinds. Painting, mostly. But she wrote poetry, too. Had a few published in some magazines I never heard of. I never really understood 'em but I could tell they were really good, y'know?"

"Uh-huh." I couldn't shake this feeling of foreboding. The beer just gave it something to swim in. Upstream, to my brain, which was pounding out SOS signals I chose to ignore. Or maybe my heart was sending them. I couldn't tell anymore. I always get those two organs confused, and I never listen to the right one. The signals they send me get jammed by too many conflicting wavelengths. Maybe that's why I love the fog and the mist. It makes me feel like a ship lost at sea, trying to follow the lighthouse beacon that seems to go out just when I'm almost safe at shore. Then the rocks break me up and I'm drowning. I have dreams like this almost every night. There seemed to be no escaping them. I was lost in these thoughts as Tommy Dodge talked Doc into refilling his shot glass one more time. I hadn't even touched the coffee he had given me and passed on another beer. I was beginning to realize it wasn't the Tommy Dodges of the world I resented. It was myself.

The rain beat down outside in a biblical deluge. Tears from heaven, like there weren't enough down here to go around. All this wetness reminded me I had to take a leak. Doc lets me use his bathroom in the back. I don't like public restrooms. For some reason I can't piss if anyone else is around. Too self-conscious, I guess. So I went to relieve my neurotic bladder, and when I came back, Tommy Dodge was gone.

"He said he'll come in and see you tomorrow, when he's cleaned up," Doc told me. "But he definitely is interested in hiring you. So you got a job, man."

Big deal, I thought. I needed the money, but Tommy Dodge had told me he was broke, so I wasn't ready to put a down payment on that yacht just yet. My tab with Doc was pretty high, though, so I nodded at him victoriously and then went to the window to watch the rain fall, thinking of a girl I knew a long time ago, a girl who sounded a lot like Rose, with one exception.

That girl was dead.

2

Blood Bank Blues

THE PHONE RANG BRIGHT and early the next day, at around 10 a.m., and since I had forgotten to turn my answering machine on I couldn't screen it out. I picked up the damn thing just to shut it up. I'd already made up my mind that whoever it was on the line was an enemy. I *hate* being woken up this early.

"Hello," said a vaguely familiar female voice. "May I speak with Vic please?"

"Yes, it's him, it's me. Whaddya want?"

"You sound like you're depressed."

"That's because I'm awake. I was feeling much better before you called."

"I'm so sorry if I disturbed you—"

"Who the hell is this, anyway?"

"This is the blood bank. You should recognize my voice by now, Vic. You had an appointment today for pheresis donation?"

"Huh? Oh, yeah." How could I forget something like that? "What time again?"

"Ten minutes ago. Would you like to reschedule for tomorrow?"

"No! No, no," I said, sitting up, suddenly wide awake. "I'll, uh . . . I'll be right down. You got a chair for me at, say, eleven?"

"No problem, Vic. You know what a valued donor you are. We always have a spot reserved for you."

I smiled, despite myself. "Thanks. What's your name again?"

"Does it matter? I'm not the one you want anyway. Have a nice day, Vic." She hung up before I could reply. I never did catch her name, after all this time.

You may be wondering why I was so hot to donate my precious bodily fluids. I'm not really such a splendid humanitarian with veins of gold. The truth was, I was infatuated with one of the nurses at the local blood bank, a red-haired beauty named Flora. My trouble was that Flora had turned down my advances repeatedly, since she was dating some bozo sax player who gigged small-time around the Bay, everywhere but in The City, since he probably sucked. I'd never checked him out, though I planned to. Anyway, today was going to change things forever, I'd decided. I had a present for Flora that she would never forget, that would win her heart for me and make her dump that loser like a bag of biohazardous waste.

Because of my occupation, I have several cameras at my disposal, so it was easy for me to complete this particular project once I'd dreamed it up. I figured the only way to win Flora was to charm the pants off of her with something so original and off-the-wall that I would make an indelible impression she couldn't ignore. I also wanted to make her laugh. I usually have no problem making women laugh, though usually at the wrong times.

So anyway, I concocted this thing I called "The Date That Never Was." I don't remember how I thought of it exactly, but once I did, I knew I had a mission. I was taking a risk, since Flora would either think I was a total nut or a romantic genius, but since everything else had failed—flowers, cards, candy, routine charm—I felt I had nothing to lose. About a week before this I had gone around with my trusty Canon Snapshooter and taken pictures of all the places I *would* have taken her had she accepted my special offer. I went to a café, the one I usually frequent, called Rendezvous, and ordered two cups of cappuccino and set them on a corner table, then snapped a picture, drank both of them in a gulp, and left. I took pictures of a bouquet of roses, assorted colors, at a nearby flower shop. I ignored the strange looks people gave me. I was used to strange looks, anyway, dating back to my early childhood. I'm a veteran outsider oddball. I took pictures of a bench in Golden Gate Park where we would have sat and chatted, and another of a phone booth where she would've called her boyfriend to tell him she'd been kidnapped by a UFO but would be back once all the tests had been performed. I took pictures of the Japanese Tea Garden, the Shakespeare Garden, a movie marquee where *True Romance* was playing, luckily, and then walked into a gourmet seafood restaurant and snapped away at an empty corner table, entering and leaving as discreetly and quickly as possible.

Once I had the requisite shots I got the film developed at this place across the street from my office that specializes in one-hour processing. I was so anxious for the developed roll of film I paced out front. When they were ready, I rushed them home and arranged them in a portfolio in the order a natural date would progress. Then beneath each photo—all of which had turned out beautifully—I wrote amusing, lightly romantic captions. For instance, beneath the photo of the café table with two cups of cappuccino on it, I wrote, "Here is the table at the local café where they discussed Art and the Meaning of Life and everything except her boyfriend." And beneath the bouquet of roses I wrote, "These are the flowers he bought for her. She loved them, but said she'd have to destroy them so her boyfriend wouldn't find out. He understood. Sort of." Stuff like that. Non-threatening, I thought, but with a point to make. Then I made my pheresis appointment, a weekly affair unless I'm out of town, and tried to wait to give it to her. She *had* to fall madly in love with me, I was convinced. Not only that, it was a lot cheaper than a *real* date would've cost me. At least a first one. Now when we were out, we'd have a lot of preliminaries out of the way. Why hadn't I thought of this sooner?

The truth is, I'm not a total nut *or* a romantic genius, exclusively. I'm a romantic nut, maybe. How I was still alone and in my thirties was a mystery even to a master sleuth such as myself.

But this would do it. No more lonely nights with Frank Sinatra. This was *it.*

The whole Tommy Dodge episode was lodged somewhere in the back of my brain, but I didn't let it get to me. I turned on my answering machine, with a message featuring Elvis singing, *"If you're lookin' for trouble, you came to the right place . . . ,"* and began sweeping and straightening up my room in anticipation of the oncoming romantic encounter. My office is the front room, and I basically live in the bedroom, which is sparsely decorated. I have a cabinet full of movies, a framed, autographed cheesecake photo of '50s scream queen Mara Corday that is sitting on my desk, a framed portrait of '50s pinup queen Bettie Page (unsigned), a framed Film Noir poster from the Roxie Theater in the Mission, a CD deck, an old turntable for my LPs, a twenty-inch TV with a VCR and cable hookup, and that's about it. Oh, and a bed. I almost forgot, since I'm usually the only person in it.

I remember when I first decided to donate blood, about six months before this. It was strictly out of boredom, believe it or not. They'd sent me this flyer telling me I'd get to watch a free video if I donated a pheresis, which means they remove the platelets from your blood while you're hooked up to this machine for about an hour and a half. It gets spun down in a centrifuge, and the red blood cells get pumped back into you. Something like that. After all those times sitting in that chair—usually I brought my own movies now—I still don't really understand what the hell they were taking from me, or why. But as I said earlier, I wasn't doing this to give anything back to humanity. To hell with mankind. Flora was my nurse that very first time, and from then on I'd been a regular donor, though I didn't always get Flora, especially after I started asking her out.

Anyway, when I first decided to donate, I had to fill out my sexual history on a form, and it was really embarrassing, since I hadn't been laid in, well, a long time. They couldn't believe it, as a matter of fact. I had to convince them I wasn't lying. I was just experiencing a personal drought. I claimed it was abstinence, when in fact it was a lack of options. The only bar I frequent is The Drive-Inn, which is not exactly babesville, and if I'm not there I'm at a local diner reading the *Chronicle* or in the Rendezvous scribbling poems on napkins and tossing them. I don't hang out in teeny-bopper meat markets. I used to, when I lived in New York. I was into the punk/New Wave scene there in a big way, and in fact much of my music now comes from that era. I'm still in love with Debbie Harry. But for setting that certain romantic mood, whether I'm alone or not, nothing beats Space Age Bachelor Pad Music, from Esquivel to Combustible Edison. The neo-surf/spy music renaissance, spear-headed by Dick Dale and The Ventures and championed by modern bands like the Aqua-Velvets, Untamed Youth, the Ultras, The Phantom Surfers, Impala, and Man . . . or Astroman?, supply me with my theme music. I also love Henry Mancini, particularly the *Peter Gunn* soundtrack, and tiki exotica music by Les Baxter and Martin Denny when I'm in that tropical island mood (typically stranded alone). Sometimes I sit in the Tonga Room at the Fairmont Hotel by myself at the bar, dreamily sipping a Mai Tai, digging the fake rainstorms, but frankly it's too depressing, because it screams for someone to share it with. As for burlesque revues at various venues, forget it. Why excite myself for no reason?

I listen the most to Frank Sinatra, the patron saint of loneliness, particularly the Capitol recordings made after Ava shredded his heart through a meat grinder, but sometimes his poetic tales of heartbroken loners strike too close to home, and I have to throw on some Ramones to regain a healthy perspective on life.

Anyway, the point I'm trying to make is that I don't meet a lot of women, since I'm either working or too tired and lazy to socialize. Really. If I just wanted to get laid—no romance or anything like that, just sex—I could. Easily. Just like that. I mean, who couldn't? The rain had cleared up and the fog had lifted by the time I set out for the blood bank. It was a scintillating sunny day, the kind that made me wish I lived in Seattle, my dream retirement destination. I hate the goddamn sun. But the fleecy cumulous clouds (my favorite kind) and the soft, cool, refreshing Pacific breeze almost made it feel good to be alive. There were a lot of Christmas decorations around now, which normally depress the hell out of me, but today, with "The Date That Never Was" tucked beneath my arm and Sinatra singing "I Believe" in my head, I was brimming with confidence and a feeling resembling complacency. Hell, I was almost happy, though I wouldn't admit it outright. I still had a few minor kinks to work out, and I was assuming Flora would be as taken with my gift as I was. I did still have that nagging sensation of fear churning in my gut like vomit in a blender, but I chalked this up to run-of-the-mill butterflies. I blocked out all thoughts of Tommy Dodge and a few other open-ended cases in favor of my immediate project, though I would need money to finance the next logical step: an actual date with Flora, followed by more dates, a courtship, a relationship, marriage, kids, divorce, remarriage, and matching grave plots. Well, maybe I was getting a little ahead of myself. After all, it was a little early in the game to be planning on a divorce. I had to be more optimistic and positive if I was going to pull this off.

Loneliness. It eats away at your reason like acid, I swear.

For some reason, despite my efforts to the contrary, in the face of my festive surroundings and my impending date with fate, Tommy Dodge did manage to creep into my consciousness, over and over. Not Tommy. *Rose.* The girl in the picture, torn and faded but still glowing with an eerie essence that induced nausea and an overall uneasiness that distracted me from my current agenda. I had to beat it, at least for the time being. Rose belonged to Tommy, anyway. As if I cared. Flora was mine. Well, *almost*. There was still that sap-brained sax player to contend with, but could he conceive of such a masterpiece as "The Date That Never Was"? I seriously doubted it, not a joker who made his living playing Top 40 at weddings and dingy dives on the outskirts of nowhere. Flora did tell me he was ambitious about playing true blue jazz, but something told me Bird's legacy would survive the challenge. I got your bird hangin', I thought as I entered the blood bank, nervous but stoic.

I was something of a celebrity at the blood bank, ever since I became a regular and began falling for Flora. Everyone knew about it, from the women up front who did the hemoglobin tests to the nurses to the lab techs to the bloodmobile drivers. I didn't care, really, though for a while I was worried I might be brought up on charges of harassment. Flora was beginning to show signs of strain. She was trying to politely deflect my amorous advances, which I perceived as persistent, not psychotic as many of her co-workers believed, and she was showing no evidence of wearing down. She'd even taken to wearing a phony engagement ring in a sad attempt to ward me off, like a crucifix for a vampire. But I saw through her flimsy ploy and came up with "The Date That Never Was" in a last-ditch, no-holds-barred effort to win her over. Games are okay for a while, but this was into overtime. I had to be decisive, and prove to her I wasn't kidding around. Time was rushing by too quickly, like a broken hourglass. I was sick of being alone. This had to work. It just had to.

I kept "The Date That Never Was" hidden beneath my arm as Denise, my official blood bank contact, took down the required information and helped me with the paperwork. Denise was a smart, attractive black woman who lived over in the East Bay somewhere with her husband and little boy. She had a wry sense of humor and was fairly savvy about the human condition, so we always chatted a bit before my appointments. She hated her job and I didn't blame her.

She was completely fascinated with my self-employment, which I kept mysterious just to tease her. She had been the one who had supplied me with a lot of background goods on Flora, who was her pal, and while she didn't encourage me she didn't *dis*courage me either. She was having too much fun watching me make a fool of myself, as was the entire establishment, but secretly I knew she admired my persistence. She was probably the only person there who didn't think I was crazy. At least, I don't *think* she did. Maybe crazy but harmless. She hated Flora's boyfriend, anyway. She thought musicians were assholes. That's only because they get laid any time they want, I told her.

"What you got there you're hiding from me?" she asked me before I went into the donor room.

"What? This? Nothin'. Just some case files."

"Bullshit. It's for Flora, isn't it?" she said, eyeing me directly.

"What makes you think so?" I grinned, blushing in a big way.

"Anyone who hasn't had sex as long as you, the desperation on your face gives you away." She laughed.

"*Ssssshhhh!*" I hissed. "Keep your voice down, will ya? I'll show it to you, but no one else."

"You know once you give it to her, the whole place will see it eventually."

"I don't care. Then it will be Flora's decision. I don't want her to think I'm trying to embarrass her."

Denise gave me a look that made me fidget in my seat. "Little late for that coy crap," she said. "Sending her flowers and shit, and now you say you want to keep a lid on it? Oh, please. I mean everyone saw the flowers when they were delivered, and of course when they ask her who they're from, she's gonna tell 'em. But then more flowers come, and candy, and cards, and then you show up once a week opening your veins and bleeding like Jesus Christ on a stick—"

"*Okay*, Denise, *okay*. I *know* all this already," I said lowly, though the girl at the front desk nearby was smiling, lamely pretending not to eavesdrop. "Now I'm not going to show it to you. So *there*."

"Fine with me. But you know she ain't here today anyway, right?"

My heart stopped, then reluctantly started up again. "*What*? Where *is* she? Out sick?"

"She's on vacation. She has a life outside of this place, you know. Unlike most of us."

My finger was hard on the panic button. I even stood up. "She isn't, like, on a *honeymoon*, is she?"

"Relax. I told you that ring is a gimmick. That fool ain't never gonna pop the question, and she ain't gonna marry someone who ekes by on what he brings home. So I gather you want me to postpone your appointment, Romeo?"

I began to pace. "I dunno . . . I guess, I mean, what's the point?"

"Helping to save lives," she said dryly.

"Yeah, yeah, yeah. Like you said, I'm Romeo, not goddamn Galahad."

"I know. You're just trying to score, and maybe toss a bone to a poor gunshot victim while you're at it. We all know your story, Vic."

"Only you think it's a comedy. Easy for you, you got a family and all. I got *this*." I pantomimed masturbation, and the girl near us burst out laughing, then caught herself.

"You sure are wound up today," Denise said with a fresh delicacy to her voice. "Sit down and relax. I'm just giving you a hard time as usual. What's with you, anyway?"

"I dunno . . . maybe it's—"

"What?"

Rose was growing in my head again. "Never mind. So when does Flora get back?"

"Coupla weeks."

"Couple of *weeks*? Where the hell did she go, anyway? Neptune?"

"Close. Europe."

My entire nervous system felt on the verge of collapse. "Please tell me she went alone."

Denise's eyes were huge as she shook her head in the negative.

"With her family?"

Denise shook her head again.

"A tour group?"

"She went with her boyfriend, Vic. Why not? It's romantic."

"I *know* it's romantic, goddamn it!"

"Will you settle down? This *is* a place of business—"

"*Shit!*"

"Vic, keep your voice down, or else. I mean it. People are staring."

I sat back down and tried to keep from hyperventilating, playing "Heart of Glass" by Blondie in my head. That song always soothes me, for some reason. I also tried in vain not to think of Flora giving head to the sax player on the Eiffel Tower while he plays the blues for his beloved. They'd both be blowing at the same time. A lot more romantic than me alone in my apartment whacking off to Bettie Page videos from Doc Schlock's library. God, I hated life sometimes. Like when I was awake.

"You want me to give it to her?" Denise asked me with some sensitivity.

"You just want to see it," I said, pouting.

"I will anyway. I'll give it to her as soon as she gets back."

"Why didn't you tell me she was going to goddamn Europe with that prick?"

"I didn't want to send you into a tailspin. Besides, she didn't even *tell* me until a few days before she left. She's been planning this trip forever. Sorry she didn't check with you first."

"If she had only waited a little while longer she could have gone with *me!*"

"I'm sure that will haunt her for life," Denise said. "Now let me see this thing you got. I have to admit my curiosity is driving me crazy. I mean what else could you possibly do?"

Now I *had* to show her. "Just look," I said, handing it to her.

I watched Denise's face as she opened up "The Date That Never Was" and read it carefully. The range of emotions on her face ran the gamut from surprise to amusement to melancholia. I figured if Flora was half as touched by it, I'd be in like Flint.

"It's . . . different," Denise said after she'd finished looking at it.

"That's *it?*"

"Well, it's very . . . unique. I've never seen anything like it. Maybe you should send it to Hallmark and make some money—"

"To hell with Hallmark!" I said. "I did it for Flora. Maybe you *should* give it to her. I think I'd be too nervous to just go up and hand her something like that. It's too, well, different. But *you* like it though, right?"

She didn't answer right away.

"What's wrong?" I asked.

"Nothing. It's a very nice thought. But it may be *too* different. Flora's from a small town. You may be too much for her."

"What the hell am I, a big city masher? I'm just being creative, for Christ's sake. You looked like you really liked it while you were reading it. And now—"

"All I'm saying is what you think is creative other people might think is . . . *you* know."

"Crazy?"

"Yeah."

"Shit." I began to pace again.

"I'll give it to her, though."

"You will?"

"Sure."

"Hey, by the way, who's that girl who called me up to remind me of my appointment? I always forget her name."

"Stephanie."

"She sure knows *my* name, though."

"We *all* do, Vic."

"So you think this will freak Flora out or what?"

"No. She is into the arts and everything, more so than me. It's very romantic, Vic. But I know you."

I shot Denise with my forefinger and winked. "So will she. Thanks. I'll get back to you."

I walked out of the blood bank feeling oddly relieved. I think it was because I didn't have to give blood again. I was beginning to get dizzy spells from my excessive conscientiousness as a donor. I needed a break. I could trust Denise. Sure, she'd show it to a few of the girls up front, maybe a few techs, one or two nurses, but that would be it. Flora would be pleasantly surprised when she returned from the Vacation That Was.

Who was I kidding? How could that pathetic little prop stand up against a lifetime's worth of romantic memories? And who was she sharing them with, at this very moment? The sax player. Off to Europe with a sax player. I sure could pick 'em. Some dream girl. I was beginning to regret I'd ever let one drop of my precious blood trickle down their cold, insensitive tubes, draining me of my very essence while I poured my heart out to one of their indifferent, callous employees. What a prize sap I was. Once again.

I was wondering what could make my day any worse when I saw Tommy Dodge waiting for me in front of my building, holding what appeared to be a letter and a postcard. He had shaved and was cleaned up, but he still beamed that aura of sadness, which I frankly wasn't in the mood to deal with. I had my own heartaches to cure. But a job is a job.

"Let's go up to my office," I told him.

"Where've you been?" he asked like I was supposed to be waiting for him all my life.

"Giving blood," I said. "Lots of it."

3

As Crime Goes By

"IT MUST BE CONVENIENT to live over a bar that shows movies," Tommy said as he sat down opposite me, my oak wood desk a welcome barrier between us. I'd picked it up at a flea market for a song.

"Like a rapist living over a whorehouse," I said. "So what's your situation, Tommy? How did you get here, and where do we go from here?"

"Well, when a club invests a lot of money in a player, like with me, they don't usually send him back to the farm to work out his personal problems. But the manager liked me, he liked Rose, and I'm a good player—ask anybody—so I plea bargained with the brass. I said, instead of booting me off the team or trading me, I'll take a year off, but I still want to keep my hand in it, so I'll go to Arizona, check into AA, clean up my act, and be back fresher than ever. I'm twenty-eight. I can't afford to fuck off too much."

"Why would they bounce you?" I asked, still thinking of Flora roaming the ruins of Rome with that sax player.

"I was a fuckin' bum. I was getting drunk off my ass, and I kept getting fined and suspended for missing practice and lousing up on the field, but ever since Rose left, I just didn't care. Everyone on the team knew why I was going downhill so fast, and they felt bad for me, but I still had to pull my weight. They all talked to the manager and the owners and everybody and they took a kind of vote on me and decided to send me back to Triple A for a season. The press made a big goddamn deal out of it. They called me 'Billy Bunt' and 'Johnny Swing' and shit, makin' fun of my name. Real fuckin' mature. I admit I'm kind of a hot dog, and anyway they're just jealous."

"Who?"

"Everybody!"

"Of what?"

"Of Rose. And all the girls. Everywhere I go, there's girls. I mean, I don't *have* to be lonely."

God, how I hated him.

"It's just that no one can replace Rose in my heart. No-fuckin'-body. *Ever*. I never met anyone like her, and I don't think I ever will. And I've known *lots* of women."

He was still hanging on to the postcard and letter from Rose, but that was all right. I wasn't ready to see those yet, and obviously he wasn't ready for me to see them. He clutched them like a mountain climber would a rope.

"How'd you hook up with Rose, anyway?" I asked.

"I met her in a bar in North Beach. Man, she was somethin'. She turned every head in the place. She came up to me and asked me if I was in the movies. She likes movies. I do too, but *new* ones. In color. Anyway, we started talkin' and hittin' it off right away, 'cause she's so down to earth, but still really smart. I respected her right away. She was with a friend, some girl, but I latched one of my teammates onto her so I could take off with Rose. We went out to a club South of Market and danced all night. Then at dawn we went down to the Cliff House, where she goes to, like, think and stuff, and write poems and draw, and we watched the sun come up and . . . it was just . . . I mean that was it. I was totally like in love with her. And she was totally in love with me. I took her to a motel room nearby and we fucked all day. But it wasn't just sex. It was special. I mean we had a real connection. Y'know?"

I nodded wearily and sighed.

"You ever been married?" he asked me.

"No."

"Why not? You a fag or somethin'? 'Cause if you are, I'm outta here. I don't deal with fags."

I closed my eyes and wondered why God had created mankind and, moreover, why He or She allowed it to go on. "I'm not gay, Tommy boy, don't sweat it. I'm just . . . picky. Or unlucky. I dunno. Let's talk about you and Rose, though, okay?" I felt weak, for some reason, even though I had not donated that morning. But in a way, I had. I was lying, bleeding and alone on the battlefield of love, and this poor schnook wanted *me* to help *him* out. I wondered how I'd find the strength to carry us both back into the trenches. Probably the fact that I didn't have January's rent was one source of inspiration. And it was Christmastime, though I had no one to shop for. I was thinking of buying a tree and decorating it anyway. I had nothing better to do. Or so I thought. In retrospect, I was already beyond the point of no return, and it had nothing to do with economics. I'd already discussed my fee and expense account with Tommy, and in spite of his financial difficulties he'd forked over the retainer and agreed to ante up the rest as long as I delivered.

"How long did this charming courtship go on before you finally got hitched?" I asked him.

"You really think it was charming?" he asked, bright-eyed.

"Who wouldn't? But moving rather quickly, wouldn't you say? I mean so far it sounds like a typical one-night stand. From what I've heard, I mean."

"Oh, I've a had a *lotta* those over the years. Fuck. I told you, Rose was different. I mean we just connected. She told me right away she'd known me in a past life. She was into reincarnation.

She didn't really have like a guru or nothin' like that. She isn't a kook. Just spiritual."

"I know the type." Did I ever. While he was describing her so many bells were going off in my head I felt like a steeple. Then I got the image of a cathedral, an empty one, except for the echoing riffs of a saxophone and the reverberating moans of a woman in ecstasy. Strangely enough, the woman in my vision wasn't Flora; it was Rose. I was getting confused and I had a headache. I wanted Tommy Dodge to go away, but I already had the retainer. Also, I wanted to see Rose in the flesh and take pictures of her in compromising positions. I won't even bother to deny the voyeuristic pleasures of my profession.

"Do you believe in reincarnation and all that stuff?" Tommy asked me, breaking the spell.

"Huh? Oh. Um, I dunno. I mean, who am I to have the secrets of the universe? I'm just small time. Can't solve the mystery of life, sorry. But I'll find Rose for you."

"You promise?" His boyish expression of neediness made me sick.

"I promise if she's in this city, or even in the state, I'll find her and—"

"And what? Make her come back to me?"

"Can't do that. I'll just tell her you have to talk to her, but I can't make her come back to you. I'm not a marriage counselor." Although I feel like it sometimes.

"But you'll tell me where she is, right?" He was getting very uptight. "I didn't give you all that money just to see where she is and what she's doing. I want you to find her and then tell me where she is so I can see her. I'll take it from there. I'm not doing this out of fuckin' curiosity."

"I got it. Now why don't you let me see that letter and postcard. And you never answered my question."

"Which one?"

"How long did you know Rose before you married her?"

"Hmm? Let's see . . . went to the motel room, fucked . . . slept a bit . . . fucked some more . . . then went to Reno. Gambled a bit, fucked some more . . . ate, slept . . . fucked . . ."

"Tommy—"

"We got married in Reno! That's right. This was a few years ago. Gimme a break. I destroyed a lot of brain cells since then. Got married in Reno, flew to Hawaii for our honeymoon, checked into the Royal Hawaiian in Honolulu, right on the beach there, Waikiki I think it is—and fucked our brains out!"

I let out a long sigh and put my face in my hands.

"You okay?" Tommy asked.

"Yeah. Just don't really need to know the frequency of your sexual encounters with Rose at this point. It's not pertinent to the case."

"Sorry," he said insincerely. "But she *was* good in the sack. Best lay I ever had, and I got a big frame of reference. So . . . how do we start?"

"Why don't you let me see that letter, Tommy."

"It's kinda personal."

"It may help me. I need to start somewhere. The postcard, too. You can confide in me. That's why you hired me. Right?"

"Okay. But don't make no Xerox copies."

"Of course not, but I may make a few notes." He handed me the letter and postcard reluctantly, watching me with intense paranoia. The letter was neatly typed and relatively brief. It said:

Dear Tommy,

I knew this day would come. It always does. What I didn't know was that I would be the one leaving. You can have any woman you want. Except me. But you'll endure without me. I need to find the answer, Tommy. If I could only remember the question. Remember the nights we spent together, spilling yourself inside me endlessly. Remember the cries of release. Remember the laughter. Remember the Alamo! I will always love you, but from afar. Our time together was the stuff dreams are made of. Time to wake up now.

Love, Rose

I went directly from the letter to the postcard. It had been postmarked in late October, San Francisco. It was a picture of Alcatraz, a typical tourist souvenir. On the back she had scribbled: "*Still haven't found a way to escape. Bring the cake, and don't forget the saw. Love, Rose.*" I was beginning to really like her. She had a sense of humor and a firm grasp of old movie lore to boot. Apparently Tommy didn't fully grasp her references.

"That make sense to you?" he asked, tearing the notes from my hand.

"Sort of. What throws me is her attitude. She seems so, I dunno. Funny."

"Funny? This seems *funny* to you?"

"No, not the situation. She just seems odd. I mean, 'the stuff dreams are made of.' C'mon. 'Remember the Alamo.' She's either really corny or really ironic."

"I don't see either."

"'The stuff dreams are made of,' that's a line from *The Maltese Falcon*. You know, the old movie? With Humphrey Bogart?" Actually it was originally from Shakespeare's *The Tempest*, but Bogey said it better, and *The Tempest* didn't do anything for me until it became *Forbidden Planet*.

"She made me watch that once," he said. "In fact . . . wait a minute. I think it was the last movie we watched on TV together. That's right. She left like the next day. I came home and she was gone. All of her pretty clothes, her many shoes, her poetry books, her artwork. Enough stuff to fill a van. Gone."

"Where were you while she was packing?"

"Me? I was . . . out."

"Out where?"

"I don't remember. Just out. What's the difference?"

"And this was how long ago?"

"About a year and a half. Lemme think . . . August before last. I was at a game, that's right. Came home and she was gone."

"Just like that. No warning signals?"

"Whaddya mean?"

"She never gave any previous indication she wanted a divorce?"

"Oh, we still ain't divorced. She's just not around. That's what's so weird about it. I mean, what the fuck is she doing?"

"That's what we're trying to figure out, Tommy boy. You ever cheat on her?"

He looked like he was going to hit me. "Fuck you," he spat.

"She ever cheat on you?"

He stood up, chest heaving. "You're crossing too many lines, buddy. You said you wasn't no marriage counselor. Let it go. This stuff ain't none of your business."

"I'm just trying to find a clue as to why she took a powder on you. Personally I couldn't care less." But then images of him "spilling endlessly" inside of her put knots in my stomach. I wished I knew why. I didn't even know this woman, although in some strange way, it felt like I did. Even her handwriting on the address was eerily familiar to me. No question about it now. I was in this for the duration. To hell with Tommy. I wanted to find Rose for myself.

"Sorry." He sat back down and didn't say anything for a few beats, looking around the room and through the blinds at the world outside, where Rose was, somewhere. "This is really killing me. All this time, and it's like she only left yesterday. And I'm not even close to being ready to go back to the Majors next season. I'm a mess, man. I really need your help." He almost started again with the waterworks.

And he'd been so good up till now. He stopped himself, though. I was glad.

"Let me see if I got this straight so far," I said. "You picked Rose up in a bar, went out, had a good time, went straight to Reno and eloped—"

"No, no. We stopped in Vallejo first and met her folks. They liked me. I was only a rookie at the time but her dad knew who I was. Then on the way back from Reno, before we went to Hawaii, we stopped by again to tell 'em Rose and I got married. Then the shit really hit the fan. She's got two older brothers, big guys, also in the Navy, who wanted to kick my ass. So did her old man. But she stopped them. Lucky for *them*."

"Why was Rose in such a hurry to get married?" I asked. "I mean, Jesus Christ. She knew you all of what, a day?"

"I told you. We had a connection. Plus she knew me in a past life. What's the big fuckin' deal here?" He really didn't see anything unusual in this. I couldn't decide if it was the booze or just innate naïveté, a polite phrase for stupidity.

"Yeah, love at first sight and all that jazz—but *marriage*? How old was she at the time?"

"Year younger than me. Twenty-three, almost twenty-four. I was twenty-four. We were young and had the hots for each other. She told me we were married in a past life but some kind of accident cut it short when we were newlyweds, so now she wanted to pick up where we left off. Made sense to me."

"It *did*? Straight up?"

"Why not? Okay, I was raised a Catholic, but I never really believed in it. Rose opened my eyes to a whole new way of lookin' at things."

I found this hard to believe. "Were either of you on the rebound?"

"You mean from like a bad relationship?"

"Yeah."

"Not really. Not me, anyway."

"How about Rose?"

"She didn't say. I kinda get the idea . . ." His eyes drifted off with his voice.

"What?"

"I think there was somebody before me. Well, lots of one night stands, but one special guy. She didn't marry him, though."

The sensation that had plagued me since Tommy Dodge first entered my life twenty-four hours before was eating me alive. I thought I was going to break out in hives. "Why not?"

"She didn't say. I didn't want to know, really. Fuck him."

"You think maybe she . . . went back to him?"

Tommy Dodge stood up, looking at me in a trance. "I never thought of that . . ."

I shrugged. "Just an idea. It would explain a few things. Maybe. Why did she stay with you for so long, though? And why marry you right off the bat—so to speak—and then stay married, what, four, five years?"

"Four, almost five. I told you already. We had a—"

"I heard you. A love connection. But just think for a second. What are the odds of something like this working out?"

He was beginning to boil over. "What are you trying to say, man? That we were *doomed*? Is *that* it?"

"Star-crossed, maybe. I mean, how well do you *know* this woman, anyway?"

He sat back down and brooded. "Just find her, Valentine. Just fuckin' find her, and I'll take it from there. You got your money, what are you so goddamn worried about *me* for? All I want you to do is find her. That's *it*."

"Okay. That's my job. I just need to have some background info to go on. There's no telling how she's gonna react to your hiring a detective to find her, though. Maybe I should lay low for a while, take some pictures. I mean, what if she isn't alone when I find her?

You want pictures of the guy she's with? How much do you want to know, Tommy?"

"Everything," he said, fuming quietly. "I just gotta know. I know Rose couldn't go this long without . . . sex. Just as long as she still loves me. That's all I gotta know. That's all I gotta know."

I didn't say anything for a minute or so. I take about a dozen of these cases a year, and have been since I started this racket four years ago, after a nowhere stint as a freelance journalist for several Bay Area rags. I had a column in a New York tabloid when I was still a kid. I wrote about the cultural underground. Little did I know I would wind up like this. At least Tommy was in a profession he had always dreamed about, as far as I could tell, anyway. But all he wanted was Rose. Even though I didn't know her, I could hardly blame him. "I'll need to see some more pictures of her," I said finally. "Some clear ones. And I'll need some more details. Who were her friends? Did she have a job while she was with you? Stuff like that."

"She had lots of artsy friends. I didn't have much to say to them. I brought home a lot of my friends for parties and barbecues and shit like that, and they all liked Rose, she was a fun girl, but I can't say they knew her much. And she worked odd jobs here and there that didn't last long. Daycare center was one. That was the last one. She wanted to have kids real bad."

"So?"

"So what?"

"Why no kids? Or did you?"

"No. No kids. We tried, but . . . I don't want to get into that now."

"Okay. What I need from you are those pictures and anything you have on her old friends. Phone numbers, addresses, whatever. Also a list of all the places she worked while she was with you, maybe even before. Whatever you have. I'll take it from there."

He seemed to be lost in some internal landscape now, but then he suddenly came back. "Whatever." He stood up. "I'll bring that stuff by later today, like around four. All right?"

I shook his hand with professional aplomb. "Sure. Anything you think will help me know her better."

"Why?"

"Huh?"

"The way you said that. You 'wanna know her better.' Why?"

"Tommy, this paranoia of yours isn't making my job any easier. Basically what I gotta do is find a drop of rainwater in a pond. San Francisco is a small city but not *that* small. She may have left by now. I need to know who I'm looking for as best I can. You want to find her, don't you?"

He calmed down. "Yeah."

"Then trust me."

"I'll be back later. With the pictures. But I don't know much about her friends. I'll see if I can find something. I got an address book that may have some names. She used to stay over friends' houses a lot, especially when I was away at games."

"Fine. I'll see ya. And don't worry. Things will work out. I just have a feeling."

I walked him out and then went into my bedroom to lie down for a while. I didn't fall asleep but I was lost in a dreamland of my own design. I played Tom Waits' song "Blue Valentines" in a loop on the CD player as I thought of the girl I once knew who was dead. Well, she wasn't *really* dead. I just pretended she was so that my separation from her would make more sense. Rose reminded me a lot of her, but I couldn't decide why beyond the superficialities. The girl I knew was named Valerie, not Rose, and I met her in New York. She was from the Midwest somewhere, she had told me, some little rinky-dink town near Chicago. She was an apprentice on the tabloid I was writing for, and admired my writing. We hit it off in a big way. We were going to be married when she disappeared one day.

I didn't rate a letter, however. Not one word. I reported it as a missing persons case to the cops, but they never found her. So I assumed she was dead, stalked and killed by a maniac. Or maybe she went back to the farm. She was a poet and an artist, like Rose, and her folks were blue-collar types, her father an ex-Marine, she had told me. She was rebelling against the constraints of a conservative background, like Rose. Valerie also loved old movies. The similarities were striking, and disturbing. I couldn't get Valerie off my mind. I was starting to forget about Flora and the sax player in Europe. All I could dream of now was Valerie, a girl I had not seen in almost six years, the only girl I would ever have married, the person who could have saved me from the loneliness that engulfed me like a bank of fog.

I wished I could solve the mystery of love for Tommy, and for myself, and for everyone. I wished I could find a way to prevent the crimes of the heart that went on and on around me like emotional genocide. I became a detective to find missing persons, and I was often successful, but the one person I wanted to find had eluded me, and I felt like a total failure in life. Despite my valiant efforts, the love criminals were on the loose everywhere, raping and maiming and destroying each other and not even realizing why, and in the end there wasn't a damn thing I could do about it.

4

Blue Confessions

I WAS A TEENAGE hound dog.

Those were the days, boy. You see, life wasn't *always* like this for me. You might say I'm the James Dean of romance—a brief, brilliant career that was abruptly, prematurely and violently aborted by a sudden and deadly crash. I guess I was just going too fast. And not watching where I was going. Now I'm a legend. A dead legend. Oh, I get around. But I'm a love zombie, an amorous George Romero reject. Late at night, lying wide awake in my bed, playing with myself for relaxation, I kept imagining Valerie as Barbara Crampton in *Re-Animator*, screaming nude and strapped to a lab table while I ate her out with my dismembered head held between her squirming legs with my own cold, undead hands. Then she turned into Rose. That was too sick, so I stopped. After a while.

My New York days were a lot different than my San Francisco ones, to say the least. I was young and naïve and the future beckoned me onward to fulfill my dreams of romantic grandeur. I was full of promise—or something. That promise may yet be realized, but so far it feels like a raw deal was pitched and signed a long time ago, and I'm just getting around to realizing it.

I think about my youth a lot when I listen to the modern rock station, which plays a lot of stuff from my heyday, which ended around the mid-'80s somewhere, peaking around the same time as *Miami Vice*. Listening to "Tainted Love" by Soft Cell or "I Ran" by A Flock of Seagulls pulls me back instantly to my glory days with Valerie. The pain is exquisite. I don't know why I listen to that stuff anymore. I should just stick to the jazz station and not torture myself with tunes from the recent past, just escape into an era where I never even existed.

But there I was, pumping up the volume as A-Ha's "Take On Me" came pouring out of the speakers of my '63 sky blue Corvair, not the ideal San Francisco car, except in terms of aesthetics. It's a beautiful set of wheels with a lovely backdrop to glide through, but those hills are murder on the clutch. I guess that sums me up perfectly—anguish in the name of beauty. Maybe I'm just addicted to loneliness, but I'm too steeped in denial to come to terms with it. Whatever. I've heard it all, and none of it makes complete sense.

I was just driving around The City thinking about Valerie and how much Rose reminded me of her. I had with me a few pictures of Rose that Tommy had left off, plus the address of the daycare center where she once worked and the addresses of friends, two in North Beach and one in Berkeley. That's all he could give me, he said. But this was plenty. Especially the pictures.

They'd all been taken in Hawaii on their honeymoon. Rose was in a bikini in two of the shots, posing on the Oahu shore with Diamondhead in the background, and wearing a long white gown and flowers in her hair in another, standing beside a giant tiki statue. She was gorgeous in a simple way. Accessible. I saw the down-to-earth quality Tommy had spoken of so proudly. Her smile set you at ease and seduced you simultaneously. There was one photo, the one with the white gown, where she wasn't smiling. Unlike in the two bikini shots, she was alone here. She looked lost in thought, pensive, deep in a reverie of a faraway time or place. It looked like a moody album cover. This was the one that got to me, despite the sexual allure of the bikini shots, where Tommy was hanging all over her, his tan, well-honed physique glistening in the sun, or maybe drenched in post-coital perspiration. She looked strangely cool and aloof in these shots, even while smiling and obviously having a good time. She was younger in these pictures, but Tommy said she still looked exactly the same. That's what threw me.

Except for the hair color, she was a dead ringer for Valerie.

I assumed this was why Rose had permeated my consciousness so completely since I'd first laid eyes on her in The Drive-Inn, but the faded quality of that photo didn't do her justice or make me realize the amazing resemblance to Valerie. I had long ago discarded all of my pictures of Valerie, and had not laid eyes on her in six years, so my memory was a bit hazy, though the touch and scent of her were emblazoned in my heart for eternity. I surmised that Rose was perhaps a relative of Valerie, but that would be too coincidental. The only other explanation went even beyond coincidence into the realm of magic. I couldn't help but ponder that possibility, however, as I set the white gown photo on the dashboard and looked at it on and off, just driving through the cool December evening, dreaming.

Valerie had auburn hair that bordered on red, and in fact Flora from the blood bank had reminded me of her. I discovered through my contact, Denise, that Flora was a patron of the arts and an aspiring artist as well, just like Valerie. I'd dated a few women since leaving New York, but as I said, my San Francisco track record left much to be desired. Before Valerie I had been something of a young stud, bedding NYU English majors who read my column and thought I was going places. I was meeting people and hobnobbing with Midtown literati, Greenwich Village bohemians, and musicians from the New Wave forefront. I once met Debbie Harry briefly backstage at CBGB, as well as David Byrne, Richard Hell, Iggy Pop, Mark Mothersbaugh, Lux Interior, Poison Ivy, and Joey Ramone.

They were all pretty trashed at the time, so I doubt they'd remember me, but so what. I remember them.

My old man was a cop in Brooklyn, my mother a cop's wife who wanted more out of life. I had a brother who committed suicide at age eighteen after catching a late show of *Dawn of the Dead*. Jumped off the Brooklyn Bridge. They said it was drugs but I knew better. It was hopelessness.

I get that feeling now sometimes when I see the Golden Gate, and it scares me.

I was a lost soul before I met Valerie, and became lost again after she disappeared. Since then I've been attracted to women who reminded me of her, physically and spiritually. Flora was the closest. Until Rose. It goes back further than Valerie, though. Valerie looked like my mother. But my mother was remote and took out her bitterness on my brother and me. Why would I want someone who reminded me of my mother? Valerie not only physically resembled my mother, a voluptuously feminine Irish beauty and class act, but she was also moody, a tormented artist struggling to find her voice, with a sense of humor that could go from witty to vicious in the blink of an eye. Most women I've been attracted to fit that description, more or less. In Flora's case I filled in what I didn't know about her with my imagination until she fit the bill, strictly out of desperation. But from the way Tommy described Rose, she was already made to order. Her letter and postcard displayed the same lost, yearning look that made me fall so hard for Valerie. Flora got that look sometimes. The crazy look. I'm a sucker for it. Call me a masochist.

My mother eventually went mad and had to be committed. She's still locked up in a sanitarium in upstate New York. My old man got shot to death in an alley while off duty. The case remains unsolved. I have my suspicions. Some day I may go back and prove them, now that I'm a licensed P.I. But I'm afraid of what I might find. That's no reason not to look for something, though.

I drove down to the Palace of Fine Arts in the Marina. In case you don't know, the Palace of Fine Arts looks like a replica of a Greek Temple. There's a museum inside called the Exploratorium, full of neat scientific knickknacks, and outside is a pond with ducks. There's a large lawn beside the pond where lovers and tourists sit and absorb the idyllic ambience. You keep waiting for an earthquake to shatter the mood. Maybe that's just me, though.

Anyway, I parked the Corvair by the lawn and walked over to the pond and gazed at it as if waiting for the Creature from the Black Lagoon to emerge from its depths and drag me to its hidden lair. Or maybe a mermaid that looked like Esther Williams, star of many of my wet dreams, guiding me down to her undersea paradise. Life can go either way.

I was almost alone since it was night and getting very chilly, and a full moon shone with icy luminescence. I thought about Tommy telling me how Rose liked to go down to the Cliff House and contemplate deep things, just as I was doing now. In a way. I was contemplating Rose's contemplation. When I pictured Rose sitting on a storm-swept precipice, she had Valerie's countenance and hair color. Rose's hair was pitch black. It could have been a dye job. But Tommy told me Rose was from Vallejo, and reared by a military family. Valerie told me she was from a Chicago suburb, raised by an ex-soldier turned preacher. They were the same age. Had the same face. Same interests.

Somebody was lying. That was easy. The big question was why, and to whom?

I would spend Tommy's retainer and expense money wholeheartedly, but this was for *me*.

The realization had been trying to break through my unconscious barrier since I'd seen that first shot of Rose, but standing there by the Palace of Fine Arts, the shock of the truth hit my brain like a two-by-four wielded by a madman. I looked at the dark silhouette of the ersatz temple and wondered what I always wondered when I saw it, whether there was a glass building standing out like architectural herpes somewhere in Greece, the result of a mix-up in blueprints. Who cares. These things happen. You expect to find something where it would naturally belong but instead find something that belongs somewhere else. This is why I have a job. People find their lovers in beds where they are not supposed to be. This is what keeps life interesting, I tell myself. The world is constantly challenging the status quo in order to keep us guessing, engaged, wondering, so we won't get too bored and jump off a bridge.

I jumped back into my Corvair and headed down Lombard toward the heart of The City. The vividness of the atmosphere intensified my heartache, for some reason. The beauty was cold and lonesome. San Francisco gives you a feeling of isolation you don't get even in New York. There's a sadness here beneath the storybook façade that is both compelling and depressing. You don't get it anywhere else in the Bay Area, either. Berkeley is simply bizarre, teaming with students and lunatics. Oakland is just desolate and dangerous. San Francisco is pretty and sad, like nowhere else on Earth, a beautiful woman dying of a terminal illness she can't understand, so she just tries to make the most of the few days she has left. She pretends to hide her sorrow with cosmetics. But I saw through it. I related to her sense of hopelessness. She was my kind of woman, all right. Doomed and determined to take me down with her. The mystery was why I would let her, why I wouldn't leave. Why I had come here in the first place. I should've gone to Portland or Seattle. Maybe later. Now I finally had a reason to be here.

Something told me if I could find Rose, I would find Valerie, and maybe even find myself and validate this whole detective business. Somewhere in this puzzle was the missing piece to my own soul, which Valerie had stolen from me when she left. To my mind Tommy Dodge was no longer in this. It was just Rose and Valerie and me, three names, two people, one big mess.

"Fade to Grey" by Visage was blasting at full volume as the Corvair sailed through the night, up and down dark streets, behind and around cable cars, past people enjoying the evening in couples and groups. There were loners, too, angry and afraid, homeless or not, and it killed me to think I was one of them. I thought I was dead until Tommy Dodge had shown me that picture. "Fade to Grey" confirmed my sense of destiny. One of my favorite songs. Fate was supplying my mission with a soundtrack. Tommy was right about karma. This was a first-class example. He was right about reincarnation, too. I had been with Valerie in my previous life, in New York, a happier existence. Then she left and I died, and woke up here in San Francisco, where she had been reborn as Rose. I had been a swinging journalist in my New York life, and a small-time PI in my present one. Rose and I would pick up right where Valerie and I left off.

I hit the gas and sped toward home in fourth gear, cops be damned. The brisk air was invigorating, the music inspiring. I was alive again. It crossed my mind that Rose might be down at the Cliff House right now, watching the waves break on the rocks, listening to the seals and gulls, thinking of me. I decided I'd look for her later, during the day, or at dusk or dawn. Those were the times she would be there. I was surprised Tommy hadn't thought to look for her there. But then he was a moron. She deserved better. Her slumming days were over. She was coming back to me.

But in spite of my self-induced euphoria, the apprehension persisted. I ignored it.

I was in a good mood when I breezed into The Drive-Inn. Doc was there as always. It was good to see him. It was Saturday night and the place was packed. Poor lost souls looking for lost poor movies, as well as each other. A few couples actually met in The Drive-Inn, but not often enough. Most of the stories were pathetic ones. I felt sorry for them, but it would feel wonderful to leave them behind forever.

"Hey, Vic," Doc said, greeting me with his customary warmth. "How's Flora?"

"Who?" I said with a broad smile as he poured my usual cheap beer from the tap.

I stopped him. "Make that a martini tonight. I'm celebrating!"

"Uh-oh," he said. "What now?"

"Why the pessimism, Doc?"

"Normally when you get like this, you're chasing another dream down the rabbit hole," Doc said. "But lay it on me."

"I'll give you the rundown on the blood bank situation first," I said, downing my martini in one gulp, including the olive. The Director's Cut of *Blade Runner* was showing on the big screen TV. Too perfect. One of my favorite movies in its most pristine form. I could hardly contain myself. I spoke to him in a stream of babble, but Doc was used to that, and he kept up even while tending to other customers. "I went into the blood bank today to give Flora that thing, you know, 'The Date That Never Was,' well, not personally, since she's in Europe with the sax player"—Doc raised his eyebrows—"but that's okay, it's all right, she'll be back, and damn sorry when she sees this thing. Forget her, anyway. Remember Tommy Dodge? The baseball player. Yesterday. Saw him again today. Showed me some pictures of his missing wife that blew my mind. Doc, I *know* this woman! I'm convinced she's the same girl who disappeared on me in New York six years ago. I mean, same face, same age, same interests. It all checks."

"Well, where *is* she?" Doc said, stunned. He dropped a glass he was washing, but it didn't break thanks to the plastic mat behind the bar. "I think maybe you're hallucinating, on the rebound from Flora—"

"*Forget* her. I'm tellin' ya. Rose *is* Valerie!"

An older obese woman, whom I saw there often, was staring at me, entranced by my story. I think she was a nurse at SF General named Beatrice. She usually rented movies with Italian mythological muscle men and Mexican masked wrestlers.

"*Your* Valerie?" Doc asked, incredulous but riveted.

"That's right. *My* Valerie. *Mine. Not* fuckin' Tommy Dodge's." Doc was pouring my third beer already and I was getting buzzed. I hadn't eaten dinner. "Jesus. Can you imagine that? A goddamn *baseball* player. What could she have been thinking?"

"Maybe she liked the way he swung his bat." Doc grinned, spreading his arms as wide as they would stretch, which was pretty wide.

"Funny guy," I said humorlessly. "Hey, can the movie bar biz and do standup, why don't cha?"

"C'mon, Vic, I'm just teasing you because you're losing it. This woman can't be Valerie. Be realistic. What are the chances of that? One in a million?"

"Ever hear of karma?"

"Shit, I got a whole section on that voodoo crap. I know all about it. But unlike a lot of people who come in here, I know the difference between fantasy and reality."

"What are you saying?"

"All I'm sayin', my man, is take it easy. Don't get yourself all worked up over a mirage. Wait till you find the woman before you start planning a future with her. And I mean, shit, even if it does turn out to be Valerie, by some miracle, I mean . . . would you really *want* her back?"

I was feeling sober all of a sudden. I hated it when Doc got rational. He took all the fun out of life. "Well . . . why not?"

"Why *not*? Vic, you're suffering from selective amnesia again."

"Again? When was the last time?"

"I rest my case."

Doc really seemed serious about this. That's what got to me. Usually he made a lot of sense with other people. But this was *me*. He wasn't saying what I wanted to hear; it irritated me.

"Refill?" he asked after a few moments as he cleaned glasses and I watched Harrison Ford dream about a unicorn.

"Make it a double this time." Damn, that sounded too much like baseball.

"What's the matter?" he asked.

"Nothin'. I'm just thinkin'."

"I don't mean to piss on your parade. I just don't want to see you hurt yourself. Especially over the same woman. You'd be renewing an old heartbreak, and for what?"

Doc knew all about Valerie. Now I regretted telling him. He was right, in a way. But Rose, or Valerie, was older now. More experienced and mature. She'd sown her wild oats, as they say. There was still a chance she loved me after all these years. I didn't want that spark of hope to die out, because my newfound joy would go with it. I didn't want to become a love zombie again. I wanted to live. So I believed in the impossible, like a religious zealot or an Elvis fan.

"I have to see for myself," I said. "But I appreciate the thought."

"Don't eclipse Flora just yet, either," he said. "I mean, you never know."

"You got that right."

I finished my second non-celebratory martini, nodded at Doc and went upstairs to my room. I listened to Frank Sinatra croon "In the Wee Small Hours" for the ten billionth time as I lay on my bed and dreamed of better nights, past and future.

5

Be-Bop-A-Ghoul-A

THE NEXT DAY I drove to Berkeley to see what I could find out. Many people in Berkeley think they know everything. I was only interested in what one person knew, and it had nothing to do with academic arrogance. Of course, I didn't know if this person was a scholar, or even a student. I knew nothing about him but his name, Bobby Bundy, and his address, a ramshackle rustic abode on College Avenue. Tommy told me the guy was one of Rose's artist pals and he dressed in black a lot, a goth-hipster-poseur, just my type. Rose had introduced them at a few of their backyard barbecues with the boys, and Bobby was always quiet and morose, alienated by the big bad athletes Tommy associated with. Rose had told Tommy that Bobby was gay, but in paranoiac hindsight Tommy wondered if that might have been a front. Rose often slept over at Bobby's after a night in the East Bay socializing with other artistic pals, and usually when Tommy was away on road trips with the ball club. She told Tommy she'd never slept with Bobby, but Tommy wanted me to find out if that was true. I didn't promise him anything, but I couldn't help wonder myself.

I was thinking a lot about what Doc had said, about whether I should even want Valerie back, if it turned out she and Rose were one.

I'd gone back later the previous night and shown him the photos. He was impressed by her beauty, and could understand the temptation, certainly, but admonished me to keep my guard up. Sure thing, I said. Like always.

I pulled up in front of the small house, which was dense with ivy and potted plants and stained glass windows and wind chimes, and went up to the door and knocked loudly. No answer right away. I rapped again and again and was almost ready to leave my card when the door opened slowly, like the lid to a crypt. It was about noon and overcast. Another storm was forecast. I felt like I was visiting the House of Dracula. I might've been. If there *were* vampires, you could be sure they'd wind up in Berkeley. And that Rose would be hanging out with them. Valerie had always had a fascination with the occult. But would she fuck Dracula? You bet.

"Whaddya want? You a cop or somethin?" said a whiny voice from within. From what I could see through the crack, Bobby was tall and thin, had black hair, a pasty complexion, wore glasses with frames too small for his face. He looked to be in his mid-twenties. He probably listened to The Cure or maybe he went the other way and was a Deadhead. He was too phony for The Cramps. In any case, I didn't like him and wanted to get this over with. I could tell right off the feeling was mutual.

"I'm a friend of Rose," I lied—well, sort of. "I've been out of town for a while and when I got back she'd moved out of her husband's place. He's not around either so I was wondering if you could—"

"Hey, man, who are you? You a cop?"

"No, man, I'm not a cop. Chill out. I'm a friend of Rose, like I said."

"How do you know me?" he said, his voice a little shaky. He was still hiding behind the door.

"I don't. But Rose mentioned you a few times. I dropped her off here once. Long time ago. After a party in Emeryville with some friends. She said you let her crash here once in a while."

"I don't remember that," he said quickly.

"How else would I know where you live?"

"That's what I'd like to know."

"Let me in and I'll explain it to you."

"No way, man. I don't know you. Just go away."

"Have you seen Rose lately?"

"No."

"You're not lying, are you?"

"Why would I lie?"

"I don't know. You tell me."

He was becoming increasingly exasperated. I like to exasperate people I don't like, which includes a vast portion of the human race. I guess I'm a misanthrope. That's what Valerie always said. Maybe that's why she left me.

"I'm closing the door now," he said, but I stuck my foot in and stopped it. "*Hey!*" he blurted. "You *are* a cop!"

"No, I told you. Just a friend. I have some important news for her that she has to get right away, or it could cost her. You can help if you just talk to me." My foot was starting to ache. I carry a .38 that my old man used to own on the NYPD. I keep it tucked behind me in the waistband of my pants. I was itching to use it on this punk, but I chose discretion.

"Man, what are you talking about?" he said, trying to force the door shut.

"Just open up, please? Or come out here on the porch. Please. Just for a minute."

There was a long pause while he considered his options. I was fingering the handle of my .38 when he wisely decided to open the door wide, and I went in.

"Thanks," I said through gritted teeth.

The place was dark and musty inside, just as I imagined. In my head Bauhaus was performing "Bela Lugosi's Dead." There was a small living room with a requisite sofa and coffee table covered with impressive tomes, hardwood floors with African-looking throw rugs, strange impressionistic artwork on the walls, and a few rooms in the back I had no desire to explore. The place reeked of marijuana and masturbation. When he closed the door behind me the sense of claustrophobia was suffocating. I felt trapped.

He was indeed dressed in black. His hair was a tangled mess, but I gathered he liked it that way. He looked anemic and pseudo-intellectual, and probably hated the sun as much as I did. We had that in common, and maybe more.

His wardrobe made me think of my own. I was wearing an early '60s Fedora, dressed in a tattered dark blue sharkskin suit with an unpressed white shirt and a skinny black tie, all of which I'd picked up in a thrift store on Haight Street. I looked like a cut-rate Tony Rome. I'm more fashion-conscious than I used to be. Valerie used to complain about my clothes all the time back in New York, when all I wore were jeans, a cheap aloha or T-shirt, and a bomber jacket. I still have my old aloha shirts, but no jeans or T-shirts, always prepared to run into her again and impress her with my sartorial evolution. I had on my best threads for this case since she was waiting for me at the end of it. Back in the day Valerie often dressed like a New Age hippie, with flower pattern dresses and sandals, or like a punk rock dominatrix in pastel tank tops and trashy leather skirts that drove me wild, so I never understood why she always gave me such a hard time. She did have a taste for elegance, even while she claimed to despise the pretentiousness of the upper class. Toward the end of our relationship she gradually began dressing like a film noir femme fatale in tight vintage dresses and high heels, and developed a taste for expensive craft cocktails in trendy nightclubs. Valerie talked the talk but didn't always walk the walk. I forgave her, though. Especially when I saw how those dresses conformed to her shapely hourglass figure. She'd fit right into the whole Cocktail Nation/neo-burlesque/retro-swing revival scene in San Francisco. In fact, maybe she was blending in right now.

Still, I couldn't help but wonder what she was doing with a phony like Bobby Bundy, and whether she approved of his wardrobe. They suited his personality—dark and dull.

"You got this place to yourself?" I asked him, more to make polite conversation than a burning desire to hear about his personal life. I felt awkward, to say the least. But I'm used to that by now, or should be. Most people I interrogate on cases are uncooperative assholes.

"None of your business," he said. He certainly wasn't making things any easier with his attitude. This was to be expected, and I guess I would act the same way toward some stranger intruding on my turf, asking a lot of questions, but it was still a pain in the ass. The PI racket isn't nearly as glamorous as I'd imagined it would be. Just a lot of legwork, mouth work, or *no* work. I needed a new life.

"I'm just here as a friend," I reminded him.

"If you were a real friend, you'd leave me alone. I got stuff to do. And I don't know you. What's your name?"

"Vic. Yours?"

"I thought Rose told you about me."

"She did, Bobby. Bobby Bundy. I was just being nice. I do that sometimes when I'm bored."

"If you're so bored, leave."

"Well, I won't be bored once you tell me where I can find Rose and deliver this message."

"I don't know. I haven't seen her in a long time. I'll give her the message if I do. What is it?"

"*Uh*-uh. I have to give it to her in private."

He made a *tsk* sound and walked back to the kitchen. His skin-tight black clothes and gangly manner made him look like a mutant insect. I scanned the living room as I followed him back to the kitchen and noticed a purse on the sofa, the floppy kind, and some women's magazines on the coffee table. Either Bobby was seriously confused about his gender, or he had a female roommate. Or an unseen visitor.

"So who's the girl?" I asked him in the kitchen, where he was pouring himself some herbal tea. He didn't offer me any, which was just as well. I'm a serious coffee man.

"What girl? I told you I haven't seen Rose in a long time. Now please, just leave me alone—"

"Some girl was here, or *is* here, unless you carry a purse and look up your horoscope in *Cosmo*."

He stared at me for a beat. I noticed some textbooks on the kitchen table. Physics and Astronomy. What a geek. Valerie wouldn't have been caught dead with a guy like this. Or so I thought.

"I have a live-in girlfriend, that okay with you?" he said. "You sure seem like a cop to me."

I shook my head. "I'm not."

"How do you know Rose again?"

"Old friend, I told you."

"And you know Tommy too?"

"Yep."

"Who did you know first?"

"Ahem . . . Rose. By far. I've known Rose for years."

"So have I, and she's never mentioned you. How come I've never met you?"

"We run in different circles, Bobby. Rose had a lot of friends in different places. That's just how she was."

"*Was?*"

"I told you. I've been out of town for a while. I miss her."

"So do I." He was mellowing out considerably. Must've been the "tea." He sat down at the table and appeared to be thinking about something distant.

"Tommy's an asshole," he said finally. "I'm glad she dumped him."

"So am I, confidentially." I sat opposite him.

"You are? Why? You want her for yourself?"

I have to say I was taken aback by that crack. "Where is that coming from? I'm a friend, that's all."

"You never had an affair with her?"

"That's none of *your* business, Bobby."

"Then you have." He sighed. "I knew it." He seemed tormented by the thought. I enjoyed it.

"What's it to you? Like you said, Tommy's an asshole."

"We could have—" he said softly.

"Excuse me? Could have what?"

"Slept together," he said in a whisper, as if contemplating it.

"Who? You and Tommy?"

He rolled his eyes at me. "Now *you're* beginning to seem like an asshole to me. What do you want, anyway?"

"I want to find Rose."

"That makes two of us. What's the message you want to give her?"

"That's personal, sorry."

"What, you tested for VD? HIV?"

"Maybe. Like I said, it's personal."

"Then why should I help you?" He was very agitated all of a sudden. "I would love to find Rose just for me."

"What about your live-in girlfriend? Would she like to find her too?"

"They're *friends,*" he said irritably. "So, yeah, she probably would."

"Then let's work on this together, shall we?"

"I don't like you."

"I didn't ask you to dance, Bobby. But we both like Rose, right? So let's just talk about her. Then I'll leave. Promise."

"What do you want from me, man?"

"Just tell me the last time you saw her, that's all."

"Why the hell should I?"

"Because if you don't, I'll drop the dime on your hemp habit."

He laughed. I didn't. "What? Pot? That's practically legal in Berkeley, man."

"Almost. Not quite."

He stared at me. "You *are* a cop."

"Your paranoia is beginning to make me suspicious." I pulled out my wallet and flashed my PI license at him. "I'm independent. Tommy hired me to find Rose. Let's cut the crap and get down to facts, okay, Bobby?"

"So you *don't* know her!" He actually seemed relieved.

"I didn't say that."

"Well *do* you?"

"Doesn't matter. I have to find her."

"Why? For Tommy?"

"He hired me. But there's more."

"What?"

"I can't tell you. Now talk to me or I'll call some friends of mine downtown and they'll come visit you sometime. They'd only do it to annoy you and only as a favor to me. Then again, if you don't tell me where Rose is, I might just kick your ass."

"Are you threatening me? You can't do that. I'll call the cops on you."

"Go ahead. There's a phone. But you won't have time to fumigate the place before they get here."

"This is ridiculous." He stood up, then sat back down. "I knew there was a reason why I didn't like you."

"Then again, I may kick your ass even if you *do* tell me where Rose is."

I'm not a big guy, five seven on a good day, but I'm solidly built and I have a lot of unresolved hostility. Also, I was carrying a piece, something I don't use except in extreme cases of intimidation or self-protection. It comes in handy a lot in Oakland, as does my fake police badge when I pretend I'm undercover. But with a geek like Bobby, a few choice clichés would be sufficient.

"You don't scare me," he lied.

"Just talk to me, Bobby."

"*What already!*"

"When was the last time you saw Rose? Start there and work backwards."

"I don't remember." He was a bad liar.

"Try."

He thought for a long time, sipping his "tea." Behind his glasses his beady eyes were darting around like pinballs. Then they obviously hit something, because his face lit up. I thought he was going to tilt. "I remember," he seemed to be saying to himself. "But if I tell you, you promise not to tell Tommy?"

"What? I told you, he hired me."

"Then forget it. I don't want Tommy to know where she is. And neither does she. So forget it. Call the cops. I don't care. I can't betray Rose like that."

I didn't say anything for a few moments. I wished I hadn't told him I was a detective hired by Tommy. I wasn't thinking clearly, trying to hurry this along so I could find Rose and confront her with her own past, embodied by myself. I'd screwed up already, but I kicked in damage control anyway, to see what I could salvage. "You're in love with her, aren't you, Bobby?"

"I thought I was. Why?" He wouldn't give me eye contact.

"What if I told you . . . I was, too?"

He scoffed at me. "You? You're only in love with yourself."

"Not only," I said. "The truth is . . . I know who Rose really is."

Bobby studied my face now, searching for sincerity. "What is that supposed to mean?"

"It means Rose isn't the person she claims to be. At least this is what I believe. How long have you known Rose?"

"Three years, about. I don't know."

"How'd you meet her?"

"On campus. She was taking extension courses in creative writing. So was I."

I pointed out the science books on the table.

"Those aren't mine," he said. "They're Lisa's. My girlfriend."

"Does she know?"

"Know what?"

"That you're in love with Rose?"

"She knows that I was. But she also knows Rose and I were friends. Nothing ever happened. It was torture, and it eventually led to a blowup. That's why I don't see her anymore. Understand?" He sat back down now.

I nodded. "Tommy thinks you're gay," I said.

"Fuck Tommy, fucking macho asshole."

"Well, there's that option. He also said Rose told him that so he wouldn't think anything was going on between you two."

He liked that. He started laughing. I didn't like his laugh. I was glad when he stopped. "That Rose. I guess he must've thought *all* of her friends were drag queens, then. Let me tell you—they *weren't*. She had some friends in the Castro and Noe Valley, and I think she had a fling with a lesbian once or twice, but Rose likes *men*. She likes sex. With *men*. Get it?"

"Got it. Hope to get more of it. So what are you telling me, though? That Rose screwed around on Tommy?"

"Big time. And I hope you tell him."

"If he asks. Should I tell him who told me, too?"

"*No!*" He stood up again, then sat back down. "I shouldn't even be talking to you."

"Then why *are* you? You scared of me?"

He rolled his eyes.

"I think it's because you want to talk to someone about Rose, because you got her on the brain. You're hooked on her, and you don't know what to do about it."

"What're you, a dick or a shrink?"

A shrinking dick, I thought. "Just a guy who wants to find Rose. Like you."

"Is this about Rose not being who she says she is?"

"I can't get into it right now. But tell me more about you and Rose. You say you could've slept together but never did. Why not? Obviously her marriage was not an issue." The idea of Valerie sleeping around made me nauseated, but I fought it. I was working.

"*Because* I loved her and she knew it. She only likes casual sex with men she'll never see again. She only thought of me as a friend. I told her how I felt and she felt bad, but she didn't return my feelings and she told me if I couldn't take the tension I should just bail."

"Why didn't you?"

"I just couldn't. I still wanted to be around her. She has that effect on a lot of people. She has this love of life that's infectious. And she's a very talented poet and painter. She's . . . stimulating. Have you met her or not?"

"I think so. In her previous life."

"Oh, so you're into that too, huh? Far East philosophy?"

I shrugged. "As far east as New York, anyway."

"Is that where you're from?"

I nodded. "That's where I met her."

"Then we're not talking about the same person."

"I think we are."

"Rose never said anything about going back east or ever living there."

"I bet there's a lot she never told you."

"I doubt it. She told me everything. We confided in each other. She was my best friend, so what do you know?" He was getting all worked up now. But he was talking. I'd pushed a button. I have a way of doing that sometimes. It comes with experience. But I'm only good at this on a case, with strangers. In intimate relationships I have a way of pushing the *wrong* buttons. Maybe if I just treated relationships like cases things would go smoother, because I'd be more cool and detached and women would find me tough and mysterious. Maybe next time. Rose already had my number, if she was Valerie, and I believed she was. I'd never met another woman who had such a lasting impact on men. She was like a goddamn virus.

"All I know," I said, "is that Rose is missing, probably somewhere in the vicinity, and a lot of people want to talk to her, but no one more than me."

"Why?" Bobby demanded. "She commit a crime or somethin'?"

"In a way," I said. "Nothing illegal, really. She couldn't be booked on anything, though apparently she's racking up quite a record for herself."

"Of what?"

"Broken hearts. She's leaving 'em in her trail like breadcrumbs. And the first crumb led me to you."

"I bet *you're* the first crumb."

"Maybe. If she's the person I think she is."

"You're really starting to freak me out, man. Who *are* you?"

"Vic Valentine, Private Eye." God, I always love saying that. I jump at the chance.

"You gotta be putting me on. This is a gag, right? Tommy's idea of a joke."

"Nope. Straight up. He hired me to find her. But fuck him, Bobby. I'm in this for myself. Now tell me what you know about Rose or I'll break your nose. I'm not kidding." I stared him down and he grew visibly uncomfortable. "I'm not here as a detective. I'm here as a person. A desperate person. Sure, after I leave you bleeding on the kitchen floor, you could call the cops on me, try to have me charged with assault, but I could always say you took a swing at me first. It happens on these cases. All the time. I'm known in just about every precinct within a hundred-mile radius of the Bay. I've never spent a night in the can, mainly because the people filing the charges are punks like yourself." I stood up now, glowering with mendacity. It never failed to amaze me what people will believe if you say it with unflinching authority. Bobby was shaking by now. "You know the difference between a punk and a bum, Bobby?" He just glared at me and shook his head. "No," he squeaked.

"Well, according to Frank Sinatra—you've heard of him—according to Frank, there are two kinds of guys in the world: punks and bums. I may not be as good as the Chairman, but I can size up a punk or a bum within seconds by now. A bum is someone who knows he's a loser and doesn't really care. He has no self-esteem. A punk, on the other hand, is someone who tries to overcompensate his inferiority complex with cheap bravado. He pretends he's something he isn't."

"Which are you?" he shot at me. I was surprised, but I rolled with it.

"Oh, I'm a punk," I said. "I have no qualms about that. And you're a punk. So what we have here is two punks. But the difference between you and me is that I listen to Frank Sinatra every day, and you don't."

"Which is he?" Bobby whined.

I moved closer and got in his face. "Neither. He's the Chairman of the Board. He's above all this. That's why he does what he does and we do what we do. But my point is that Frank would probably be on my side in this. And Frank would tell me to beat the hell out of you until you told me what I wanted to know."

"You're crazy," he whispered.

"There're two kinds of women in the world, too," I continued, unabated, "and we both know what kind Rose is. But we forgive her, don't we, Bobby? Because we know at heart she's just a nice little farm girl, until something or someone turned her around and made her what she is today." Bobby was sweating now, and I was loving it. I went on, making it up as I went. I had him right where I wanted him. "Now if you don't tell me where she is, or where you *think* she is, I swear to God, I'll do something very unprofessional to you. And Frank Sinatra and the cops will back me up. Oh, and you're right about one thing. I *am* crazy." He believed that more than he ever believed anything.

"L.A," he whispered. "I ran into her in Santa Cruz when I was there with Lisa about six months ago, and she said she was going to L.A."

"You're lying. Tommy got a postcard from her postmarked San Francisco six weeks ago."

"Then she came back. All she said was that she was going down there to visit some friends."

"Who?" I asked.

He stared at me, glassy-eyed.

"*Who?*"

"She . . . She has a kid down there by some other guy. I don't know the dude, I swear. But I know she has a kid. She showed me a picture. I swear that's all I know, man. Now leave me alone."

My adrenaline rush went down the drain. "She has a kid?" I backed off Bobby and sat back down. "You sure?"

He nodded.

"How old?"

"Not very. One, I think, by now."

"Who's the father?"

"Some guy. Older guy. She met him a few times when she went with Tommy on the road to L.A. She would screw him in the hotel room while Tommy was playing ball. They'd both be balling at the same time, but not with each other."

"So who's the guy, Bobby? His name."

"I don't know. He's a sculptor or something. I think he lives in Venice. In a way, I *want* Tommy to know, because it would kill him. Tommy's sterile, you know. He and Rose couldn't have kids and she wanted kids real bad. That was her dream in life, to raise a kid. I really wanted to give her one, but she wouldn't let me. She kind of *let* herself get knocked up by this guy in L.A. The guy is like fifty-something and had never had children, so he went for it.

The baby lives with this old dude and some other woman, though. I don't understand it. It's a weird set-up. Rose told me she was going down to L.A. to get her baby and raise it herself now that she is free. Everyone knew about it except Tommy, that bastard. I hope you tell him. His ego will be shattered. Serve him right."

"It smells like sour grapes in here," I said, sniffing the air for effect.

"It didn't before you showed up," he shot back.

"How the hell could Rose hide her pregnancy from Tommy?"

"That's one reason she left, man. She was three months pregnant when she split."

"And he didn't know?"

"I don't think so. She didn't want to hurt him. She's left him before. Lots of times. They had this open relationship, sort of. He would bring home women and fuck them in their own bed, while Rose was out with friends. She'd go home and find some groupie walking around the house naked."

"How do you know?"

"She told me. She didn't care much, since she fucked around, too, though Tommy didn't have a clue. He's *such* an idiot. I never knew what she saw in him, except she said he was great in bed, and that she knew him in a past life and had some karma to work out with him. *I* don't know. I started to get into that Far East trip when I knew her, but after being with Lisa, who's such a scientist, I got out of it again. I think I was only into it so Rose would like me more. It didn't work."

"You said Rose didn't want to leave Tommy, so that's why the baby was being raised in L.A."

"At first. All the other times Rose left, me and her friends were glad, but we didn't push her. She would leave town and write Tommy letters that she sent to us so we could send them to Tommy, so they'd be postmarked locally. She went to New Mexico a lot—Santa Fe—just by herself. Or to L.A. When she got pregnant she became confused, and almost had an abortion, but the guy said it was okay. Rose wants to be a mother but still have her freedom. I tried telling her that was impossible. She didn't want to lose Tommy, but she knew the truth would kill him. So she left him, and the baby was born down there, I think. Then she came back here. That's when I ran into her in Santa Cruz with Lisa."

"Was she living there?"

"No. In The City. She loves it here, but that postcard you got, that you know about, could have been sent from one of her friends here. She could still be in L.A., man. With her baby. But I don't know. I haven't heard from her since Santa Cruz. I lied when I said Lisa and her were friends. Lisa is very threatened by her."

"I'm in shock," I said softly.

"You don't seem so tough now."

"I could still kick your ass," I reminded him. "But later. Right now, I'm just not in the mood." I got up, ready to get the hell out of there. "Where's Lisa now, anyway?"

"At work. Why?"

"Just curious. Where does she work?"

"None of your business."

I shrugged. "You're right. I don't really care, anyway. But you're lucky."

"I am? Why?"

"You're not alone, kid. It's hell out there."

He didn't say anything. I started to leave, then he said, "You really love her, huh?"

I shrugged again.

"So who is it you think she is, anyway?"

I opened the door and breathed in some fresh, cool air. "I don't know anymore," I said, and I left.

6

The Big Scream

NO MATTER HOW MUCH you think you know, there's always something going on that you don't—but should. So you can plan your life accordingly. In my case, I never find the missing piece of significant information until it's too late. Like with Flora, going off to Europe with the sax player while I was investing all this time and energy in winning her over. And now this. Rose had run off and had another man's baby while married. I kept staring at the white gown photo, wondering if this was indeed my Valerie. My Valerie. What a joke. Why did I need this? I thought about giving Tommy his money back and telling him Rose was dead. I was beginning to die inside all over again, killed twice by the same woman. And I couldn't even call it murder, really. I set myself up. It was suicide. I may as well have followed in my brother's footsteps and jumped off a goddamn bridge.

After leaving the House of Dracula I'd driven down to Telegraph Avenue and sat in a café, sipping a latte and wondering what to do next. I looked at street people and saw a possible future for me. I couldn't stay in this line of work, especially now. It was killing me. The main reason I'm in it (besides being otherwise unemployable) is because of my connections with the SFPD. An old friend of my father lived in San Francisco and was a police captain. He'd helped me obtain my PI license when I'd expressed interest in the profession after moving west, initially aiming for Portland or Seattle since I dig that cool, cloudy climate. But I'd missed my target by a few hundred miles. If I'd wound up in one of my initially intended destinations, none of this would be happening. Fate.

I became a PI partly because my old man was gunned down under mysterious circumstances and I wanted to find out why. I got nowhere with my amateur "investigations" but was already hooked by the notion. I didn't want to work for wages, and I knew something about surveillance from Pop and his cronies. My column was canceled and my writing gigs suddenly dried up, so I decided to try my luck out west. I settled in San Francisco because I was told there were more opportunities there for writers. I was misinformed. There's a glut of aspiring authors and journalists in the Bay Area, and the competition was just too fierce. I couldn't find work in my chosen field, so I looked up my father's friend on the force and he helped me set up my own independent business. I could've just joined the SFPD (or NYPD, for that matter), but we all knew I wouldn't last long. I'm not a team player. I hate taking orders or conforming to a system. Plus I'm too chickenshit to be a real cop. Soon after helping me out, this police captain pal of Pop croaked from a heart attack, and I was left completely alone in The City.

I stuck with the PI gig until I no longer had to supplement my income with odd jobs, some writing, some menial. I met Doc Schlock on a case, actually, one of my first. I was working out of a cheap hotel room in the Tenderloin at the time. He ran a small cult video store in Oakland. He called me one day after seeing my ad in the *Tribune*. It was a simple case. He wanted me to find his mother. I found her the same day, wandering the mean streets of West Oakland, delirious. She was old and going senile. I retrieved her from danger and Doc and I have been best pals since.

When he made his move to The City, he told me about a vacant studio above The Drive-Inn, his new name for an old pub he'd acquired, which he was in the process of renovating. The rest you know already. Again, it was Fate, I guess. Doc had reported his mother missing to the cops before calling me, but had no luck. I found her within hours. Things like that made me believe in Fate even before this Rose business. I felt compelled to continue my search for her in spite of the encroaching agony.

I left Berkeley in the late afternoon and returned to The Drive-Inn. Doc wasn't there working the bar, one of his hired hands was, a sexy young punker chick with lots of messy green hair, not her natural color, I surmised. Her skin was like ivory, she was built like Yvonne "Batgirl" Craig, and she wore lots of mascara and lipstick and fishnet stockings with miniskirts and skimpy blouses showing off plenty of creamy cleavage. She screamed trouble from head to toe. I like danger, but not when it's that obvious. Her name was Monica.

"How about a drink, Vic?" she asked, snapping her gum seductively. "I'll make it nice and stiff."

"Uh, that's okay, maybe later. Here." I handed her a note to give to Doc explaining I'd be down in L.A. for a few days and I'd talk to him when I got back. Monica took the note and gave me a wink I felt in my crotch.

Then I called Tommy Dodge, who answered his phone on the first ring. He sounded bombed, but that was his business. "Tommy. Vic. I just talked to your buddy over in Berkeley."

"The faggot?" He belched. A true American archetype.

"No, he's straight, turns out, but he never boffed Rose. He wanted to but she turned him down."

"How come? *Gotta* be gay then."

"Because she loves *you*, Tommy boy."

He bought it. "Oh. So where the fuck is she then?"

"L.A. maybe. I'm going to check it out. I'll catch a red-eye flight tonight. It'll be on your bill, plus car rental."

"*Wait* a minute. L.A.? What the fuck is she doing down there?"

"That's what I intend to find out, Tommy. If you still want me to."

"What makes you think she's down there?"

"Bobby told me."

"But he's a fag, what does he know?"

I sighed. "Whatever. Listen, that's a pretty good lead after only one day's work. So you should feel encouraged."

He didn't respond right away. Then he said, "I guess. So what are you gonna do when you find her? Fuck her?"

Whoa. I hoped that was the booze talking. "Uh . . . no. I'll just call you, of course."

"I want you to put her on the horn right away. You hear me? As soon as you find her, Valentine. You got that?"

"I know my job. So no beef about the extra expenses, right? Tommy?"

"Huh? No. Whatever it costs, whatever it takes. Just *do* it. I don't care if you gotta fly to Tim-buk-fuckin'-tu, just find her and bring her home to daddy." He hung up on me. I had the idea he was getting ready to hurl anyway. *Whew.*

Poor bastard. I almost felt bad when I hung up. There was no way I was telling him if I found Rose. Not right away, anyhow. The first priority on my agenda was to talk to her myself, find out why she'd left *me.* My second plan was to win her back for *myself.* If that failed, then I'd go straight to plan three, which was to hand her over to Tommy, then head straight to the nearest bridge.

I called the airline and booked a red-eye to LAX. I still didn't even know the name of Rose's baby's father, since Bobby couldn't— or wouldn't—tell me, but I had another idea.

The daycare center Tommy had told me about, where Rose had worked, was over in Sausalito. It was 4:30 p.m. when I called them and they closed at 5:30. I told a woman on the phone I was a PI and needed to talk to her about a former employee, Rose Dodge.

She'd never heard of a Rose Dodge, but she had once employed, briefly, a Rose *Myers*.

That settled it. Valerie's last name was Myers.

I told the woman it was of vital importance I speak to her right away about Rose. She couldn't hang on the phone since it was a busy time of day, but she promised to wait for me to show up and we could chat in person after the place closed up.

It was rush hour on the Golden Gate Bridge, so I didn't get into Sausalito until almost 6 p.m. It was drizzling lightly, and the ominous cloud cover promised a downpour.

On the way over I thought about what I would say to Rose, I mean Valerie, once I caught up with her. Rose Dodge. That was not the name of an artist. No wonder Rose kept her last name. But what was her first name, really? Valerie or Rose? Or something else, even? I decided that would be my first question to her. The rest would just come to me.

I was practically hyperventilating by the time I got to the daycare center on the far end of Bridgeway Drive, past the restaurants and boutiques and pier with its quaint houseboats. I thought the woman in charge, a Mrs. Parsons, would be able to help me because Tommy had told me Rose was still working there the day she left, as far as he knew. She had left work that same morning, in fact. Or so she had told him. I'd find out soon enough.

I realize now how impulsive I was behaving, booking a flight to L.A. before I even had a solid lead. And Rose must have sent that Alcatraz postcard from within The City, personally, because Tommy confirmed the handwriting. It also looked like Valerie's handwriting, I realized later. But at the time, I just wasn't thinking clearly. People in my profession aren't always as calm and collected as they seem in the movies. We're human. We screw up. But things went my way anyway. I had this faith in Fate that was guiding me. Whatever it was that was steering my course, I hit pay dirt at the daycare center.

I had the white gown photo with me, which I kept partly to show people on the case, and mostly for me to dream about. I showed it to Mrs. Parsons, who had long silver hair but only looked about forty or so, rather attractive in an aging hippie sort of way, and she instantly identified the girl in the photo as Rose. We were standing inside the daycare center, which was small but cozy, and gazing out at the rain.

"Her husband kept calling us frantically the day after she quit," she told me, "but all I could tell him was that Rose had left without giving any notice. To be honest, I didn't even know she was married. I was quite stunned."

"Rose never mentioned Tommy Dodge to you?"

"No, never. I knew she was pregnant, but—"

"*You* knew?"

"Well, certainly. She was three months along when she left."

"She ever say anything about the father?"

"Yes. But . . . I don't want to betray her confidence, although she didn't tell me like she had anything to hide—"

"Mrs. Parsons, you can imagine the emotional state of Mr. Dodge. It is very important I find her. To be honest? I don't plan on giving Mr. Dodge all the facts. I mean about the baby and all. He just wants to know she's okay."

"Well, I know he's a sculptor, his name is . . . let me think. Luke Bradshaw. No! Brandon. That's it. He lives in Venice. I know because he called here for her once, and she told me his name so I'd know it if he ever called again. But he never did. And she told me they weren't married, so . . ."

"Hmm. Any idea why she'd confide in you?"

"We were friends. She was on a spiritual path, and so am I, and we share a love for all children." She spread her palms.

I nodded, swallowing back puke. "I see. Mrs. Parsons, when he contacted you, did Mr. Dodge give you any indication that he knows about this child in L.A.?"

"No, not at all."

"And you knew he wasn't the father?"

"He just claimed to be her husband, he gave me his name, which wasn't her name, and he told me he was a baseball player. She'd never even mentioned him to me. She only talked about Luke, and even then, very little."

"Is she . . . how should I put this . . . emotionally attached?"

"In love? With Luke?"

I nodded. She saw right through me.

"I don't know." She smiled. Then after a pause, she said, "Are you sure Tommy Dodge is the only man who wants to find her?"

"No, I do. It's my job."

"I understand," she said, still smiling.

I picked up the familiar odor of incense. Valerie used to burn it all the time, especially when she first got into the Hindu thing, as I called it. It wasn't really Hinduism, exactly. She'd just met some people in Greenwich Village who turned her on to Indian philosophy, and she selected whatever parts of it appealed to her and adopted them. That's how she was. That's how all people are. They choose whatever is comfortable for them, whatever answers their own personal questions, and then they just believe in it. Personally, my faith in anything metaphysical had died out until now. I was on a quest for the truth, and I felt guided somehow. It's difficult to explain unless it's happened to you. In retrospect there was a chance I was forcing this faith in order to survive, to have something to live for, like everyone else seems to. It doesn't matter now.

Mrs. Parson was exceptionally nice to me, and offered me some refreshments. We chatted a bit more, and I learned her husband was a carpenter and she had three kids. I told her I envied her husband.

"Why?" she said, eyes twinkling flirtatiously.

"He has a very beautiful wife and a nice family," I said. She was pretty sexy, actually. Even while talking to her politely I couldn't help but wonder what kind of lover she was. She was dressed in loose-fitting clothes but I could tell she had a knockout figure. I kept flashing on the rape scene in *Straw Dogs,* but fought it. I really, really needed to get laid, but not like that.

"Maybe what you're looking for is just around the corner," she said sweetly, making me feel slightly guilty over my lurid imagination. "You never know."

"Yeah, whatever." I shrugged and clogged up my mental sewer. Enough vulnerability in front of a stranger, anyway. "I should get going. Thanks for your help. Luke Brandon in Venice. I'll find him."

"Do me a favor. If you see Rose, please don't tell her I told you," she said, leading me out.

"Mrs. Parsons, why did you tell me?"

"I just have a feeling about you," she said. "I trust my instincts. Just don't make me regret it."

"Oh, I won't. Thanks again. Good night."

When I walked back into the cold, windy night, the lights of Sausalito were glimmering brightly in the rain. The Christmas decorations seemed especially appropriate over here in Marin, which is very woodsy and has a New Age-meets-old-world feeling that reminds me of Christmas any time I'm here, throughout the year. But the wet neon also made me feel sad and lonesome, and I couldn't wait to get the hell out of there and take a nap at home before catching my flight.

I packed two of my vintage sharkskin suits, one blue, one gray, and my '40s gumshoe-style trench coat. Apparently it was raining in L.A. as well. Fucking *Blade Runner* for real. I brought my Don Johnson Ray-Ban Wayfarers anyway, because I liked the way they looked on me. I always wore them, even in dense fog, especially while out on a case. I don't like people to see my eyes. Inside I'm a marshmallow, Valerie had told me. A burnt marshmallow. I didn't want anyone to know that, and my eyes would give me away.

I got the usual hassle at airport security about my gun, but I had allowed time for it. My late police captain friend had supplied me with a travel permit for it, but I had to "prove" I was on official business. This usually meant running a bullshit check on my PI license, then calling someone at SFPD for verification (more friends of my old man, though strangers to me—favors from beyond the grave). If none of this worked, I pulled my phony cop badge, which was riskier. But it usually worked.

An hour and ten minutes after leaving SF International I was in the City of Angels. It was raining lightly, less so than in the Bay Area, but the cold front was probably following me down the coast. At least the smog would be cleared out. Fog, good. Smog, bad.

I rented a dark blue BMW since Tommy was footing the bill anyway, and drove to the nearest motel, checked in, and slept until around 8 a.m. Then I went out and drove into town and ate at Rae's coffee shop on Pico in Santa Monica before heading down to Venice.

Venice is sort of like Berkeley on the beach. The houses are old and filled with struggling artists and potted plants. Cafés are abundant, and the politics lean decidedly to the left. The main difference was the women—much prettier and sexier, wearing bikinis even in cool weather, riding around on roller-skates and bikes, usually surrounded by hunky males, though. I know I sound superficial. But at least I'm also transparent.

I didn't pay much attention to anybody as I stood in a phone booth on the pier and looked through the phonebook for Luke Brandon. *Bingo.* I dialed his number right away. It was almost 9:30 a.m. by now, and the rain had stopped and the sun was barely breaking through the gray skies.

"Hello?" said a friendly, masculine voice I hated immediately.

"Mr. Brandon?"

"Yes?" he said tentatively.

"This is, um, a friend of Rose?"

Long pause. "Yes?"

"I'm in town for a few days and she gave me your phone number to look her up." I felt very awkward, unlike when I usually pull this ploy.

"Who is this?" he asked politely.

"My name is, uh . . . Vic. I'm a friend from up in the Bay Area, and—"

"Where are you now, Vic?"

"On the pier. Where are you?"

He actually gave me his address, which was only a few blocks away. He didn't mention whether Rose was there, but it almost didn't matter. In the background I'd heard a scream. A baby scream. I had to see this child for myself. It was a piece of Rose I could never share with her, the result of a bond with this Luke loser that would last forever. She was permanently linked with Luke because of this kid. They had shared the ultimate human experience, blending their bodies and producing something magical and sacred, something I would have loved to have shared with her, if only she had given me the chance.

By the time I reached his house, which was tiny and surrounded by a picket fence and a massive flower garden, I had worked myself into quite a frenzy. I was in no shape to greet anyone, but I knocked on the door anyway and a tall, robust, fifty-something guy answered. He reminded me a bit of Kirk Douglas, actually—squinty eyes and cleft chin and wavy gray hair. He had his shirt off and was wearing jogging shorts. He was very muscular and appeared to be sweating, like he'd been working out. He wasn't breathing heavily, though. He was very relaxed as he shook my hand and led me inside. He even smiled as he shut the door and then hit me squarely on the jaw, sending me reeling into a weight machine in the middle of the room.

As he came at me again I got up and took a swing at him but he ducked and then connected with a one-two combo to my rib cage and face. As I went down the second time I could already feel my left eye swelling, and I was spitting blood. He really seemed to be having fun until I managed to reach for my .38 and stick it in his smug, stupid face. He chilled out quickly and I backed him up to the wall, the barrel sticking in his left nostril. I could only see him out of my right eye. He was grinning. I couldn't hear a baby now, only the sound of my own heartbeat.

"This how you treat all of Rose's friends?" I asked him, cocking the piece for effect, though he didn't seem fazed.

"Only you," he said proudly. "I had an idea you'd show up."

"How the hell is that?"

"One of Rose's friends up in Berkeley called me yesterday, said you'd been there pushing him around. He asked me to give you a warm welcome for him."

"Bobby," I said.

"Yeah."

"He said he didn't know you."

"Surprise! He lied. Now put that mean thing down, will you? I'm through welcoming you, anyway. Really. You got the gun, right? I'm unarmed. Now just put that mean thing away."

Trying to stare him down with my one good eye, ignoring my physical pain, I uncocked the .38 and stuck it back in my waistband. Luke was still smiling like he knew something I didn't. From another room came a female voice.

"Is it okay to come out now?" she said.

"Yeah, hon," Luke said, and from the bedroom emerged a thirty-ish Asian woman, dressed in sweats, her long black hair in a bun. She was very pretty but cold, and she eyed me with steely suspicion. "Sweetheart, this is Vic. Vic Valentine, Private Eye. Like Kookie on *77 Sunset Strip*, only shorter. He says he's a friend of Rose. Vic, this is April. That's not her real name. I forget her real name. Couldn't pronounce it anyway. But I met her in April, so now that's what I call her."

"Charming," I said. Then I heard the baby in the bedroom, crying out for attention.

"Rose's kid," I said patly.

"Mine too," he said.

"Where's Rose?"

"She doesn't want you to know," he said.

"How do you know?"

"Bobby told her you were looking for her, and she freaked out. She doesn't want Tommy to know about Samson."

"Samson?"

"That's our son. April's, too. We share."

I was feeling dizzy and unattractive. April kept staring at me with apparent disgust. "What the hell are you looking at?" I snapped at her.

"Watch your tone with my wife, Vic," Luke said.

"Your *wife*? This is getting complicated."

"Not really. April can't have kids. Had her tubes tied back wherever she's from because she was a hooker when she was a kid. She regrets it now, but too late. I made her a citizen and all she can offer in return is mind-blowing head, which works for me. But not a family. Rose wanted a kid, I wanted a kid, April wanted a kid. What's so fucking complicated about that?"

"Tommy wanted a kid, too."

"Who gives a shit about that drunken bum?"

"Rose does. She's still married to him."

"Only on paper. She can't stand the bum now."

"She likes punks now, I take it."

"Bobby told me about that." He laughed. "Jesus. Frank fucking Sinatra. Who listens to that has-been any more?

"I do."

"You're an anachronism, Vic. Look at you. A walking fucking cliché. Vic Valentine, Private Eye. What a fuckin' joke. Talk about a bum. Which am I?"

"Neither. You're a jerk-off."

He laughed uproariously. He was so obnoxious I seriously considered blowing his brains out there and then. Big loss to the planet that would've been. I couldn't help but stand there and wonder why Rose kept getting involved with these lame-brained jock bastards. Luke was big, like Tommy Dodge, and was probably hung to his knees, had to wrap it around his waist. Other than that, I couldn't see it. I never thought Valerie was as shallow as this. But here he was, the father of her only child. I couldn't understand it.

"I want you to leave," April said to me suddenly, her disdain as thick as her accent.

"Not even a cup of coffee?" I said.

Luke laughed again. "Sure. Make him some coffee, and put some brandy in it, make a man out of him. Sit down, Vic. You look like shit. Go on, sit down. I won't hit you any more. You're too pathetic."

I was feeling pretty weak, so I plopped down on an easy chair and looked at the sculptures, mostly unfinished, around the room. The place was more like an artist's studio than a house. The sculpted figures looked like twisted human beings in torment, many of them copulating couples. The effect was surreal. I felt like I was going to pass out, but that would've been dangerous under the circumstances. April hadn't gone to make my coffee yet. She'd gone into the bedroom and quieted the baby. Samson. I guess if he had a sister they'd call her Delilah.

"What is April, Chinese?" I asked.

"Filipino, I think," Luke said, going into the kitchen and fixing brandy-laced coffee. "Met her in Kauai soon after the baby was born. I hired her to come up to my room and suck my cock in celebration. Didn't want to put my dick in a whore since I was a father now and all. She was so damn good at it I decided to keep her. I had her checked out by a doctor, then married her on the spot, brought her back here, and she's been keeping my pipes squeaky clean ever since. Cream?"

"Ah . . . no thanks, Brandy's enough. So now April is Samson's surrogate mother, as well as your resident skank, right? A live-in nanny who puts out. How convenient."

"Watch your filthy mouth. That's Samson's other mom, like you said."

"Bobby told me Rose was coming back here to be with her kid."

"Sometimes she does. She's a wandering spirit, that one. Best lay I ever had too." I cringed. He looked out to see if April had heard that last line, but she was still in the bedroom. "April is the second—a hot piece of ass and a wonderful mother. Two beautiful women. I'm a lucky man."

"You still fucking Rose?" I asked him.

"Shut up," he said as April came into the room, holding Samson, who was calm now. He was a big kid, and had Valerie's auburn hair, and big blue eyes. I felt oddly removed, and depressed. He did look like Rose.

"Nice looking kid," I said sadly. Luke served me some spiked coffee. "You *are* a lucky guy," I told him.

"What do you want with us?" April asked flatly. She seemed like a very bitter person. From what I already knew of her history, I couldn't blame her.

"Nothing with *you*. Tommy hired me to find Rose."

"Why?" she asked.

"He loves her. He's a wreck without her."

"Good!" Luke exclaimed, pacing around the room, massaging his pecs and fondling his genitals. What a he-man. "He deserves to suffer, after the way he treated her."

"What are you talking about?" I said.

"That fucker screwed around on her every chance he got. Then if she complained, he beat the living daylights out of her. If I ever meet him, I'll make him shit his own teeth."

"You want his address?" I said.

Luke laughed again. What a happy guy. "Naw. I don't get up there much anymore."

"Sure," I said. "So Rose is on to me, huh."

"Thanks to that pussy," Luke said.

"Bobby? I take it you don't get along with him."

"I've never actually met him. He used to call Rose here after the baby was born. She still stays with him when she's up there . . ." He caught himself. But it was too late. "I mean, she *used* to. Not anymore."

"She in L.A.?"

"I told you, I'm not going to tell you."

"What if I asked you at gunpoint?"

He laughed. He really got a big bang out of me. "You'd have to shoot me, and you wouldn't, so forget it."

I sipped my coffee thoughtfully for a few moments, watching the baby, who was staring at me from April's arms. "Does Rose know my name?" I asked.

"I guess. What's the difference? She know you personally?"

"I think she does."

"You *think* she does?"

"She used to, before she changed."

"Changed? From what to what?"

"Never mind." I stood up, feeling wobbly. "I gotta go."

"What's the rush, Vic?" Luke said. "Stay a while. You just got here."

"I get the distinct impression I'm not welcome," I said, pointing to my swollen left eye and bloody mouth.

He snapped his fingers at April. "Hon, get him a cold towel. C'mon, *move* it." She set the baby down and complied. "What's Vic stand for, anyway, Victor?" Luke asked me.

"Today? Victim," I said.

More laughter. What a pain in the ass. "You know? You're a funny guy."

"How'd you meet Rose, anyway?"

"At a ball game. Dodger Stadium. Met her at the hot dog stand, took her to my van, and fucked her in the parking lot. Then we became an item whenever she was in town. Now enough of that," he said as April returned with a cool towel, which she gave to me. I sat back down as I wiped the bloody residue from my face and gently patted my left eye. "Sorry I slugged you so hard. You're not as bad as Bobby made you out to be. How'd you find us so damn quick?"

"Woman Rose used to work for gave me your name."

"Yeah? That was sloppy of Rose to do that. But maybe in the end, she *does* want to be found."

I went into my pocket and handed him one of my cards. "Do me a favor. If you see her, just give her this. Tell her if she feels like it, to give me a call sometime. *Any* time. Tell her this card is like a coupon that will never expire."

He thought for a second, then took the card. "Okay," he said. "I'll do that, Vic. But I doubt she'll call you."

"Whatever," I said, putting down the bloody towel and rising to leave. I headed for the door, and Luke followed me.

"You gonna tell Tommy about Samson?" Luke asked, barring the front door.

"No," I said. "No point to it. He just wants to see Rose. I'll let *her* tell him."

"Promise?"

I nodded.

He slapped me on the shoulder, and I flinched. "You know something? I like you."

"What a relief," I said as I walked out. Just as I did, the baby Samson let out a big scream, but the door slammed behind me and there was nothing I could do about it.

I checked into a motel on Ocean Avenue in Santa Monica, just to relax and get cleaned up. I showered and stared at my black eye and bruised lip. All in the name of love. If Rose knew my name, she knew who I was, and either would or would not want to see me. The fact that we both lived in the same city would be too much of a coincidence for her to ignore. But maybe she was too ashamed to see me, or maybe she just didn't care anymore. With all this fucking she'd been doing, I couldn't have been more than a dim memory. There was no guarantee she'd been carrying a torch for me like I was for her all these years. In fact, it looked like this had been an unrequited affair from the start. She never loved me. She used me, for whatever purpose, and then went on and used other men, like a leech woman from a B movie. A real femme fatale. Doc was right. I should've forgotten about her a long time ago. I should've told Tommy what I knew, even about Samson, then let him do what he wanted, hand it back to him.

But I didn't. I had to see this through to the end, bitter as it may be. There was too much coincidence here for me to ignore, too. There was a reason for it, I was convinced. I was a pawn in someone else's game. I had no choice.

Since this whole trip was on Tommy's expense account anyway, I decided to enjoy myself and have a nice little vacation on his dime, and maybe stake out the Brandon house in Venice to see if Rose showed up. I called Tommy from my motel room and told him I had a line on Rose but it would take a while to follow it through, so I'd be down here for a few days. He was loaded and barely understood me, so it worked out.

Then I drove into Hollywood and treated myself to dinner and martinis at Musso and Frank's, a real class joint and a local landmark, then got drunk in this dark bar nearby called the Burgundy Room that had a picture of Frank Sinatra behind the bar and lots of his music on the jukebox. I played "Witchcraft" and "One for My Baby" a few times, flirting with slinky women but getting nowhere. My black eye and fat lip didn't help, even though I felt like Mad Max in *The Road Warrior*. I took in a movie on Hollywood Boulevard, which I barely remember, something noisy, and then drove back to my motel in Santa Monica and slept into the late morning.

The following day I drove into Venice and kept tabs on Luke's place. I saw him leave with April to go jogging, saw them come back. But I had the feeling they knew I was there, and Rose would be warned away for a while. The futility of the situation was eating away at me like AIDS. My immune system was down. The virus called Rose was slowly killing me, even though I'd been infected long ago.

I spent two more days and nights hanging around the Brandon house before I decided to call it quits and head home. I took a train back north with nothing to show for my journey but a big bill and an ugly secret I decided to keep to myself.

7

Sax and Violence

WHEN I GOT BACK into San Francisco there were a few messages on my machine from Tommy, asking me where the hell I was and what the hell was I doing, and one from Doc, telling me to be sure to contact him the moment I got back. There was also a message from Denise at the blood bank. Flora had returned sooner than expected from Europe, and Denise had given her "The Date That Never Was." I was back in the saddle, though Denise had not mentioned Flora's reaction. I decided to be optimistic, just so I'd stay away from the bridge.

There were also a few hang-up calls. It was hard for me not to hope they were from Rose.

After I unpacked and got cleaned up, I went down to The Drive-Inn to see Doc. I felt like one of The Bowery Boys, recounting their latest misadventure while lounging around free-loading in Louie's Sweet Shop. Doc wasn't Louie, though. Oh well. But he was glad to see me, and vice versa.

"The man," Doc said, pouring my beer. "Back from Tinseltown. Any luck?"

"Not really," I sighed. "I met Rose's baby." More like *Rosemary's* baby, I thought.

"Her *what?*"

"Her *baby*. She has a goddamn kid. Can you beat that?"

"By Tommy?"

"Nope. Some old dude. Well, fifty-something. Real asshole. She sure can pick 'em."

"What's the story? You tell Tommy, or does he know already?"

"Naw, I'll let Rose tell him. If she wants to. I don't want to alienate her by hurting Tommy needlessly. Not that I really give a damn about Tommy, y'see. I just don't want to piss Rose off."

"You mean Valerie."

I nodded. "They even have the same last name. Myers. It's *her*, Doc."

He shook his head. "Like fuckin' Amelia Earhart falling out of the sky right into your lap. One in a million shot you'd wind up in the same town."

I smiled. "Not really. I knew she loved it here. I originally wanted to move to Seattle, as you know, but I think something in me drew me here instead. She told me she'd visited San Francisco as a kid and wanted to live here someday, so . . . here we are." I never told Doc I felt like I was living in self-imposed exile in the Bay Area, still not feeling quite home here, even after all these years. It contributed to my incessant restlessness, like I could never go home and find inner peace. The Space Needle still beckoned. Maybe Valerie/Rose and I could move to Seattle together when this was all over and start fresh, even though neither of us had ever been there. Well, I haven't. But that was part of the appeal. Someplace new and different, far away from my aching loneliness, which I hoped to leave behind some day, as if it was a portable object easily disposed of via distance, rather than an internal malady that I carried with me wherever I went.

"Ah, I get it," he said. "So you moved all the way out here hoping you'd run into her by some slim chance. Unbelievable."

"Like I told you, I knew that friend of my father, who helped me out with my new career path, so there were more practical reasons, but . . . I guess so. It was instinct. Or something."

"Or something."

"I always have my reasons, Doc."

"You mean excuses."

"Whatever," I said with a shrug, suddenly weary of this subject, even though I'd brought it up.

"But then Tommy Dodge hires you to find her. Now, that *is* some weird funky freaky shit."

"Right? But I've been thinking . . . maybe *she* turned him on to me. I mean maybe she saw my ad in the paper one day, and . . . *I* don't know."

"You mean this could all be some kinda set-up?"

"I don't *know*, Doc. I mean if it's Fate, what's the *point*? It makes more sense that it would be a set-up. I'm not the one who changed his goddamn name. And I always kinda hoped she'd see my business ad in the paper and look me up."

"You had this planned all along, in a way."

"In a way. She walks among us on this island Earth, after all. So I figured I'd run into her again someday, somehow, with a little luck, and a little scheming. Now that I'm *this* close, I've *got* to find her."

"Could be she *wants* to be found."

"Things are going too easy, too soon."

"Except for that shiner. That's a whopper. How'd you get that?"

"In the line of duty, pal. Actually, Rose's L.A. boyfriend gave me this to remember him by."

"Nice guys she runs with. She's trouble, Vic. Black widow style. Find her, satisfy your curiosity, then leave her *alone*. And *move*. I'd miss you way up there in Seattle, but I'd rather visit you there than in a loony bin. Or a graveyard."

I put my head in my hands and sighed. "Can't promise that, Doc. It's the *loneliness*, man. It's killing me."

"I hear ya. But there's lotsa other women out there, Vic. *Millions*."

"So how do you meet 'em? Jesus, I just want *one*. Is that too much to ask?"

"Yeah, but you want the wrong one. Let her go. You know, I never told you this, but Monica thinks you're cute."

"Huh? The punker babe? What is she, nineteen?"

"Twenty-two. She's a bartender for Christ's sake. And she's very mature for her age. What the hell, just have fun for a change. Stop being so deadly damn serious all the time. You'll burn yourself out before you're forty, drop dead of a broken heart."

"So? Who would miss me?"

"*I* would, sucker."

I felt bad now. "Thanks, Doc." I looked up at the big TV screen, where *Tarantula* was playing. The giant arachnid in question was pulling a Peeping Tom on lovely Mara Corday. Beside the TV, Doc had written on a chalkboard: TODAY ONLY!! JOHN AGAR FEST—TARANTULA, REVENGE OF THE CREATURE, THE MOLE PEOPLE, AND THE BRAIN FROM PLANET AROUS!!! I loved this crazy place. But I couldn't call it a reason to live, or even home. Despite Doc's friendship and the cozy comfort of old movies, I felt spiritually destitute. It was all just a flimsy, fluffy escape from bleak reality. My desire to see Rose only increased with each waking moment. I just couldn't help myself, much less anyone else. Yeah, yeah, I know. Boo hoo fuckin' hoo. But that's the way I felt, anyway.

I was in a major funk when I left The Drive-Inn and went back upstairs to call Tommy. He wasn't there so I left a long-winded message summarizing my trip, leaving out all the details about Samson and Luke and telling him that friends of her had informed me that Rose had been down in L.A. but she had returned to Frisco; they weren't sure what area. It was highly unethical of me to string him along like this, but I just didn't care anymore. I was spending Tommy's money freely and not giving him what he was paying for. I felt slightly guilty, but I slept deeply just the same.

The next day was the day before Christmas Eve, and as usual I was mired in holiday malaise. I owned a copy if *It's a Wonderful Life* that I usually tortured myself with around this time of year, but not this year. Doc even broke down and played Christmas-themed double bills, like *Miracle on 34th Street* with *Santa Claus Conquers the Martians,* and *White Christmas* plus his favorite, *Black Christmas.* It was sickening. As a kid in Bensonhurst (home of the Mafia and *The Honeymooners*) this used to be my favorite time of year, even when we got lousy presents or *no* presents or the folks were fighting because my old man spent Christmas Eve out in some dive, drunk with a floozy. I just dug the festive ambience, the snow and lights and carols and all that jazz. Manhattan and Brooklyn were at their most charmingly Runyonesque this time of year, at least to me. What a sentimental sap I had been. I was too young to see through the gaudy façade and manufactured nostalgia and accept it as the massive commercial scam it really was. Now as a hip, jaded adult, I had Santa's number, all right. Fat fucking phony. He was just the jolly front for this cynical racket. Needless to say, my holiday spirit was indeed a ghost that didn't even have the energy to haunt me anymore. It had passed on to another dimension. R.I.P.

I went down to Rendezvous to soak up some of the pleasant atmosphere, drink some spiked eggnog, listen to the carols on the sound system by Nat King Cole and Peggy Lee and Dean Martin, hoping the bright blinking lights and pretty decorations would cheer me up, rather than give me a migraine. Rendezvous is in Technicolor year-round anyway, all purple and green, Space Age shiny and retro-futuristic, like something out of *Forbidden Planet* or *The Jetsons* or a special guest villain's themed lair on the old *Batman* TV series or *Ren and Stimpy's* house, with Googie-style décor and furniture. It was more L.A. than San Francisco, in a way, but maybe that's why I could escape into it so easily, feel like I was someplace far away, even another planet. Actually rustic, New York-style coffeehouses were all the rage in L.A. these days. A few years ago you couldn't get espresso in L.A. unless you had it imported. Now suddenly they were Seattle South. I guess it was a funky new trend or something, though they claimed it was their invention, I bet, so they'd retain their avant-garde, trend-setting image. Whatever. The eggnog and decorations perked me up slightly, and I saw in the *Chronicle* that one of my favorite bands, the Aqua-Velvets, was playing at Bottom of the Hill, while Bud E. Luv was at Bimbo's 365 Club in North Beach, and Mr. Lucky and Kitten on the Keys were at Club Deluxe in the Haight-Ashbury. I wouldn't make any of these cool gigs. I had work to do. Plus I was tired of sitting at the bar by myself, surrounded by horny hipsters on the make. I hate being one of those loner guys in a crowd, moping in the corner like a serial killer scoping out his potential prey. I'm antisocial by nature, but when you go to a nightclub or a movie theater and ask for one ticket, people wonder about you. Hell, I wonder about myself. Maybe I was just being too self-conscious, but in any case, I didn't enjoy attending public events solo. Easier just to stay home with a Doris Wishman video and jack off. That way no one thinks you're weird, because no one *knows*.

I just needed a date, and then all my problems would be solved. Or so I thought.

My next plan on the case was to stake out Bobby Bundy's Berkeley abode, since he was obviously in active cahoots with Rose and there was a chance she'd show up there sooner or later. I also was in the mood to roust someone, especially after my humiliating encounter with Luke Brandon, and Bobby was my leading candidate. I just needed to sublimate my frustration into some mindless mayhem.

That same day I got my chance, and it wasn't with Bobby. But if felt even better.

The blood bank was open on a shortened schedule for the impending holidays, so I went over to see Denise and hopefully Flora. This had turned out to be a nice diversion from the Rose business, and anyway I felt so low nothing Flora could say or do could make me feel any worse. I was impervious to pain at this point. I'd experienced so much of it lately I'd built up an immunity to it. The truth was my apathy was merely a phony phase, a survivalist reaction, but it didn't matter.

Denise was there, practically waiting for me. She smiled brightly as I came in and sat down. Fortunately it was slow and she had a chance to chat with me. I told her my black eye was an accident, then we got down to it.

"Mission accomplished," she told me. "Flora was only on a ten-day tour, after all. I'd lost track of the time. She just got back yesterday, and I gave her the thing."

"So?" I couldn't help but beam like an idiot. "What did she think?"

"She thought it was . . . interesting."

I waited for more, but Denise just looked at me with this silly smirk. "And? That's it? It wasn't a science project. I don't want a *grade*. Just a reaction."

"Well . . . she asked me to give you *this*." Denise went into her desk and pulled out a slip of paper, which had on it an address down in Palo Alto, in the South Bay, an almost totally unknown territory to me. In all my years here I'd never even been to Palo Alto, not even on a case. I knew it was the home of Stanford, and I heard there was a really cool old movie house there that showed classics, but all suburbs struck me as holding tanks for extra people. There was written the name of a dinky jazz club on University Avenue near the campus, called The Note Pad. Cute. And written at the bottom was a time: 10 p.m.

"What's this?" I asked.

"She wants to meet you there tonight."

Whoa. "You're kidding. Is she here now?"

"No. She still has a few vacation days she decided to take for the holidays. I gave her 'The Date That Never Was' over at her apartment in Alameda."

"If she lives in Alameda why does she want to meet me down in Palo Alto?"

"Does it matter, Casanova-on-wheels? You got a car, right? Jesus, I thought you'd be bubbling over. What's with you?"

I was taking this pretty lightly, considering all the work I'd put into this pursuit. Maybe I was just burned out on the whole thing by now. Or distracted by recent revelations. "I've been working on a case," I said. "It's a tough one, that's all I'll say."

"Sounds like you could use some R & R," Denise said. "Here's your shot."

"What *else* did she say?"

"Not much. I was on the way to work when I dropped by to see her. She called me when she got back into town to ask about her schedule and some other things because her boss is out sick—"

"Okay. Oh boy." My usual anxiety was beginning to kick in.

"You're welcome," she said dryly.

"Oh. Sorry. Thanks, Denise. Really. I mean it. I'm just a mess these days."

"What's the matter with you? You look beat. You got a place to go for the holiday?"

"Ah . . . naw. I don't care about that stuff. Just another day to me."

"You sure? You're welcome to come over for some turkey."

"Where is it you live again?"

"Walnut Creek, though I'm moving soon, can't afford it."

"Gee, that's really nice of you, thanks Denise. I usually go over to Doc's. But thanks."

I gave her a kiss on the cheek and left with my ticket to heaven.

It was a dark and stormy night as I drove south down the 101 and exited at University Avenue, entering the densely collegiate thicket of Palo Alto, which was prettier than I imagined it would be, far less funky than Berkeley, with lots of grand old houses and tree-lined streets, reminding me of some of the fancier towns in

New Jersey, especially with the ubiquitous Christmas decorations. It was nicer than a lot of other small towns I'd been to around the Bay, which just seemed like randomly populated excuses to build another Taco Bell and Target.

During the drive I was more preoccupied with Rose than Flora, though. Was Valerie Rose, or was Rose Valerie? Had she lied to me about being from the Midwest, or had her folks moved there from California? Or vice versa? Valerie had told me her old man was an ex-Marine and a preacher, about as Republican as you can get, which always sounded deliberately stereotypical to me, like she was making it up. In any case, both Rose's and Valerie's fathers had allegedly been in the military. I decided that Rose had made up Valerie, rather than vice versa. I would operate under that assumption until I found out the truth, anyway.

Tommy had still not returned my call returning his calls, which seemed odd. Maybe he was dead, which would solve a few problems for me, except for my fee. He was bankrolling this investigation, even if I was really only doing it for myself. He was probably in a drunken stupor, or maybe a coma. I didn't let it bother me. I had a date with Fate.

I pulled up in front of The Note Pad right at 10 p.m. The fact that I could find parking so easily reminded me I wasn't in The City anymore. I felt strangely confident. Elmer Bernstein's opening theme to *Sweet Smell of Success*, one of my favorite flicks, reverberated in my head as I strutted toward the club, my Corvair looking beautifully distinctive sandwiched between two SUVs. Almost all cars manufactured after 1975 were as bland as the population that consumed them. My dream car is a 1957 Thunderbird, powder blue with a white interior, but my precious Corvair was as close as I could get, and anyway I didn't want to hurt its feelings, just like you never tell your date how you wished she looked like Ann-Margret. Ideals are meant to remain out of reach, I guess.

I was dressed in a dark green sharkskin suit with a white shirt and thin black tie and shiny, pointy black shoes, like a Rat Pack reject or one of the Jets from *West Side Story* going to the dance at the rec hall. I thought I looked quite devastating myself. I decided I was there for Flora, not Rose or Valerie or Ann-Margret (though actually, Flora always remind me of her, at least as embellished by my imagination). Flora has been the girl of my dreams until just recently when she was supplanted by a phantom from my past. Actually, the whole situation felt anti-climactic, like the day after Christmas, when you were surrounded by toys you were already bored with. I hadn't had the chance to play with this one yet, though. Maybe tonight I'd really get lucky for a change. I tried to get in the proper mood and approach this opportunity in the right spirit, adjusting my attitude along with my tie as I walked inside.

As soon as I entered The Note Pad, my attempt at a positive posture collapsed. The place was small and noisy and dark, like most other dives, but all decked out for the season, which gave it a special glow. I saw Flora sitting at the bar smoking, alone. She wasn't quite Lana Turner, but she'd do. She smiled and waved when she saw me in the doorway, casing the joint. My familiar tension was beginning to kick in as I approached her. It was either too dark or she was too drunk, but she didn't even mention my black eye.

She looked radiant, which was partly attributable to the alcohol making her face flush, but mainly because she was not in a nurse's uniform and her natural beauty was free to express itself. She was dressed in a long flower pattern dress, like Valerie used to wear, only more formfitting, and she had on bright red pumps and sleek nylons. Her legs were crossed gracefully and she dragged on her cigarette with the style of a '40s sex siren. I was madly in love with her all over again. In this light her eyes looked violet, like Elizabeth Taylor's, rather than their usual hazel. I was ready to dump the Rose case by the time I sat next to Flora at the bar.

The joint was packed with pretentious putzes and academic androids, and on the small stage a four-piece band was jamming

Christmas carols. They were supposed to sound like jazz but it came off more like Muzak to my well-trained ears. I felt like I was crashing a complete stranger's wedding. Why the hell had Flora asked me to come all the way down here? Alameda was a lot closer—and more exciting.

Then it hit me: the long-haired Joe Blow wailing on the tenor sax. Her boyfriend. When she blew him a kiss and waved and he winked and waved back there was no room left for doubt. Then she pointed me out to him, and he grinned and waved at *me*. I expected Rod Serling to step out of the shadows any second and introduce tonight's episode of *The Twilight Zone*, featuring a hapless detective trapped in a bar with his dream girl and the love of *her* life, who was the sax player on the stage. The detective didn't know it yet, but he had accepted an invitation to his own personal hell, conveniently located in Palo Alto, California. He was imprisoned here for eternity, watching his dream girl make love to the sax player, while the detective sat in a cheesy dive loaded with half-witted hipsters and scholastic snobs and tried to act entertained. Perfect plot. Like the kind you get buried in. But hadn't I seen this one before? Was my life going into perpetual reruns already?

"Who's that?" I asked Flora as if I didn't already suspect, just to make polite conversation.

"Joey," she said, casually confirming my fears. "Thanks for coming, Vic. It's nice to see you in the *real* world."

Ah, so *this* was the "real" world, I thought. All my life I'd been wandering around Disneyland, apparently. "Joey? Like Joe Blow?"

She actually laughed. She had a sweet laugh. I wanted to kill her, but she was too pretty to ruin. Maybe later, after a few drinks, she wouldn't look so hot, and I could strangle her with a smile on my face. With my luck, she'd look even better.

"No, Joey Link," she said. "My fiancé. I showed him that thing you made me? 'The Date That Never Was'? He thought it was brilliant, and he wanted to meet you."

How about my new project: The Life That Never Was, I thought. That would go over even better, I bet. I downed a shot of bourbon I'd ordered, then requested a whole bottle from the bozo bartender. "He did? You're kidding me?" I said, stifling a belch.

She shook her head, and her long, dark, red hair whipped about so daintily I almost grabbed it so I could yank it back hard as I bent her over the stool and fucked her in the ass. I realized that would never actually happen. "And of course I loved it. You're very creative, Vic. Wonderful imagination. I hope we can get to be good friends."

"Your fiancé, you said?" I drowned another shot, and my face was hot and blushing. I was also fighting back tears I hoped she wouldn't notice. Like always, I wanted to ride this situation out with some dignity. As usual, I knew I'd blow it somewhere down the line. I was merely procrastinating.

She held up her cute little finger and flashed the phony engagement ring at me. "Remember? I showed you at the blood bank. He proposed officially in Milan, though. It was very romantic."

"Wished I coulda been there. Congratulations," I said, downing shot number three, then just swigging out of the bottle.

"Have you been to Europe?" she asked me. "It's wonderful. I wished we could have spent more time there, but we're on a budget. Musicians don't make much, but he's very talented. He'll go places. And he'll have me."

"I could suggest a few places," I mumbled like Marlon Brando in *Guys and Dolls.*

"Pardon?"

"Nothin'. Joey Link, huh? Too bad he isn't missing. He'd be famous."

She thought for a moment, then got it and laughed much too loudly. She really was plastered. "Oh, the Missing Link. Right. You are such a funny guy, Vic."

"That's what people tell me. Hey, can your boyfriend play 'My Funny Valentine'? He could dedicate it to us, to me, I mean."

"Maybe," she said seriously. "I'll ask him during the break, okay? This set is almost over."

"Oh no! And I was enjoying it so much! So your name will be what, Flora Link?"

"Um-hmm." She was trying to make eye contact with Joey on stage again, but his eyes were closed as he poured his passion into a solo riff in the middle of a touching rendition of "Jingle Bells." Some people were slow dancing to it, then began to bop again once the solo was over and the band picked up the beat. Joey looked over at us and pantomimed drinking, meaning he would join us during the break, I guess. Whoopee. Then the band broke into "Blue Christmas," completely desecrating it. It was nauseating. Flora seemed to be really digging the scene, though. I was close to throwing up all over my dream date, induced by the music and my sour mood. I decided to swallow back my puke, at least for the time being.

"Flora, can I ask you something?" I said once she had stopped staring starry-eyed at her honey and remembered I was there.

"Sure, Vic. Anything." I could barely hear her through the din inside my brain as well as out.

"Why did you invite me here? Really. Straight up."

She took out another cigarette and lit it thoughtfully, then pulled away with that crazy look in her eyes, which I'd always found so seductive. Except now it scared the hell out of me, like it always should've. "I'm not sure," she said finally.

"You're not sure? Really? I mean, think of *my* position, how awkward this makes me feel. I mean . . . you know what I mean, Flora!" She was just staring off into space, with the crazy look glowing in her eyes like maniacal neon. "What I mean is—I *like* you. You *must* know that by now. All the flowers and cards and stuff . . . you *know* I like you. Shit, the whole blood bank knows it.

Even Joey must've figured it out by now. And he wants to *meet* me? C'mon."

"Well, we didn't think you were serious," she said suddenly, in a somewhat irritable voice.

"You didn't think I was serious? You thought I was devoting all this time and attention to you as a lark? Like I had nothing *better* to do?" I downed the rest of the bottle of bourbon in a gulp. I was completely blitzed by now, slurring my words but still making perfect sense, at least to me, which was a lot more than I could've said for Flora at this point. "I don't believe you," I said, eyes lowered on the bar.

"I don't appreciate you saying you wished Joey would drop dead," she said coldly. "He's the love of my life. You have no—*hic!*—no right to say that." She was so wasted now she was wobbling on her stool.

"Thanks for inviting me, Flora," I said as I stood up, determined to just walk away from this set-up. I didn't know if Flora was just toying with me or what, but she was too bombed to tell me now, so I'd find out later. Or never. I don't think she knew herself. I don't think she even noticed me heading for the door. She was about to pass out. Then the set ended abruptly, or seemed to since my sense of time and perception were a little off. I thought I heard the voice of Louis Armstrong singing "Cool Yule" but I could've just been imagining it at that point. I followed this bad impulse back into the bar and up to the stage. I knew what I was doing but it was like I was in a dream and could do anything I wanted with impunity, so I didn't care about the consequences of my actions. It was *my* dream. And Joey Link was in it. I wanted him out. Suddenly I felt as tough as Rocky Sullivan in *Angels with Dirty Faces*. I marched boldly up to the stage, through the throngs of mingling morons, grabbed Joey by the lapels Cagney-style, then proceeded to beat the hell out of him with his own saxophone.

The memory is hazy, to say the least. I remember few details besides Joey's bent saxophone, his bleeding nose, Flora's screams, band members climbing all over me and holding me down, a big black dude, who I assumed was the bouncer, tossing me out the door, some sirens, cops, bright lights, some harsh words, Flora sobbing on my behalf and refusing to press charges, the back seat of sterile cop car, a drunk tank with two stoned Mexicans wearing Santo and Blue Demon masks for some reason (unless that was part of my delirium), then some bad coffee in the morning and a stern warning to stay sober and in any case out of The Note Pad forever. I'd been 86'd from a club I wouldn't normally be caught dead in.

They wouldn't have to tell me twice.

8

Creature from the Hack Saloon

MY MOTHER'S MIDDLE NAME was Violet.

This may mean nothing to you, but I couldn't help but consider this fact as I drove back to civilization the morning after the Flora fiasco. Flora. Rose. Violet. Talk about a flower pattern. Maybe from now on I should stay away from women with names derived from any kind of plant life. But then Rose had fooled me. She'd told me her name was Valerie. You just never can tell.

"YOU'RE ALL CRAZY!" I shouted out the window of my Corvair, partly still drunk and partly hungover as hell. "THAT'S WHY WE STALK YOU AND SEXUALLY HARASS YOU IN THE OFFICE!" I continued as I sped up 101. "BECAUSE YOU'RE ALL FUCKING CRAZY, OUT OF YOUR FUCKING MINDS! AND WE LET YOU WALK AROUND FREE! YOU'RE *CRAAAAZY!*"

A CHP on a bike pulled me over. I was cited for speeding. I'd been doing around ninety during the course of my harangue.

"You married?" I asked the stone-faced cop.

"Yeah. Why?"

"You happy?"

"Yes, why? You think I'm sexy?"

"Funny guy. Maybe you got a sane one." I belched. He asked me to get out of the car. He gave me a sobriety test. I failed. He called a black-and-white to take me to the Daly City PD while they impounded my Corvair. I was booked on a DUI. Nice day I was having already. It was Christmas Eve, too. One I'll never forget. A call to a friend of a friend at SFPD got me my wheels back, but I still had to pay the ticket and go to traffic school. Like they would teach me a goddamn thing about women.

For some reason I wasn't in the mood to go to Berkeley that night and post a watch over the Bundy place. At that point I didn't care if I ever saw Rose again. Let Tommy have her. They deserved each other. I was through with women, I decided. At least for the rest of the day.

I cuddled up with some eggnog and forced myself to watch *It's a Wonderful Life* until I retched. I couldn't tell if I was reacting to the bourbon or the flick. It didn't matter. I was beyond the point of giving a damn. Belch, fart, vomit. I had no self-esteem left at all. No shower, no shave. Eat ice cream and corn chips in bed watching TV, jerk off to pictures of women who were in their prime forty years ago. Who cared. I had no life. What was the point of trying. All I wanted to do was sleep.

The phone rang about 8 p.m. that night, just as I was drifting off. I thought maybe it was Daly City PD calling me after they'd pulled my sheet and found a number of prior offenses swept under the rug by my deceased police captain friend. Believe me, going from one police station to another—literally driving from one to the next—would make anybody paranoid. Or I thought maybe it was Flora, calling to tell me how much she'd enjoyed our evening, wanting to know when we could do it again, hopefully soon. I'd never see her again, I thought at the time. No more blood donations from *this* sap. I'd given my quota for a lifetime, and then some. They'd drained my *heart*, the bloodsuckers. Flora may as well have been goddamn Vampirella. I would miss Denise, though. Maybe it was her, calling to tell me what a fool I'd been, and that she wanted nothing to do with me ever again either, regretting her part in this whole sordid mess. It wouldn't quit so I finally answered it.

I gruff male voice said, "You Vic Valentine?" It was no one I knew.

"Yeah, so?"

"You the guy lookin' for Rose?"

"Who *is* this?"

"My name is Simon Brewster. I'm a friend of Rose. Can you meet me at Spec's Bar in, say, half an hour?"

"I guess. North Beach, right?"

"Yes. I live on Telegraph Hill. I'll just walk down in twenty minutes or so. You'll be there?"

"I'm in the Richmond. But . . . I gotta . . . I'm kind of a mess—"

"I'm not asking you for a *date*. I just want to talk about Rose. You want to or not? I can go either way."

I bet. "No, no, I mean, I'll be right over. How'd you get my number?"

"Ad in the paper, where else?"

"How'd you know I was looking for Rose?"

"I *know*, okay? *Everybody* knows."

This was getting interesting, but frustrating. I was perking up considerably. "*Everybody*? Like who?" Was this in fuckin' *Time Magazine* or something?

He grew impatient. "Look, it's Christmas Eve and I'm offering to help. Take it or leave it."

"We can wait till after the holidays, if you want—"

"I'll be there in half an hour. I'm wearing a red turtleneck sweater and I have a beard. If you're not there within an hour I'll assume you're an asshole and forget about it. Bye." He hung up.

I looked like hell, but so what? I threw on some casual threads and my trench coat and raced, or rather, drove carefully over to North Beach. No more soused *Speed Racer* shenanigans from *this* boy.

I could've lost both my driving and my PI licenses in one fell swoop. Next time I would. I needed my wheels. My Corvair was my baby. I still had a court date for the DUI in a month, but I tried not to let that aggravate me. I had bigger fish to fry, and the grill was just getting warmed up.

Simon Brewster. That name sounded familiar. I rolled it around my tortured brain as I drove around North Beach trying to find a goddamn parking space, with Leonard Cohen ironically singing "Everybody Knows" on the radio. Finally I had to settle for a lot, shelling out three fins for the privilege. Simon Brewster. I walked down Columbus, crossed Broadway, and ducked down the alley to Spec's, which was right across from City Lights bookstore and Vesuvio Cafe, two Beat landmarks, and in between them was an alley where Jack Kerouac used to heave after a drunken night on the town. Simon Brewster. Spec's was a classic hole-in-the-wall, one of my favorite bars in The City, along with Top of the Mark, which I could never afford. Another night, another bar. And I generally prefer coffee to beer and bourbon, believe it or not. Then I recalled. Simon Brewster was a friend of Rose in North Beach that Tommy had told me about. I realized this as I walked in and saw him at the table in the back. I had his address on a slip of paper at home. Somewhere. But now he'd caught up with *me*. How convenient. How suspicious.

The joint was jumping with hack poets and their cut-rate muses, plus yuppie poseurs from the Financial District wallowing in designer angst. A lot of them dressed like they'd just caught a swing band up the road at Bimbo's 365 Club, an elegant vintage-style supper club that featured a lot of burlesque acts, with naked mermaids a major part of its motif. Some live ones even swam in a tank behind the bar. I dug that place and resented the fact these well-heeled heels had dates to bring there and I didn't. And they thought they were so goddamn hip, which really killed me. They figured if they rubbed shoulders with struggling artists in a bar like this it would eventually rub off and save them the trouble of giving up their cushy lifestyles in exchange for authentic integrity. Still, definitely a different scene than where I was just the night before, which seemed so long ago already. At least the old-time bartenders had the class to play Dave Brubeck on the sound system, over the distant, echoing howl of Allen Ginsberg. Thank God.

Appropriately enough, "Take Five" was playing as I took a chair next to Simon Brewster, who I swear could've played Santa Claus in the Macy's Day Parade. He was around Luke Brandon's age, maybe a bit older, but much kinder and gentler in appearance. He had a no-nonsense air about him, though, and he was reading something by Lord Byron when I sat down beside him. He nodded without looking at me, finishing whatever passage in no big hurry, and then he closed the book after marking his place.

He was wearing grandpa glasses, which he took off to study me. His eyes shone with avuncular warmth. He actually seemed like a nice guy who wasn't going to hit me anytime soon. I was relieved. "I was almost ready to leave," he said in his gravelly, smoke-choked voice. He was obviously a heavy smoker, or had been at one point.

"Cross-town traffic and no street parking," I said. "Gimme a break, here I am. And frankly I feel like shit."

"You look it. But then so do most men who've given their hearts to Rose." I didn't say anything. He didn't give me a chance. "Look at me," he continued. "Would you believe I'm only twenty-five?"

We both laughed politely. "So what's the story, Simon? Tommy told me about you, you know."

"Oh? What did he say?"

"Nothin' much. Just that you're a friend of Rose. Tommy hired me to find her."

"Yes, I know."

"Yes, you know. Of course. Who told you?"

"I'm not at liberty to say."

"Rose."

"I'm not at liberty to say," he repeated in his level tone. He was beginning to bug me in a big way all of a sudden. Suddenly Eartha Kitt was singing "Santa Baby." More Christmas carols. Damn.

"Simon, no one's on trial here," I said. "I thought you wanted to help me?"

"I do."

"Why? How? Simple questions."

"With simple answers. Because I feel Rose must be stopped from hurting herself and others any further. In a way, *she* is the one on trial, or will be, once she gets nabbed. But she's running away from herself, and has been for years."

"How do you know all this? Who are you to her?"

He took a sip from his Cognac on the table. "I believe that I, and not this Luke Brandon character, am the father of her child."

"Excuse me," I said, getting up and heading directly to the bar, asking for something, anything, a double shot of it, fast and hard, quickly. I wasn't even sure what he poured, looked like whiskey, when what I really needed was a suicide cocktail, equal parts dynamite and cyanide. I gulped it, tossed a few bucks on the bar, and returned to the table.

"Go on," I said, suddenly coughing up a storm.

He talked right through me. "Rose and I had relations on a regular basis, right up to the time her child was conceived. Samson, I believe his name is."

"I met him a couple days ago."

"Oh? Down in Venice?"

"You been down there?"

"No, I've never met Luke, the purported father."

"You should sometime. Great guy."

"Really?"

I pointed to my black eye.

"Oh," Simon said. "Yes, that's about how I pictured him." He sighed. "Rose always was attracted to the macho element. She liked the primeval feel of a big, muscular body on top of her. She said it made her feel protected from the world."

"Nothing personal, Simon, but you don't seem like her type."

"Neither do you."

"What makes you think I want to be?"

"I heard that you thought she was someone you used to know, under an alias or something."

"Oh, you heard that? Listen, Simon, you better tell who's telegraphing my every step in this thing or—"

"Or what?"

"Or . . . goddamn it, Simon."

"You'll shoot me?" He laughed softly. You could tell I really intimidated the hell out of him. "Okay. I'll give you a clue. *I'm* a bum."

"Shit. Bobby. The human megaphone."

"When did Frank Sinatra come out with this bum and punk theory of yours?"

"Never. I made it up. So Bobby put you on to me."

"Somewhat."

"Somewhat? Just shoot straight, Simon, will ya?"

"I'm already talking more than I'm supposed to."

"What the hell's that supposed to mean? Is a safe gonna fall on your head outta nowhere? Next you'll tell me Rose has Mob ties."

He didn't say anything, just watched me with bemusement.

"She *doesn't*, does she?"

"Not to my knowledge."

"Bet she fucked a bunch of 'em, though."

"Could be."

"Could be Samson's old man is the Mafia."

"You mean when she was in New York? That was a long time ago."

"She told you she'd been to New York?"

"Of course. She left home for the Big Apple when she was barely eighteen."

I sat back in my chair, stunned by a revelation I already knew. I guess I'll never completely get over it. "That's where I met her. But her name was Valerie then. Valerie Myers."

"Really? She never told me she'd changed her name at any time."

"Take it from me, pops. She did." I downed the rest of my drink. I was in palookaville all over again, the only place I was welcome. "That's why I want to find her."

"Does Tommy know this?"

"Not unless someone's told him, like Bobby, that little fink. Wait till I get my hands on him."

"Tommy isn't very bright."

"No kidding," I said. "I've heard from several sources that Rose was about three months pregnant when she left, and Tommy didn't have a clue."

"Oh, I think he knew. But he also knew it couldn't have been his, because he was sterile. That was a clinical fact. It was one reason he slept with so many women, before and during his so-called marriage."

"So-called?"

"They never actually tied the knot. Not on paper. I thought you knew that."

"What? Wait. Tommy has a ring. I saw it."

"Purely symbolic," Simon said. "It means nothing. There was never a legally binding ceremony. Rose wanted to be able to come and go as she pleased."

"As it were."

He shrugged and sipped his Cognac. I just sat there, stunned. Billie Holiday was serenading us with her sadness during the silence. Talk about a pregnant pause.

"I don't get this," I said finally. "First I find out Rose left Tommy to have this kid, but she didn't officially divorce him because she loves him. Now I find out they were never even hitched to begin with. Meaning Tommy has no legal hold on Rose."

"Exactly. But she may go back to him someday. She wants that door to stay open."

"Why?"

"Who knows. She told me she has some karma to work out with him."

"Jesus Christ." My head was spinning. "Why won't someone just give me the straight dope on this?"

"That's what I'm trying to do, Mr. Valentine."

"Call me Vic."

"Short for Victor?"

"Sometimes. So what makes you so sure you're the father if Rose was sleeping with all those other guys?"

"She told me Luke only indulges in the acts of fellatio and cunnilingus. And quite a lot of both, from what she said. He has issues with actual intercourse. He's afraid he'll catch a disease. Although apparently he sometimes made an exception for rough anal sex, at least in her case. On the other hand, I ejaculated deep inside of her sweet vagina quite frequently and fluidly, condom free."

"*Jesus*, TMI, Simon!"

"It was pure bliss—"

"Shut the fuck *up*, already! Anyway you're full of shit too! Bobby told me she basically set Luke up to be the father of her child!"

"That's not what she told me. And I knew her . . . intimately."

I was feeling *really* nauseated. *Again.* "Then why the hell is the baby down there with Luke and that Filipino whore?"

"What Filipino?"

"Luke has a wife. Or what he calls a wife. More like a live-in prostitute who babysits on the side. I don't know any more. All my traditional notions of love and marriage have been chucked down the sewer."

Simon sighed. "That's probably why, then. Rose wants her baby to have some kind of structural family background, and she knows, being an old poet, I can't provide her with that sort of stability."

"You're a poet now? That doesn't surprise me, actually."

"And a painter, of sorts. Not as talented as Rose on either count. She came to me as a student. I was her tutor. But then she began to teach *me*. What does Luke do?"

"Besides eat pussy like it's going out of style? Lifts weights and sculpts. Maybe not in that order. Maybe he sculpts his own barbells."

"Ah, the best of both worlds."

"Meaning?"

"It sounds like Luke possesses both an artistic spirit and an animalistic body. Rose's ideal was someone who was both physically and mentally stimulating."

"Where does a jock like Tommy fit in, then?" Or me, for that matter.

"He had the right body. I had the poetry. You can't always get everything you need in one package. She's still searching for perfection though, I'm sure. That is her downfall, because pursuit of an ideal that doesn't exist can only lead to tragedy. Are you familiar with the Byronic hero?"

"Not exactly."

"You've heard of Lord Byron, I trust?" Simon asked.

I nodded at the book on the table. "Praise Lord Byron and pass the ammo, I always say."

"I am beginning to suspect that's the one thing you have in common with Rose, perhaps the single element that attracted you to one another. You both feel ennobled and emboldened by an essentially impossible quest, romanticizing your solitary situations and justifying iconoclastic attitudes and antisocial behavior as necessary sacrifices made in the name of your hopeless missions. You wear blinders that block out the rest of society, rendering their suffering and aspirations relatively petty and inconsequential compared with your own cynical, selfish interests."

"Are you through?"

"Never."

"Well, I tell ya, Simon, not to sound ironic, but I've never been accused of being Byronic. *Moronic*, yes, on more than one occasion. But I'd have to be *bionic* to put up with all this shit in the name of a fantasy. Valerie—Rose—was, *is*, very real. She's not a figment of my imagination. She's flesh and blood, a part of my life, not a dream."

"Then where is she?" Simon challenged. "If she's so real, why can't you touch her, feel her? In the end, there is no difference between a dream and a memory. Both are intangible mental images with little bearing on the reality of the present."

"Memories and dreams both matter, Simon. One reminds you of where you've been, the other guides you to where you want to go."

He shrugged again. "Semantics," he said simply.

"Semantics, romantics, Byronic, iconic—whatever, dude. Listen, I'm blown away by your psychological prowess, Simon, no kidding, but all I want you to do now is level with me and save the barroom psychiatry for someone who really needs it. Besides, I got a friend I can talk to already."

"A trained psychiatrist?"

"No. Even better. Bartender. Although I do call him 'Doc.' At least bartenders have no ulterior motive."

"Except they still take your money."

"At least it's cheaper than a real shrink. And they actually offer something substantial in return."

"You are a very jaded young man, my friend."

"I'm not your friend, pal, but yeah, I'm jaded as hell. If you won't help me, fine. If you're just yanking my chain for your own sick amusement, as I'm beginning to suspect, I'm outta here. I can't take much more of this."

"I see Rose still has quite a hold on you."

"Her grip is loosening, trust me. It's hard to carry a torch for a dame when she keeps pissing on it."

"So you *do* still love her. My, my . . ."

"It's the booze talking."

"Perhaps, but real people are listening. You should tell it to be quiet or it will give you away to the wrong person some day."

"Spoken like a true wise man. Two more and we'd all go visit a manger. But Rose's conception wasn't immaculate, was it, Simon?"

He shook his head and smiled. "Quite dirty, in fact. I know. I was there."

I suddenly wanted to belt him, but considering my recent experience, I held back my violent impulses. "None of my business. The truth is . . . I have some unfinished business of my own with Rose, or Valerie, that predates this soap opera. I think maybe she's setting me up."

He raised his eyebrows. "Really? For what? A knock-off, as they say in gangsters' parlance?"

"She killed me years ago. I've just been wandering around like a zombie ever since."

He laughed softly. "Welcome to Club Zombie, Mr. Valentine. Cheers." He polished off his Cognac.

"Jesus," I said, massaging my weary eyeballs. "*Ow!*" I'd forgotten about my black one. I needed rest more than anything at this point, including sex. I can't even sleep like a normal person. "You make me feel so anonymous," I said. "Just another heartbroken stiff in Rose's private cemetery."

"You turn an interesting phrase. Ever do any writing?"

"Some, back in New York, but I don't want to talk about that right now."

"You are a man of unfulfilled promise. I know. I recognize myself in you."

I looked at him, his ruddy complexion, his graying beard and thinning hair, and I was terrified. He was a vision of my possible destiny, the goddamn Ghost of Christmas Future, staring me in the face, warning me. I did not want to become an old geezer sitting alone in a bar dwelling on a wasted past with a dwindling future for compensation. I had to get a grip on myself. Simon Brewster was a monster created by Rose, the mad scientist, experimenting with men's hearts and souls, extracting their precious fluids, and then discarding them like used test tubes. I had to break the spell. But in person, with her, face to face.

"I have to say, you've made this the most depressing Christmas Eve in many a moon," I told Simon as the spins started to set in, as much from exhaustion as alcohol consumption.

"Don't blame me for that," he said. "I'm just trying to help. You had a head start on your depression long before I called you. If you can't take the truth, stop looking for it. Now you want to find Rose, or don't you?"

"I don't know anymore." I was sounding more and more like Tommy Dodge. "I mean . . . yeah. Call me Byronic, but I gotta see this thing through to the end. It's too late to turn back."

"If you really believe she's setting you up, she'll come to you eventually, even if you do nothing. Perhaps *especially* if you do nothing. Maybe you're playing into her hands by knocking yourself out this way."

"You really think she's that kind of person?" I asked sadly. "She didn't use to be."

"People change. And perhaps she isn't the person you think she is."

"Maybe she never was."

"Exactly."

"So what can you tell me that will help me find her?"

"She's in town, I know that much."

"Where?"

"I'm not sure. When we spoke she wouldn't give me her exact location, because she was afraid I'd tell you."

"Wait. You spoke to her recently?"

"This afternoon, in fact."

"Then she knows I'm looking for her?"

"Obviously."

"Why didn't you just say that?" He was a cerebral bully. I'm always getting my own ass handed to me, one way or the other.

"I wanted to get a reading on you first, see what kind of person you are. I don't want Rose hurt."

"You mean physically?"

"In any way. I'm not a fan of aggression. I'm quite passive. Too much so for my own good."

"Simon, what do *you* want?"

He looked around at the walls decorated with thousands of Beat-era souvenirs, obviously recalling better times. "I want her to accept responsibility for her actions. To come clean with everyone. Even Tommy. Even you."

"Why?"

"Because I care for her, and she is destroying herself by destroying others. Can't you see? She is not a bad person, or even a selfish one, not really. She has a good heart. But her blindness is ruining her potential, both as a person and as an artist. She is a lost soul, and I'd like to see her found."

"You sound like her father."

He smiled. "More like her mentor. *And* the father of her son."

"You're really sure about that?"

"Positive. And she agrees."

"So how do you feel about Samson being raised by Hercules down there?"

"That's what Rose wants, and I understand. She wanted the child, not I. She was hoping I would supply the necessary creative, intelligent genes. She did say I was like the father she always wanted. Hers was a right-wing bigot."

"Yet she still slept with you."

"Vigorously."

"Didn't you feel used?"

"Blissfully."

I mentally blocked out any disgusting images of this unholy union. "Whatever. I should get going. I'm getting dizzy. Do me a favor? If you hear from Rose, please call me." I handed him a business card, even though he already had my number. In more ways than one.

He took it. "Perhaps. But she *is* in town. That's all I can tell you."

"Better yet, tell *her* to call me."

"I'll tell her you called me, looking for her, and gave me your number. That will be the story when you find her. Agreed?"

"Sure." I stood up and grew lightheaded, but maintained my balance. "We'll be in touch, Simon. And thanks. You've definitely changed my take on things."

He nodded and went back to his mental masturbation and Lord Byron.

I went home to my physical masturbation and Bettie Page. I tried whacking off to an old video of her changing in and out of dominatrix duds, with the sound off and Screamin' Jay Hawkins on the turntable, but my heart wasn't in it. I was exhausted but couldn't fall asleep, wondering who Rose was sleeping with on Christmas Eve. Santa? His elves? His reindeer? Then I started wondering about things like the nature of intimacy. Rose obviously didn't love any of the men I had met in her sexual wake. At least, not in the soul mate sense. She had told me *we* were soul mates, in her opinion, because we had so much in common. At least back then, when she was an aspiring writer (in addition to artist) and I was on my way. I used to tell her she looked like a Vargas girl come to life—and she did—and she'd pose for me in seductive lingerie, driving me insane with desire and loving her power over me. We watched old movies together, like she did with Tommy, apparently. We went bowling.

To the Museum of Modern Art, and the Natural History Museum, my favorite childhood haunt. To the racetrack. The local Edward Hopper-type diner. Even to ball games. Valerie always did like sports, and men with hard bodies, but she never really gave me a hard time about my own less-than-Greek physique. She liked my looks, even though I wasn't big and muscle-bound. She was cheesecake even if I wasn't exactly beefcake. Beef jerky, maybe. We were together almost four years, nearly the length of her bogus marriage to Tommy. We lived together for three of them. We were officially engaged at one point. I still had my ring. I wondered if she still had hers. Probably not. She was never as sentimental as I am. We didn't have *everything* in common, after all.

As I lay there, I started wondering about just how faithful she had been to me back in New York. She had often talked about having kids someday, when she was ready, I assumed by me. Now the thought of having a family terrifies me. Strange how things turn out. *Too* strange. Many men had known the intimacies I shared with her, which seemed to cheapen my memories of her. Images of Luke and Tommy and Simon and the Harlem Globetrotters having their way with her tortured me all night. I finally jerked off and came several times in a row just thinking about all these men fucking her, imagining myself in their position, which was easy to do, since I had been at one point, so I could somehow be a part of these remote, alien trysts, assimilate and merge them into my own sacred recollections. But it wasn't just the sex. It was the affection, the quiet talks, the shared secrets, all things I had once revolved my entire life around, scattered to the four winds, which howled outside my window until I finally fell asleep and slept well into Christmas Day.

9

Slay Belles

WHEN I DID WAKE up it was nearly three o'clock in the afternoon. I forced myself to get up despite that feeling of dead weight I get sometimes when I first open my eyes. It was just my usual depression intensified by the holidays, so I tried to beat it and salvage something out of the day. I showered, shaved, and put on some decent clothes and my trench coat, plus my Ray-Bans, since the sun was shining brightly, not that it mattered. I'm always in a fog.

I walked down to my favorite café, Rendezvous, which was bustling with the usual crowd of artists and students and local loners like myself, despite the holiday (open for a shortened schedule, though—even pagans want to celebrate Christmas at home), and read the paper while I sipped a latte. It was very relaxing. I felt something bordering on contentment. It was nice just to sit and take it easy and not talk to anyone or beat up anyone or get beaten up and grilled by a bunch of cops. I thought about Flora and realized what an ass I'd made of myself, belatedly. I'd really blown that one for good. Just as well. She loved another guy. And she had a flower name. No more flower names. Well, after Rose. I still had to talk to her in person, and I had to tell Tommy *some*thing. After all, he was buying me Christmas coffee, and then some.

I went back to my office to check messages. One from Tommy: "Hey fuckhead, where the fuck you been? I'm in Pennsylvania with my family. My parents and my cousins and my brothers and sisters. And aunts and uncles and grandparents. I'll be back in a few days, after New Year's, the *day* after, and you'd *best* have something for me. What the fuck am I *pay*ing you for? Oh yeah, Merry Christmas." *Click.* He sounded drunk as usual.

The next message was from Denise: "Hey, lover man. I talked to Flora, and she *never* wants to see you again. She was too upset to give me all the details. What's up? Call me tomorrow. Merry Christmas, Vic. Hope we can bail you out of this one, but it looks *bad*." At least Denise and I were still on speaking terms. Then there was one last message, from Doc: "Yo, my man, come on over tonight. I got a surprise for you. Bring some wine or somethin'. Merry Christmas, my man." After that someone had called and hung up. My heartbeat pumped like an Uzi hoping it had been Rose.

I called Doc and told him I'd be over in the early evening. He lived in the Sunset, near UCSF. He had a nice place, top story of an old Victorian, full of movie memorabilia. He wouldn't tell me what the surprise was, and at the time I didn't really care.

I decided to drive down to Union Square and walk around looking at the decorations and listening to street musicians play carols. I sat next to the big Christmas tree in the center of Union Square, near some old bums. Two pigeons were copulating passionately beneath the tree. Everyone but me, I thought, feeling sorry for myself like a loser. Well, everyone but me and the two bums, unless they had a thing for each other.

I arrived at Doc's place around seven after steeping myself in solitude. We generally got together Christmas night, unless I was out of town on a case. He usually spent Christmas Eve over in Oakland with his senile mother. I was expecting it to be just him and me, but it wasn't. Monica was there, the green-haired punker babe. Doc had set me up.

She answered the door, dressed in a tight crimson sweater and a short black skirt with black leotards and spiked pumps. She was a petite but curvy girl with large pointy breasts and a pretty perpetual pout and big emerald eyes that matched her hair, so she was *always* ready for Christmas. Like I said earlier, she looked like a punk rock version of Batgirl. She was definitely Batman bait. I felt a familiar fluttering beneath my utility belt. Why was Doc doing this to me? I guess I deserved it.

"Hey there, come on in and join the party," she said with spooky seduction, like Elvira, Mistress of the Dark. I have to say Little Elvis had perked up considerably, despite the previous evening's rigorous workout. I called my pecker Little Elvis sometimes, since it'd been hiding underground for so long, presumed dead. That's why I rehearsed it on a regular basis, so it'd be ready for its big Comeback Special, if and when. Elvis' *real* Comeback Special was broadcast around Christmas 1968. Maybe mine would be a yuletide rebirth as well. My jumpsuits were back at home, though. Oh well, might just have to play this gig raw and acoustic. But then maybe I was getting ahead of myself. I tried not to think of Monica's nude body spread eagle on my bed like some sleazy Eurotrash sexpot from a Jess Franco flick, as I wished her Merry Christmas and went into the kitchen, where Doc was putting the finishing touches on supper.

I'd bought a bottle of red wine, courtesy of Tommy Dodge, which I set on the dining room table, then I chatted idly with Doc and Monica while James Brown sang Christmas carols on Doc's stereo. I actually felt good for a change. Doc was showing Monica his collection of autographed Pam Grier memorabilia. I noticed she kept casting furtive, flirtatious little glances my way as Doc droned on proudly about his prized possessions.

Finally we sat down to supper. "I was telling Monica here you're a bona fide private detective," Doc said as he started slicing the turkey. "Just like in the movies. But for real."

"We were watching *Kiss Me Deadly* the other day at the bar," Monica said, staring at me like I was Mike Hammer in the flesh. I was ready to nail her, that was for sure. I was feeling pretty horny all of a sudden. Funny how opportunity can inspire ambition, more so than vice versa.

"I can't say my life is quite that exciting," I said. "But close!" I quickly added. We all chuckled politely.

"Monica graduates next year from SF State," Doc said, passing around the various dishes. He was an excellent cook. It was quite a spread. Besides the turkey with stuffing, there were black-eyed peas, collard greens, fried chicken, mashed potatoes with gravy, apple-sauce, a huge garden salad, cranberry sauce, corn bread, and the promise of two desserts. He learned all this from his Southern-bred mother, he told me.

"What's your major?" I asked Monica, watching her work a turkey leg, trying not to imagine it was my cock.

"Art," she said perkily.

"That's nice," I said.

There was a long pause.

"So where are your folks?" I asked her, and it was like a bomb fell. "Sorry if it's a touchy subject," I then said to the shell-shocked pair, both staring at me, making me even more self-conscious than usual.

"They're dead," Monica said finally. "I killed them," she added with a morbid giggle. "But we won't get into that. It's Christmas. Let's talk about pleasant things, okay?"

Jesus Christ, I thought. Christmas with the Addams Family— or worse the Manson Family.

I nodded. "Fine with me." Then no one said anything for a while. This was beginning to feel decidedly awkward. My horniness was getting stronger and I was getting weaker by the minute. And this was my best shot in, well, a *while*. I'd never given Monica more than a passing dirty thought; she just looked too obviously like trouble, and I got enough of that already. But I trusted Doc, and also I was lonely and desperate, a lethal combination. Like Doc always said, when the dick gets hard, the mind gets soft. My heart was like a rock, however. For once I thought I could just bang a babe and not get all emotional with her. I wouldn't be able to take Monica seriously, not with that emerald mane, too much like William Shatner as Captain Kirk fucking that alien green girl on *Star Trek* (also played by Yvonne Craig!), and she looked like she only had casual sex in mind anyway. I decided to let the good times roll.

Doc broke the silence with some tales of his own background. His real name was Curtis Jackson, a life long aficionado of comic books and exploitation movies, which was obvious when scanning his flat. After dinner but before dessert he took Monica and me on a tour of his crib, which I envied, since I was into all the same stuff, but I didn't have the space or income for a museum like this. He showed us his collection of *Famous Monsters of Filmland* magazines, boxes of classic comics (mostly Marvel), Aurora monster kits (both in the box and assembled for display), vintage Mego superhero action figures, and shelves and shelves of videotapes. He also had quite a stash of old 8mm Castle films as well as stacks of 16mm prints, along with original movie posters and lobby cards from the '30s through the '70s. He had perfectly preserved his childhood, which he never talked about, but I got the idea it wasn't too happy. He was a geek that got picked on a lot, from what I gathered, plus he was dirt poor. This massive hording was sort of his revenge against life. I felt kind of sorry for him by the time we sat back down for dessert.

"Don't you ever get lonely?" Monica asked him sweetly, but eyeing me as she said it. We'd been playing eye-ball all evening. Little Elvis was feeling confident and ready to take the stage.

"I got friends," Doc said happily, but that was it. Like I said, he never talked about his love life, not even with me. He changed the subject, predictably. "Vic, tell Monica about when you were a writer in New York."

She looked at me wide-eyed.

I was ready to take full advantage of her enthusiasm. "I wrote about music, mostly. Punk and New Wave, and avant-garde art and movies—cult, grindhouse, like Doc stocks—and underground literature. Stuff like that. But I gave it up."

"Why? I *love* that stuff. I *love* Dario Argento and what's his name, Lucio Fulci. I watch *Zombie* all the time in the store; the customers get sick of it! You mean that kinda stuff, right? And I *love* punk! You must like The Cramps, right?"

"Oh, of course."

"And how about David Lynch? You like him, right? I *love Twin Peaks!*"

"Absolutely. *Blue Velvet* is one of my favorite flicks. Sometimes I think he's secretly directing my life, from a screenplay by Rod Serling, with a Henry Mancini soundtrack."

She considered that theory rather more seriously than I intended it, then suddenly said, "Russ Meyer! Just getting into his movies. I think *he's* directing *my* life!"

I hoped, since I was now *in* it. I tried not to stare directly at her tits as I said, "*Faster Pussycat, Kill! Kill!* Tura Satana rules, right? Russ was an Oakland boy, you know."

Monica reached over for a high-five, inadvertently or perhaps strategically showing off her own bountiful bosoms, which I tried not to notice as I returned the gesture. I had her in the palm of my hand, literally, replacing Little Elvis for a change.

"How come you don't write about that stuff anymore?" she asked me. "Must be a market for it."

"I'm not sure," I answered truthfully. "It's very competitive, for one thing. Also, I wanted to try something new and different. So I did."

"I like trying new and different things," Monica said with a smile. I looked over at Doc, who was beaming. He winked at me.

Later in the kitchen, while Monica was in the bathroom doing whatever she was doing, I got Doc alone as he was cleaning up.

"This *is* a surprise," I said to him.

"Merry Christmas," he said. "I had a feeling you two would hit it off."

"I still need to talk to you about what happened with Flora in Palo Alto the other night."

"You saw her? In public?"

"For the first and probably last time." I heard the toilet flush. "I'll fill you in later. Also, I met a guy who says *he's* the father of Rose's kid. He also said Tommy and Rose aren't even really married. I can't—"

"Forget that shit for now. You got your hands full right here. Go for it, my man." Monica walked into the kitchen just then, smiling with carnal coyness.

Of course Doc had it worked out that Monica, who lived in the Mission District and come over via MUNI, would get a ride home with me. And naturally I wanted to show her some clippings of my old column, which featured interviews of some people she may have actually heard of, like William Burroughs and David Bowie, both of which were very brief, but sufficiently impressive. I drove her to my place and took her upstairs. The band was playing the intro for Little Elvis' first appearance before a live audience in ages.

"You like Elvis Presley?" I asked Monica as she walked around my office, checking out the framed autographed photo of Mara Corday that I displayed proudly on my desk, taking peeks into the bedroom now and then. I was going through my CD and LP collections in there. "Come on in," I said to her. "My scrapbook is in here."

"I like Elvis *Costello*," she said, walking in. "You ever listen to any *new* stuff, like Nirvana or Pearl Jam? I like that, too."

"Not really into grunge," I said, rifling through my West Coast jazz LPs. "But I would like to live in Seattle some day. I really like coffee.

And rain. How about Chet Baker?" I'd already lost her. I should've borrowed some Jimi Hendrix from Doc.

"Wow, a real life detective's office," she said, still pacing around the other room. "The guy in *Kiss Me Deadly* lived in his office, too."

"Ralph Meeker as Mike Hammer," I said. "I'm just Vic Valentine as himself." I decided Esquivel was too esoteric for her, Martin Denny too exotic. I briefly considered the Aqua-Velvets or the Mermen, because she seemed like she'd dig surf music as much as I did, but instead I went for the throat: "How about Sinatra?" I was trying hard to set the perfect mood. Or else I was just delaying the actual act by prolonging the seduction process. I was out of practice, and nervous as hell.

She was way ahead of me, though. She came in and sat on the edge of my bed. "Vic Valentine, Private Eye," she cooed dreamily. "That's good enough for me. Hey, you got any pot?"

"Aw . . . no, no I don't. How about a martini? Wait—I can't make that either. Out of both vodka and gin. I may have some beer." My seduction techniques suddenly seemed hopelessly antiquated. If this were 1962, I'd already be inside of her.

"Okay!" She was already pretty tipsy from all the wine at Doc's place. I was a bit woozy myself, though I never touch wine. I went to the portable fridge and pulled out a Corona and popped the top, then came back to the bedroom and handed it to her. So much for classic style. But regardless of the method, the goal was always the same: get 'em tight to make 'em loose. This was just like the old days, when I would seduce young groupies with my literary prowess and star connections. I was living again. I put on an LP and Frank started crooning.

"What's *this*?" she asked, screwing up her face as Frank sang "All the Way."

"Frank Sinatra," I said. "I thought you said he was good enough for you?"

"No, I said *you* were." She set down her beer on the floor and hopped up from the bed and flipped through my LPs real quick. "Here. Play *this*." She handed me a Sex Pistols album I forgot I still had, since I never played it anymore. I didn't really want to make love to Sid Vicious and Johnny Rotten screaming about anarchy. But then this wasn't love, I reminded myself. It was hardcore sex with a hot young groupie. Lust, not love. I put on the Pistols and when I turned around, she was completely naked and lying on my bed, smiling slyly at me. I guess I finally chose the perfect music. I hadn't even shown her my clippings yet. They were all yellow and depressing, anyway. This wasn't the old days, after all. I was just old, but there was Monica, the same age as the others had been over a decade before. I was like one of those pathetic old guys who tries to recapture his youth by banging young girls. So what. I'd tried sincerity and romance. It didn't work. The Space Age Bachelor lifestyle was a myth. Live and love for the moment, *in* the moment. Dive in, Vic. *Drown.*

I quickly tore off my own clothes and turned off the light, since I didn't want her to notice my slight love handles, then climbed on top of her, voraciously slobbering all over her perfumed body, making her giggle and moan. Her skin was soft but firm, her nipples large and hard to my touch. She was the voluptuous drive-in doll of my dreams, Mamie Van Doren and Anita Ekberg and Marla English and Yvette Vickers, all rolled into one curvaceous package. I was so anxious I forgot to get a jumpsuit for Little Elvis. Anyone who was this easy had to be infected with *some*thing. I almost didn't care. Infect me, I thought. This would probably be the last time I ever got laid anyway. It's not like I was going to donate any more blood. *Infect me.*

After some intense French kissing, my busy tongue and lips worked their way down the length of her ululating figure, all the way to her feet. I sniffed and kissed her soles and sucked on her purple painted toes, then licked my way back up to her pussy, which by now was dripping with desire. I kissed her warm, fleshy thighs, then I went down on her hungrily. Even her pubic hair was dyed green. Like chewing on moist moss, but I did so with relish. She didn't want me to stop, grabbing my hair and groaning, pulling my face even deeper into her juicy crotch, wrapping her legs around my head and shoulders and bucking with ecstasy, arching her back with amorous athleticism. I immersed myself in her femaleness, her lusciousness, her scent. I massaged her breasts as I licked away at her vagina, which was gushing. She finally came screaming, in tandem with the Pistols. And she went on and on and *on,* my heavy breathing muffled by her insatiable muff. It was a good thing The Drive-Inn was closed and I had no neighbors. Someone might call the cops. It must've sounded like I was stabbing her to death. In fact, penetration of paradise was my very next plan. . . .

I climbed up and was kissing her belly and tits and throat and face passionately, ready to plunge my throbbing wood deep inside that green bush and spray her internal garden with my penile pesticide, when she suddenly stopped me and sat straight up, staring off with that look in her eyes. The Crazy Look. Little Elvis was about to explode, all ready to break into his first number, and now *this.* What was it? Sound check? Security problem? WHAT?

"I can't do this," she whispered. "I'm sorry." She slid out from under me and began getting dressed.

"What are you talking about?" I said, my boner hanging in mid-air like a missile with an aborted launch. "You just had like a two-minute orgasm in my *face,* and now you gotta *go?* What about *me?*"

"Men are so selfish," she said irritably. "You're all the same. Take what you want then leave like nothing happened."

"What the *hell* are you talking about? *You're* the one who's leaving! I *live* here!" I was frantic now, but my raging hard-on was still lingering, rigid and red with impending release. "I don't get this! What did I do? What did I *not* do?"

"I'm sorry," she said again, putting on her bra. It was like I'd unwrapped a Christmas present and now it was being re-wrapped and taken back to the store, just as I was about to enjoy it. "It's not you. It's me. Can't we just be friends?"

I wiped the residue of her vaginal juices from my mouth. The scent of her was permeating my nostrils and brain. "Monica. Look at me. What am I supposed to do now?"

"Jerk off," she said simply. "But do it in the bathroom. I'll wait in there." She took the rest of her clothes with her as she walked into the office, leaving me there alone with Little Elvis, just like old times. I went into the bathroom and put him through a record short solo rehearsal, shooting all over the sink within three quick strokes, even though my pecker was still aching from last night's maudlin masturbation marathon. Little Elvis had been rejected by an audience that once adored him. Maybe he'd been gone too long and was no longer appreciated. The fans had moved on without him. They merely satisfied themselves with his talents, then sent him back to Disgraceland. His services were no longer needed. All that remained were memories.

I washed my grimy hands and wiped my glistening genitals with the same towel, then went back to the bedroom and got dressed. When I walked into the office, Monica was sitting patiently behind my desk, staring out through the blinds at the misty night. "This is a cool place," she said as if in a trance. "I hope there aren't any hard feelings."

"There's not a hard anything now," I said. "Monica . . . why? What happened? I have rubbers somewhere, if that's it—"

"Oh, I never use those. They chafe me."

"So . . . what then? Why change your mind like that after you've already gotten off? I mean, I have to say, I feel a little used."

"I'm leaving," she said in a huff, heading for the door. "Men are all alike. Doc was wrong about you. He said you were different."

"Monica, wait," I said, catching her by the arm. She offered no resistance, but didn't give me eye contact, either. "Monica . . . I thought you wanted to, *you* know. All the signs were there, I thought. Especially when you took all your clothes off and lay on my bed. How could I misread that kind of signal?"

"I figured that's all that you wanted," she said coolly. "And I was right. I just wanted you to like me. But then after I came the feeling left me and then it was just you and me naked and I realized that's the only reason you want me. I mean, you don't even *know* me. You'd never call me, you don't care about my personal life. You didn't even ask me about *my* art." She started to cry, and I held her. "You don't even know my last name," she said, whimpering on my shoulder.

"What is it?" I asked.

"Ivy."

I froze. The flower pattern. *Goddamn it.* I should have known. I should have asked. "Really?" I said. "Monica *Ivy?*"

"Yeah, why? You don't like it?"

"No, no. It's . . . nice. Perfect, in fact. Just perfect." The Sex Pistols album had ended and we just stood there in each others' arms for a while. Then we started kissing, necking, first gently, then passionately. Little Elvis was called back out of his dressing room, sore and weary as he was from all that rehearsing. I should have known I couldn't get intimate with someone without it becoming emotionally complicated. The last name would have tipped me off, but now it was too late, I was in too deep. Well, almost. We kissed and I wiped the tears and mascara from her pouty face. She was leading me back into the bedroom by the hand when the phone rang. I let the machine pick it up. It was after midnight, probably Tommy. I'd talk to him in the morning.

Monica Ivy and I were back on the bed making out, undressing each other again, when a voice sliced through the mood like a machete. It came from the answering machine in the office:

"Hello, Vic . . . it's me . . . Rose. I . . . I don't know what to say to you. I thought you might be home, since it's late . . . I'll call back. Merry Christmas, Vic."

I had already run into the office, but she hung up just as I picked up. I played back the message, over and over, while Monica stood in the bedroom doorway, half naked and pouting. "Who's that?" she asked.

"Um . . . a client, very important client . . . from this case I'm working on . . . and I don't know how to get in touch with her. *Shit!*" I was barely aware of Monica now. I paced back and forth in my boxer shorts, listening to the message, again and again, as if there was a secret clue buried somewhere in those few precious words. But it was her voice, all right. Valerie's. A voice from the past. It was like hearing from a ghost.

"Maybe I should go," Monica said tentatively.

"Maybe you're right," I said with abrupt detachment. "I mean, I barely know you. Let's go out first sometime, somewhere, and talk. I'll see you in The Drive-Inn and uh, we'll set a date. A *real* one. Okay? I promise." I was helping her get dressed and leading her to the door at the same time. I sure was being nonchalant and less than gallant, especially so soon after my stab at sensitivity, but I couldn't help it. Rose had spoiled everything, once again.

I called a taxi for Monica and then stood vigil by the phone, waiting.

10

Pillow Stalk

ANOTHER SLEEPLESS NIGHT ENSUED, but this time, I kept my hands off myself. I tried blaming my insomnia on Doc, somehow. The Marquee de Sade, setting me up with this flower child from Hell. Green hair, like ivy. *Poison* Ivy. Like the Batman villain. I'd mixed it all up. If she hadn't been there I probably would've made it to the phone in time to talk to Rose. No. The machine would've picked it up and I probably would've slept through it. I wasn't expecting her to call so soon. This was all happening too damn fast. My life had been one long, listless lull, then *bang, bang, bang*. Well, *almost* bang, bang, bang. Flower power. It was crushing me.

At least I had Christmas behind me, always a relief. In a spirit of forced optimism and fabricated hope for the coming new year I changed the message on my answering machine, from Elvis' "Trouble" to Frank's "That's Life." I used the part where he sings, *"You're ridin' high in April, shot down in May, but I know I'm gonna change that tune, when I'm back on top in June!"* But this was still December, and next month was January, so I changed it again. *"I'm a fool to want you,"* Frank sang, *"I'm a fool to need you . . ."* No, too desperate. I didn't want Rose to know I was longing for her. I wanted her to think I was over her, and just looking for her to tie up a few loose ends. She had taken my hardcover edition of *The Catcher in the Rye* with her when she vanished. I wanted my goddamn book back. Nothing else. That was it.

I finally settled on me just saying, "This is Vic Valentine, *please* leave a message, and where you can be reached, thanks," over Duke Ellington doing "Creole Love Call." That used to be one of Valerie's favorite tunes. Maybe it was one of Rose's, too. In any case, she'd get the message.

I didn't leave the office that whole day. I watched movies— *Laura, Phantom Lady, Out of the Past, Criss Cross*—from my personal noir collection. I sat restlessly staring into space listening to isolated tracks from various jazz LPs by Gerry Mulligan, Chico Hamilton, Art Pepper, Miles Davis, Dizzy Gillespie, Quincy Jones, and Stan Getz. I ordered out for a pizza. The phone did ring several times, and each time I was disappointed.

The first call came from Doc downstairs, around one in the afternoon. "So how'd it go?" he asked me.

"Just tell me one thing," I said to him. "How'd her parents die? She really knock 'em off or what?"

"What makes you ask that?"

"She's the Bad Seed all grown up, that's why."

"What?"

"Nothin', forget it, just kidding. Actually, it was . . . interesting."

"That's *it*?"

"I'll tell you more when you tell me how her parents died, Doc."

"Well . . . it's pretty ugly. Murder-suicide, up in Santa Rosa. That's where she was raised. She was about fourteen and came home and found her folks dead on the floor. It was in all the papers. I remember reading about it."

"I don't."

"It was before you got out here. Anyway, she's a little screwed up, but a nice kid, wouldn't you say?"

I felt kind of guilty now. "Yeah, she just needs . . . needs some loving, I guess."

"No shit. Did you give her some?"

"Doc, take it easy. Jesus. What am I, Mister Kiss Kiss Bang Bang?"

"I helped you out, Mr. Bond. The least you can do is give me a field report."

"Doc, what the hell is this, one of those late night phone sex hotlines? You just horny or what?"

"Always."

"Then why don't *you* do her?"

Big pause.

"Doc?"

"Well . . . I can't hide this from you. I already did."

"*What?* When?" For once Doc had shocked the shit out of me.

"Last night, for one. She came over to my place from yours. She's still here, in fact."

"Wait, for *one*, you said. Meaning—"

"There've been a few other times. So what? We're not an item. Just two lonely people. And you're lonely too. I talked to her about you. You both have a lot of pain in your pasts, I thought you could share some suffering. And help each other heal. Is that so wrong? Vic?"

"I'm here." I didn't know how to respond. In a way, I was glad to hear Doc was getting some. But not from Monica.

"You upset?" he asked.

"No, no. Just . . . you didn't take *advantage* of her, did you? I mean—"

"Vic, you know me better than that. Come on. We're buddies who sleep together once in a while. 'Friends with benefits' is the trendy phrase for it. She has no problem with it, I sure as hell don't, and neither should you. It's just *sex*, man. Think of it as free physical therapy between consenting adults."

"So she must've told you how last night went with us, then."

"Well, yeah, though she didn't say much about whether you actually did the nasty. I thought she just came over for a rich chocolate dessert after a light meal that failed to fill her up. She did say you got a mysterious phone call and kicked her out, which didn't sound too gracious."

"I didn't kick her out, for Christ's sake! But I did get a call. From *Rose*."

"*What?*"

"I'm waiting for her to call back. She left a message but no way to reach her."

"That's incredible. This is getting weird. And good."

"For you, maybe."

"Are you glad? You found her!"

"Not really. She could've been calling from anywhere. Maybe she won't call back. Ever. I'm goin' crazy just sittin' here."

"I bet. I should let you go, then."

"Doc."

"Yeah?"

"Um . . . nothin'. Just thanks for thinking of me. I'll talk to you later."

"Okay, no problem, my man. Just keep me posted. And you're sure you're not pissed about Monica, right? I was just trying to help. She really likes you, you know. You could have a great little friend there."

"Yeah, yeah. No problem, Doc. Thanks again."

After I hung up I went into the bedroom and lay on the bed, beating my raw meat thinking about Monica sucking on Doc's big black cock. I couldn't get over it. At least it temporarily took my mind off of Rose. Rose. When she'd called, she'd identified herself as Rose, not Valerie. But the voice was unmistakable. When I came I thought of her, and no one else. Then I started up again, picturing all kinds of crazy crap. In one fantasy scenario, we were both rutting werewolves in that bestial campfire sex scene in *The Howling*.

The phone rang again around five, snapping me out of my ribald reveries. I was spent from whacking off so much, thinking about my close call, so to speak. This time it was Tommy, back in Pennsylvania.

"*What the fuck's going on?!*" he yelled. "*Where's Rose?*"

"I'm not sure," I said. I felt terrible, lying like this, but I did it anyway. "No strong leads."

"I want my fuckin' money back. This is fuckin' bullshit."

"Tommy, let me say a few things, okay? For one thing, don't *ever* leave a message on my machine again and call me a 'fuckhead.' Got it? Two, these things take time. I've talked to a few people who knew her. I know she's in San Francisco."

"Fuck, *I* knew that! This is *fucked*, man. You're getting me nowhere. I want my fuckin' money back. I'm coming back in a few days, and I want my money back, you hear me?"

"Even without the phone, all the way from Pittsburgh. Calm down, will'ya? Thing number three: I talked to someone who told me you and Rose aren't legally married."

No response.

"Yo, Tommy?"

"Who the fuck told you that?" he said finally.

"Never mind. Is it true or what?"

"No."

"No, you're not married, or no, it's not true?"

"What the fuck's the difference? I'm paying you to find her, aren't I? None of your fuckin' business, how's that?"

"So you still want me to find her?"

"YES! Fuck!"

"Then I won't be giving you your money back, some of which I've spent. L.A., remember?"

"For what? What did you find out?"

"That . . . she lives there sometimes."

"Yeah? Is there . . . she got a guy or what?"

"*A* guy? No. No one special."

"Okay, then how about a *bunch* of guys?"

I took a deep breath. "Not that I know of. I'm not inquiring about her sex life, just her whereabouts."

"All right." He was coming down from his rage fit now. "Whatever. But if you don't find her soon I'm pulling the plug, got me?"

"Be patient."

"Fuck you, 'be patient.'"

"Also, Tommy, I heard Rose has left you before this, and that you fucked around on her and beat her. Any truth to this, any of it?"

He got wound up all over again. "Who in the FUCK are you talking to? This is totally like fucked up. I didn't pay you to dig up dirt on *me*, so back off."

"Just tell me this, then. What was the longest she's left you before this?"

"I dunno. Month, maybe. Two months."

"And she always came back."

"Always. We're soul mates. She told me."

I cringed. "What?"

"She said we were soul mates. Connected on the inside. She said we always would be, no matter what."

"That's just what she told . . ." I stopped and caught myself.

"*What?* She TOLD you something? You *talked* to her?"

"No. No, no, of course not. I meant—*you* told me that. Already. What I need to know. What I meant was . . ."

"What?"

"Nothin'. I lost my thought. Give me your number there and I'll call you if anything pops up."

He gave me the number and a few more threats and then hung up. I'd forgotten all about Monica and Doc now. I went back and lay down, thinking about Rose telling Tommy that they were soul mates. That was much more powerful than sex. That was true intimacy. How could she say that to a bonehead like Tommy? And how many soul mates did she have, exactly? Doc could screw Monica from now till Armageddon, and I bet he'd never whisper in her ear, "Baby, we're soul mates." I didn't care anymore how many cocks had thrust into Rose's pussy. Penises and vaginas eventually rot away with the rest of the body. Exchanging bodily fluids was no more intimate than donating blood to a stranger in the hospital. It all blended together and washed away some day. But souls are eternal. Emotions linger longer than the smell of sex. When you're on your deathbed, you'd recall who touched your heart, not your genitals.

Even Rose's baby wasn't the ultimate shared experience. He was only flesh and blood, after all. And I wasn't sure whose. Maybe she wasn't, either.

But what the hell, I thought as I lay there in the dark. It could be souls rot away with the body, too. What did anything matter in the long run, except memories? And they only lived on in corpses that couldn't talk.

As the night progressed, I grew more and more morbid. My contemplation of the ephemeral nature of the Universe was once again interrupted by the ringing of the telephone. It was around 8 p.m. Denise from the blood bank.

"I thought you'd never want to talk to me again," I said.

"Why? Ain't no skin off my neck," she said. "What happened, exactly?"

"I'm not sure. The whole thing is a little fuzzy when I think about it. What did Flora tell you?"

"She just called me up yesterday morning all bent out of shape. She sounded like she'd been crying. She felt bad about something. All I could make out was that you beat up her boyfriend and she never wanted to see you again."

"That kinda sums it up, actually."

"Why'd you beat up her boyfriend?" I could tell Denise was amused by the situation, rather than turned off. She was enjoying this.

"He was *there*, I dunno. She invited me to this club and he was there. I got drunk quickly and she sorta pissed me off. It felt like a set-up."

"Your whole life is a set-up," Denise said. I could hear her smiling.

"No kidding."

"That was dumb, Vic."

"In retrospect I must agree. But it was just one of those things. The heat of the moment. I guess I just cracked."

"Well, I wouldn't come around to the blood bank for a while. But you wanna hear something funny? You remember Stephanie?"

"Who? That's right. The girl who calls me for my appointments. What about her?"

"She misses you. I think she has a little crush on you herself."

"Is she cute?"

"Not bad. Big breasts, pretty face. Young."

"What's her last name?"

"Huh?"

"Her last name, Denise. What is it?"

"Um, lemme think. I forget. What's the difference, anyway?"

"Denise, find out her last name or forget it."

"Flora's right, Vic. You *are* crazy."

"Flora said that?"

"*Oh*, yeah. *Long* time ago. The other night just confirmed it. Listen, my husband is on me to get off the phone. But lay low for a while. Maybe this thing will blow over. Flora's a nice girl. She probably feels bad you were hurt."

"Tell her not to lose too much sleep worrying about me."

"I'll do that. Come by and see me in a few weeks, though. I'll try to talk to her in the meantime, smooth things out."

"Thanks, Denise. You're a peach. Happy holidays and all that jazz."

"You too."

By this time I was sick of talking on the goddamn phone. I lay awake waiting for it to ring, though. Around 2 a.m. I finally drifted off in front of *Ren and Stimpy*. I awoke around ten the next morning, got up, made myself some coffee, scrambled eggs, and toast, and continued my phone vigil.

I knew I couldn't go on like this indefinitely. Eventually I'd run out of food, or would just need some fresh air. Even though I didn't plan on going out that day, I shaved and showered and got dressed, like I was getting ready for a big date. I sat there all day, all dressed up and no place to go, and no one to go there with. There were plenty of places I could've gone, should've gone, but if Rose wasn't there, I wasn't interested in them.

I got a couple of calls that day from potential clients I blew off, telling them my schedule was too hectic. It was stupid. This was a slow season and I needed all the work I could get. My priorities were mixed up. All I did was eat, drink, sleep, watch movies, and jack off. The absolute basics.

Two more days like this went by. Tommy would be back soon, and I had nothing for him. I should've been staking out the Bundy house if nothing else. I had a score to settle with that punk anyhow. And I would. As soon as Rose called. Something told me she would.

It was the middle of the night, around 1:30 a.m., and I was watching *Niagara*, a Technicolor melodrama with plenty of unintentional laughs, starring Marilyn Monroe at her most stunningly beautiful. Her character, a femme fatale named Rose. That's when the phone finally rang. I knew before I picked it up on the fourth ring who it was.

"It's about time," I said when I picked up.

There was no immediate response. I waited. Then: "It's been a long time, Vic."

"Tell me about it." I tried sounding cool. I don't think I did. My voice was quivering. "So . . . is this Rose, or Valerie?"

She laughed softly, and I could feel my heart melting. God-damn, she had me already. "Rose. It always was, even in New York. My hair is black now, though. It really is brown."

"Auburn."

"You say auburn, I say brown."

"I say eye-ther . . ."

"You say ee-ther . . ."

"Let's call the whole thing off!" I laughed then stopped. This was too strange. Old feelings and words came pouring out too fast. "Where are you?" I asked gently.

"I . . . I can't tell you that now. I'm sorry. I shouldn't even be calling you, but . . . I just couldn't resist."

"Why?" I said. I felt tears well.

"Why couldn't I resist calling you? Because . . . old times and all that. It's funny how things turn out. We're so close, after all this time. Geographically, anyway."

I paused, then said, "I miss you." I regretted it immediately, but it was out.

"I know," she said. "I'm sorry." The softness in her voice was killing me. "Things aren't the same now, Vic. My life is different. *I'm* different . . . it just wouldn't be good to see you again. I'd rather remember it like it was."

"You would? Vanishing on me without even a goodbye?" There was an edge to my voice now, but I couldn't help it. I couldn't contain ambivalence that had been building for so long. "It's hard for me to remember the good times without thinking of that. I don't see how you can, either."

"You're bitter. I shouldn't have called . . ."

"No, wait! Please don't hang up. Please. Please . . ." I slumped down to the hardwood floor of my office, completely at the mercy of this voice on the telephone. My loneliness wouldn't allow me to act aloof and detached. I needed her, and she knew it now, whether I wanted her to or not. "Please, Valerie," I whispered into the phone, eyes closed.

"Rose," she corrected me gently. "It's Rose, Vic. Valerie doesn't exist anymore."

"Did she ever?" I asked.

"Only to you, and the people who knew her back in New York."

"Why, though? I don't understand."

"It's . . . hard to explain. I just . . . I wanted my life to change direction from where it was going, and I didn't know how to do that without changing *everything*—who I was, my whole identity, which was wrapped up in this little girl named Rose, raised in small towns here and there, living with people who suppressed her, people whom she loved as family but could never relate to as people . . . surrounded by rednecks and cowboys and bigots. I needed to be around people like me, artists or whatever. I needed to be someone else for a while, or rather, live inside someone else's skin, someone who could blend in freely with my adopted culture without being judged, so I was finally free to be and express myself, who I was, deep down. And then after I'd been that person for a while, the one I invented, I wanted to move on, shed that fabricated skin, so that fake outer imposter had to die, so the real inner me could live and flourish without hiding anymore behind a façade. You understand?"

"Um . . . no."

"I *knew* you wouldn't. Listen, maybe this was mistake. It's like we're reviving the dead. It should stay buried."

"No," I pleaded. "It's not dead. Not as long as we're both alive. Just talking to you now . . . it is sort of like a resurrection. I was dead, Val, I mean, Rose, until I found you again. Jesus, this sounds so corny and soap opera. I just don't know how else to put it."

She was quiet for a moment. Then she said, "How could you still love me after everything?" It sounded like she may've been crying a little, which made me feel better, in a way.

"I don't know," I said. "But . . . I do."

"Did you tell Tommy about us?"

"No way. I won't even tell him I talked to you until—"

"Until what?"

"Until we've resolved this."

"Resolved what?"

"Come on, Val. Rose. Whatever. You owe me something after all this time."

"What do you want me to do?" She was starting to get upset now, but that was inevitable. "Come over and sleep with you, a farewell fling?"

"Okay," I said.

"I'm *married* now."

I had to laugh. "I know better than that, and you know I know. You and Tommy aren't legally bound. Your pal told me a few nights ago."

"Which one?"

"The fat one. Simon."

"He's not fat."

"Whatever. He told me *he's* the father of your kid, too, *not* Luke Brandon. Rose, what are you *doing*?"

"This is really starting to bug me now—"

"*Bug* you? I can't believe this. The girl I knew had a heart, a conscience—"

"*I didn't call you so you could lecture me on my morals!*" she shouted.

"Then why *did* you call me?"

"Because. Because I wanted to hear your voice."

"Not what the voice had to say, though."

"Same old Vic."

"At least I'm consistent."

"And boring and predictable."

"Don't make this ugly, okay? Let's just talk, can we, please? I've waited for this conversation for six years."

"That's too bad. You should've been out living your life instead."

"Like you? Hurting people?"

"I'm hanging up now—"

"*No!*" I yelled, standing back up and pacing with the phone. "No way. No more running, Rose. Just talk to me."

She was obviously crying now, but her tone was angry. "It's pointless. Hopeless. You're in love with a dead person, or a figment of your fucked-up imagination or something. Valerie is gone. I'm *Rose.*"

"Rose from the dead."

"Don't pull this glib shit on me, either. I know you."

"Oh, do you? Since when? I'm not the same old Vic, either, you know."

"It sure sounds like it. Judgmental, wise ass—"

"I'm older now. I'm burned out, to be honest. I don't care as much anymore. I don't want you back, Rose."

"Then what *do* you want?"

I have to admit she had me there. "I'm not sure."

"Whatever it is, it won't include me."

"Not even as a friend?"

"That's impossible and you know it. Too many lines have been crossed."

"I don't think you know what you want, either," I said.

"Who the hell *does?*"

"I don't care. Just clear a few things up for me, then."

"Like what?"

"Why'd you leave me, for starters?"

"I didn't. Valerie did."

"Oh, Jesus Christ."

"That's the truth. I killed Valerie. That was the only way to break free of . . . Of . . ."

"Me?"

"My whole life back there. I wanted to be just Rose. Start over again, but as *myself* this time."

"You know, you're beginning to sound schizo. I told Tommy you had the symptoms—"

"If you're going to insult me—"

"I'm trying to understand, goddamn it! Give me a break, will you?"

"You accuse me of being insane and you expect me to—"

"I don't expect you to do anything but tell the truth!"

"I'm trying! If you'll just shut the fuck up and listen!"

"I'm listening."

She got herself together, put her emotions back in order, then said, "I don't have a split personality. And I'm not disguising myself to fuck with anyone's head. This isn't *Vertigo*. I'm not Kim Novak and you're not Jimmy Stewart. Stop romanticizing everything all the time. This is me now, accept it or forget it. Even if my name had always been the same, or my hair color or anything, I'd still be different from the person you knew in New York. Even living together I hid parts of myself from you, and those parts wanted to breathe, so I had to leave, to set them free. Our karma had finished."

"Oh, don't hand me that crap, please! You can't blame everything on karma. Sometimes you have to take responsibility for your own actions, in *this* life. And anyway, what happened to all that soul mate talk? Or did you trade me in for a new soul mate, like Tommy? Or Luke?"

"Your bitterness is turning me off," she snapped.

"Just answer me, please."

"I don't have a soul mate. No one does. I realize that now. We're all independent fragments of the same whole, from the same source."

"Hole? Like a black hole?"

"Whole. With a 'w.'"

"I don't get you."

"That's why we can't be together. We've grown apart. Shit, we did a long time ago. I don't even know why we're talking."

"Because beyond all this hocus-pocus mumbo-jumbo there are tangible human feelings to deal with, okay? I'm a *person*, not a fragment. I'm a whole entire person, with emotions and reactions. I'm not a goddamn machine you can turn off and on at your whim. Nobody is. Not even Tommy, your so-called husband."

"He *is* my husband, whether you want to accept it or not."

"Legally?"

"Morally. In my heart."

"You still love him?"

"Yes. Even before I met him, I loved him."

"What?"

"I saw him play in New York against the Mets. I saw him playing and something moved me. He was on the San Francisco team and I took it as an omen. Then we met in a bar in North Beach. It was Fate. I'd always felt I would have to return here one day, after everywhere I've lived in my life—"

"Wait, slow down here. First, you saw him from the stands at a ballgame, and then fell in *love* with him?"

"I said I was *drawn* to him. Then when I met him in person in that bar here I realized he was the same guy I'd been watching that day, who moved me and made me realize I had to come back here. It all made sense."

"To who?"

"To me."

"You fell for some lug named Tommy Dodge watching him, what, hit a home run—"

"Actually it was a double."

"*Whatever!* Jesus Christ! Then you decide to dump me and come out here because Tommy Dodge hit a double?"

"You're looking at it wrong. I'd already made up my mind to come back to the Bay Area, without you. Something about him just . . . oh, forget it. This is hopeless. I should go."

"Wait, please. Please shed some light on this for me. I deserve that much since I'm the one who got told to hit the showers once Tommy stepped up to the plate."

"What do you want?"

"Walk me through this. You saw Tommy at Shea Stadium while I was someplace else. He touched you somehow, whatever, you moved out here, ran into him, decided it was karma, married him in Reno, had *another* man's baby, left Tommy without divorcing him, he hires me to find you, you find me instead . . . now I don't know what the hell's going on."

"It is odd that he hired you," she said softly.

"Karma?"

"Could be."

"But isn't everything?"

"Well . . . yeah."

"And you didn't help karma along somehow?"

"What do you mean?"

"I mean this whole situation is weird, to say the least. Almost deliberate. Like a set-up."

"What are you saying?"

"I guess what I'm saying is . . . I don't trust you now."

"That's your choice. I'm being as honest as possible. You're too much in denial to deal with the truth."

"*What* truth? Okay, you told me you, or Valerie, was from outside Chicago, raised by an ex-Marine preacher, and Tommy told me you were from Vallejo, a Navy brat."

She was laughing now. "They're *all* true. Sort of. I did live near Chicago when I was young. My father moved around a lot. He used to be a preacher, had a lapse of faith and gave it up. And he was never a Marine; he was in the Army. I did embellish that a bit, I admit, but what's the difference? By the time he got to Vallejo he was retired and doing some kind of government work. Vallejo was a cheap place to live at the time. We always lived just outside major cities, in affordable suburbs, but close enough to go into town when we wanted to. I went to New York straight from there, because even San Francisco seemed too provincial for me at the time, plus I wanted to get as far away from it all as possible, my family and everything. I wanted to be a real writer or artist or something, not just marry some asshole like my father and become a tormented housewife like my mother. I wanted an all-new life—can't you understand that? I wanted to put Rose away for a while until I could decide who I wanted her to be. So I became Valerie, who was *part* of Rose, of me, but not *all* of me. But after a few years of hiding from myself, I couldn't do it any longer. So Valerie died, and Rose was a complete person now, ready for a real life after gestating in this cocoon I'd concocted. I simply outgrew it, just like I outgrew my youth. Now I'm finally, completely me, and I don't have to run or hide anymore. That's why I found the strength to come back here, because I knew no one could ever oppress me again."

I'd been doing a slow burn thought that whole explanation, or confession, or whatever it was. "You know what really scares me?" I said. "That all this makes perfect sense to you. Revolving your life around baseball games and bopping around the country having babies—"

"Fuck you," she said. "This *was* a mistake."

"Don't you even care that someone, namely me, got hurt while you were out fucking around?"

"That's *my* responsibility?!" she shouted. "You're a grown man, or should be, or will be when you actually grow up."

"You're not making sense. At all. You're not really even married, are you? It won't change the way I feel, one way or another. Just tell me."

"I told my parents Tommy and I were married, so we could live together. Then it was like we were married. We never had an actual ceremony, but so what?"

"And he couldn't give you children, so you had one by someone else without telling him."

"I *did* tell him."

"He knows about Samson?"

"How do you know his name?"

"I met him. In Venice."

"When?"

"Few days ago. Luke didn't tell you?"

"I've only talked to Bobby and then I called Simon to meet you, so he could tell me what you looked like. I had to be sure it was you, that you weren't pretending to be Vic Valentine, the one I knew, to smoke me out of my cover. Bobby wouldn't tell me what you looked like. He's a hurt little child sometimes. He wants to destroy me and you and anyone else he can take with him. I won't be speaking to him again. But now you tell me you've spoken with Luke."

"I thought he'd spoken to you about me. He told me you didn't want to be found."

"He lied. *He* doesn't want me found, by Tommy or anyone. He's very possessive. That's why I can't be with him. So Bobby told you about Luke, and about Sammy. That jerk. I'll have to call him after all."

"Seems like you can't trust anybody these days," I said pointedly. "Nothing or no one is what they seem to be."

"Welcome to the world, Vic."

"Bobby did tell Luke about me, though. Then Luke beat the hell out of me."

"That's probably because Bobby told him who you said you were to me."

"I really didn't tell Bobby much."

"He's paranoid and jealous. So is Luke. *Men.* I'm sick of them!"

"So what about Tommy? And Samson?"

"I'm thinking of going back to Tommy once I get Sammy away from Luke and that bitch."

"Wait. Luke is *keeping* Samson from you?"

"*Yes*, that bastard."

"How come?"

"He's trying to blackmail me into going back to him by holding Sammy hostage. His name is *Samuel*, not *Samson*. I wish Luke would stop calling him that. He's even renamed him, that fucking creep."

I sighed deeply. "What a mess."

"I know."

There was a silence for a while. Then I said, "If Luke is married to April—"

"He isn't. If he told you that he's lying. She wants to, if only to get a green card, but he's putting her off until I come back to him, which I won't, even though Sammy means the world to me."

"Would Tommy take you back even with another man's baby in your arms?" I asked her.

"I hope so," she whispered.

"Rose . . . let me ask you one thing, and try not to get upset."

"I'll try."

"Who *is* the father? Really?"

Long pause. "I'm not sure."

"How many candidates?"

She thought. "Five."

"*Five?* Tommy's sterile, right?"

"Yes," she said painfully.

"Luke, Simon—who else?"

"No one you know, don't worry about it."

"Rose, you're killing me."

"How?"

"Your promiscuity. You weren't always like this."

"No."

"Were you faithful to me?"

"Hmm . . . mostly."

My stomach churned. "*Mostly?* What the hell does that mean?"

"I don't want to get into that now, probably never. It doesn't matter, anyway. It's all in the past. Let it go, Vic. Just let it go."

Silence. "Hold on," I said to her, then I went into the bedroom and got a pillow and returned with it so I'd have something to rest my head on as I talked. "Okay," I said when I returned.

"Vic?"

"Yeah?"

"It *is* good to hear your voice."

"It's good to hear yours too," I whispered. "In spite of everything."

Silence.

"Rose?"

"Yes?"

"Do you . . . do you ever think about me, or did you?"

"Yes."

"Really?"

"Yes. That's why I called." The tenderness in her tone was dissolving the tension, slowly. "I still think about you. I was sorry I hurt you. I still am. But . . ."

"But what?"

"I don't know. Sometimes I think I'm so together and others . . . I'm just confused."

"Me, too. Rose?"

"Yes?"

"Do you still love Tommy?"

"Yes."

"What about me?"

"I . . . I'm fond of you."

"Gee."

She laughed delicately. "I wouldn't mind seeing you again . . . sometime."

My heart jumped. "Really? When?"

"I don't know. I'll call you if I . . . get the urge. Right now I have too many problems to work out on my own."

"Like Sammy?"

"That's the big one, yes."

"I could help you, you know."

"How?"

"I could get him back for you. I would, too."

"You don't have to do that."

"I want to."

"Why?"

"Because. He means a lot to you, I can tell. Why does Luke have him to begin with?"

"When I told Tommy about the pregnancy, he flipped out and called me a slut, even though he screwed around on me all the time. We had a fight and then kind of made up, but I knew Tommy was holding it against me. So I talked to Luke and he said I could stay with him until I worked things out with Tommy. But he was lying. He hooked up with this other woman as a ploy, I think to make me jealous, but it backfired. I told him to give me Sammy back, but he wouldn't. Since we're not married I wasn't sure what legal steps I could take, so I don't know what to do now. I can't go back to Tommy until I figure it out."

"I'll help you," I said, though I didn't know why.

"Even though I might go back to Tommy?"

"I love you, Rose. I want you to be happy. I want . . . I want you in my life, somehow. Even if you're just my friend."

She was crying again. I was glad. "Oh, Vic . . ."

"But we'll both keep Tommy out of this until it's settled. Okay?"

"Okay. But what are you going to do?"

"Go to Venice and come back with your baby. Then you'll *have* to see me."

"So you do have ulterior motives."

"Don't we all?"

"I can't pay you."

"Just be my pal."

"I'll try. If you can forgive me."

"I'll try, too. Tell me where you are, though."

"Vic . . . I can't. Not yet. I need time to be alone."

"All right. Whatever. But how can I get in touch with you if I come back with Sammy?"

"I'll get in touch with *you*. When should I call you?"

"Give me a week at least. A week from today. If I'm not home, leave a message."

"Vic?"

"Yeah?

"I love you." She hung up as soon as she said that, but I would coast on those words all the way to Hell and back. If I made it back.

11

The Secret Snatch

THE HUNTER HAD BECOME the hunted, and the prey was praying. I didn't book my flight to La-La Land right away. I waited till New Year's Eve, in fact. I needed time to brood, to think. I wasted almost half the week I'd given myself to get Samson, or Samuel, back from Luke, but I knew it wouldn't take long. Like Luke had pointed out, I had a gun, he didn't. Unless he was lying. *Always* that possibility. But the real danger that kept me looking over my shoulder was coming from Rose's direction, and I wasn't even sure where she was. She had artfully dodged (so to speak) my suspicions that she was setting me up all along, playing cat and mouse with me, and of course she was the pussy, but in a way this no longer mattered. Soon I would have something she wanted, something tangible and precious, and we could barter on this basis. I tried to make up my mind just what it was *I* wanted, needed from her after all this time. She had been right when she told me that she was a different person now, regardless of any superficial changes. She hadn't elaborated on her promiscuity, during or after our relationship, which led me to believe she was somewhat ashamed of it. I gathered she was only experimenting with men, as I had hypothesized to myself earlier. I didn't tell her this, though. Later, I thought, when I saw her in person, something I strongly believed she had planned all along. But from what starting point, I could only guess. I was no longer in control of the situation, if I ever had been. Intentionally or not, Rose was weaving a web around me, and I was so desperate for her company I was actually helping her spin it.

I was dipping into my savings now, investing my own cash into this enterprise, with no promise of any reward other than some of Rose's precious time. I guess I seem pretty stupid to you. And if I don't, then you're worse off than I am.

I brought Doc up to speed, calling downstairs to make sure Monica wasn't around. I needed to avoid her for a while. I didn't want to lead her on. I can't hurt people like they've hurt me. Well, not emotionally. If I had the chance, I'd cause Luke and Bobby and other people from throughout my life serious physical damage. But knowingly hurt someone's feelings? I just can't do it. I'm not sure why.

Doc sounded strange to me when I went to talk to him about my conversation with Rose. He was rather remote, and it bothered me.

"I really don't give a damn about Monica," I told him, looking up at the big TV screen where Michael Landon was turning into a werewolf and terrorizing a sexy gymnast. Doc was hosting an all-day American International Pictures marathon, featuring many of my all-time favorites: *I Was a Teenage Werewolf, I Was a Teenage Frankenstein, Blood of Dracula, How to Make a Monster, Invasion of the Saucer Men, It Conquered the World, The She Creature,* and *The Amazing Colossal Man.* The bar was lined with losers and loners, all lovelorn, with nothing better to do than sit there and stare at vintage monster movies while getting hammered, recalling the more carefree days of childhood, watching weekend fright fests on the tube. And there I was right alongside them. There seemed to be no escape.

"She knows you don't care about her," Doc said coolly.

"I didn't say I don't care about *her*," I said. "I mean about your thing with her."

"Ain't no thing, my man. I told you. She's all yours. Really."

"Not yours to give away, Doc. She's her own property, right?"

"Spare me the politically correct shit, Vic, please. Especially coming from an unapologetic misogynist like you."

"How am I a misogynist?" I asked defensively. "I *love* women!"

"As long as they do what you want them to. All I'm sayin' is that Monica actually digs you. You're not chasing a fantasy. She's *real*. Take it from me."

"I can vouch for that too, Doc." I cringed, thinking about both of us suckling the same spectacular pair of bosoms. It was just getting too much like some hippie sex commune around here all of a sudden. "Anyway, I told you, I got business elsewhere."

"You mean with the Spider Woman?"

"Don't call her that. I love her."

"I can see it in your face, man. She's sucking the life out of you, I'm telling you. Don't go back down there, man. I got a bad feeling about this."

"Jesus Christ, Doc. You sound like the prophet of doom. I'm just trying to help her."

"But for what?"

"Friendship."

"Aw, shit. You know better than that. There ain't no friendship going on there. Forget the love thing, she's not even treating you right as a friend. She's playing with you, man."

"No, she's not. I thought she was, but she's not."

"Then why won't she tell you where she is?"

"She has her reasons."

"Like she's nuts."

"Oh, and Monica isn't? I wouldn't be surprised if she bumped off her parents, and made it *look* like a murder-suicide."

Doc looked at me with a coldness I'd never seen in him before. "She doesn't deserve that, man. Don't take this out on her. She's a good kid, and she thinks you're the cat's pajamas!"

"Oh yeah? Then why that crack at Christmas dinner, that she offed her own folks?"

"It's her way of dealing with the pain, man, by joking about it. Just forget it. Go to L.A. Let Rose screw you over again. I don't care anymore."

He walked away to tend to other customers. I finished my beer and left.

I didn't talk to Doc again before my New Year's Eve flight, which took off from SF International at two in the afternoon. By 4:30 I was back in my old Santa Monica motel, but a different room. I went to Dolores' Restaurant in West L.A., right near the Nuart Theater, and had the eggplant florentine. Then I drove directly to Venice in my rented Cadillac. If nothing else, I travel in style. Especially in an image-conscious town like this—and someone else was footing the bill. I even wore my shades after sunset. I wasn't just trying to look cool. My black eye was still healing.

The lights were out at the Brandon house, but I was ready to wait for him to return. Fireworks were blazing across the sky from the Pier, and people all around my discreetly parked Caddy were having a good time celebrating the holiday. Luke would probably be drunk as hell when he got back. All the better. But where was the kid, I wondered. At a babysitter's? Surely they didn't take little Sammy along with them to the party. But then Luke seemed like the type of guy who would do something like that. I checked the chamber of my .38. Full.

Green, blue, red, purple, white, pink and orange explosions lit up the windshield. The loud booming and yelling seemed distant despite the proximity. I was thinking about what Doc had said. He was right. What the hell was I doing there? And how was Rose celebrating New Year's Eve? Not alone, in any case. Like me.

I turned on the radio and a DJ who called himself Happy Harry Hard-On (I could relate to that alliterative moniker, except for the "Happy" part) was introducing a song—"Everybody Knows," by Leonard Cohen. *Again.* Different town, different station, same old tune. It's like it was following me around on this case. I almost turned it off, but the lyrics spoke directly to me, so I had to listen. I began to cry. Some tough guy I was. Raymond Chandler would spit on a sniveler like me. Hell, so would I.

I sat there until well after the last firecracker had popped, listening to the radio and wasting the battery. Midnight came and went. What if they were out of town? I could have wasted this whole trip. And Tommy would be back in two days, demanding information or a refund. I didn't plan on giving him either, but I couldn't string him along forever. I needed the baby in order to see Rose. I would wait here for days if necessary. I wasn't leaving town without that kid.

June Christy was singing "Midnight Sun" a little late, at around 1:30 a.m., when I made out two silhouettes moving toward the little house. I was parked down the block, across the street, so I couldn't be sure until the two figures walked through the picket fence and past the flower garden to the front door that it was indeed my quarry. I didn't notice a baby, though, and I was worried. In any case, I got quietly out of my Caddy and walked up to the house just as the lights went on in the front room. I hadn't pulled my gun yet. I decided to wait on that, try to reason with them, before I resorted to threats I wasn't sure I could back up. I'd never shot anyone before in my life, but I was willing to break a precedent on that cold, clear night, the first morning of the New Year, actually. I'd start if off with a bang for a change.

I crept stealthily toward the door just as it was closing. I jumped up on the porch and pushed it back open, scaring the hell out of April who was standing behind it. She screamed as I entered.

"I don't believe it!" Luke exclaimed. He seemed happy. He was drunk. I was tired of dealing with drunks. Why was everyone loaded all the time? It was as if everyone I met pumped themselves full of some sort of anesthesia. All that pain. But I wanted Luke to feel his—*and* mine.

"Oh, you remember me," I said, taking off my shades and putting them in the pocket of my trench coat, revealing my shiner as a reminder of my previous visit. "Even with my shades on. I'm touched. In the head, anyway."

"And I did the touching," Luke said, grinning. "Come back for a touch-up job, did you?"

"I'm calling the police," April said, heading for the phone. Then I heard Sammy cry out from the back room. The bastards had left him all alone while they went out. Nice family values. There was no question now—Sammy was coming with me.

"Wait," Luke said to her. "Let's see what Vic Valentine, Private Eye, has to say for himself." He moved closer to me. I could smell the booze on his breath from where he stood. He was grinning at me. I think he liked me. Too bad the feeling wasn't mutual.

"I'm here for Rose's baby," I said patly. "She told me you're keeping him from her. She wants him back. *Now.*"

Luke burst out laughing. He actually doubled over, in tears. Then he recovered and said, "You know, Vic, I'm gonna miss you."

"I'm all broken up myself we can't have a life together. Just hand over the kid."

Sammy screamed from the back room, and April went to him, shutting the door behind her.

"I'm not leaving without that kid," I said adamantly.

"Then make yourself at home," Luke said, "because that brat stays here."

"Why? You don't give a damn about him. You just want Rose, and you can't have her."

"What makes you think so?" he asked with a wrinkled brow.

"She told me herself."

"Oh, she did, huh. You spoke to her. In person."

"Well, on the phone. The point is, she doesn't want *you*, she wants her kid."

"He's my kid too, Vic."

"No hard proof of that."

He grabbed his own crotch and growled with a grin, "I got your hard proof right *here*."

"Not according to the mother. And she should know."

He moved closer to me. "What the hell does *that* mean?"

"Ask Rose yourself."

"I don't like what you're insinuating, mister." Then he lunged for me. I dodged, but he landed a strong, swift blow to the side of my head. I wavered and he gave me a wicked rabbit punch with his elbow. I fell as any rabbit would and began coughing for some reason. I felt dizzy. I thought of my gun.

"You know, Vic," I could hear Luke saying behind me, "I think I have you figured out. You *like* pain. See, I'm doing to you what Rose will do to you. Again and again and again. You just keep coming back for more. You like it. Admit it. You're one sick fuck."

Then he kicked me around my left ear. I heard bells and a baby screaming and Luke laughing and something that sounded like the "Hallelujah" chorus. I kept thinking of my gun. "Rose is lying to you," Luke continued, somewhere around me as I crawled around in pain, my favorite sensation. "She loves me, but I can't settle with just one woman. April knows that and respects it. But Rose, she's selfish. She doesn't want the responsibility of a child or a relationship with a mature man. She clings to Tommy because he's a boy she can manipulate. Not me." He kicked me again in the groin, and I groaned. "*No* one tells me what to do. Samson is mine, because April can take care of him, and Rose doesn't even want to. She doesn't want that kid. She had a fantasy of motherhood saving her from herself, but she'll never change. She wants a quick fix for her whole life, to live over again in a new body she created, see. But Samson is his own man. He's not a fucking guinea pig. He's a man in the making. And April and I will make him that way. He needs a real *mother*. Now . . . can I help you up? I think it's time for you to leave."

I reached my hand aimlessly into the air above my head, and he took it and pulled me up. As soon as I was on my feet, he slugged me again in the face. I felt something burst in my mouth, like my tongue, as I went back down.

"See? You *like* it!" He beamed. "You're a glutton for punishment. From me, from Rose, from *any*body! You *knew* I'd hit you again, you sucker! Vic, I'm sure gonna miss you. Now when you leave for the last time as this will be, I'm gonna hafta go out and *buy* me a punching bag. Having you around was saving me money and giving me a great little workout besides. But now—"

"Fuck it," I said, pulling out my .38 and shooting Luke in the fleshy part of his right thigh.

He yelped and went down to his knees, smirking. "Vic," he moaned, "I'm proud of you. You stood up for yourself, for once. Didn't think you had it in you. But now you'll hafta kill me. You up for it?" He lunged at me like a wounded bear. I aimed at one of his sculptures and blew it to plaster. He stared at the remains, squinting with disbelief. April was screaming along with Sammy in the back. "You should aim for the kneecaps next time," Luke groaned with a grin.

"Good advice for once," I said. "Just stay put or I'll take you up on that."

Training my gun on Luke, who was kneeling on the floor, holding his bloody leg, I backed up to the bedroom door, shot off the doorknob, and went in. April was on the phone, ostensibly with the cops. I hit her once with the gun on the side of her head. She went down, but was conscious. I was in a bad mood. I tore the phone line out of the wall and then cradled Sammy, who was wrapped in a blanket, in my arms, and walked out of the bedroom. Strangely enough, April didn't protest.

"You're in big trouble, mister," Luke said to me weakly. "This is a crime. You can't just shoot people and kidnap their children. You'll be put away for this." He wasn't smiling now.

"*You're* the one who kidnapped Rose's baby," I said to him, heading for the front door. "And I shot you in self-defense while retrieving him for my client. She hired me to get her child back. I believe she'll back me up on this. She'll tell everyone who the real father is, and it isn't *you*. You have no hold on this kid." Sammy was strangely quiet in my arms now, staring at me with his big blue eyes. I cradled his head and shot one more sculpture to bits before I left.

"FUCK YOU!" I heard Luke yell as I ran down the street and into the Caddy, which I'd rented under a false name, the alias I always use—"Chumpy Walnut." No one ever hassled me about it, which is strange, I guess. I always like to see if I can get away with it, and I always do. So far. Anyway, I'd arranged to drop the car off in Frisco. With Sammy in tow I raced directly for Highway 101 without even checking out of my motel. I had Sammy, so I had Rose.

As I drove north with Sammy asleep in the seat beside me, I thought about a lot of things. I was hoping people thought the gunshots had been firecrackers. The further I got with no sirens behind me, the surer of this I became, and I relaxed a bit. I also knew I'd have to go to my place before I dropped the rental car off up in the Bay Area. I looked awful, all swollen and bloody once again after a visit to the Brandon house. He was right. That *would* be the last time. It felt good to plug him like that. I never realized how good it would feel to shoot someone you don't like. I'd have to do that again sometime, I promised myself. In the meantime, I had a few problems to concentrate on. Once I had fixed myself up at my place, what would I do with Sammy? He woke up somewhere around Santa Barbara and wailed for most of the journey. I'd done him a big favor taking him away from those bogus parents. But how would I feed him? What do you feed a one-year-old? Milk? Baby food? Ice cream, I thought. I stopped off and bought a pint and fed him some Rocky Road, the same flavor as the highway we were traveling. The stuff dribbled down his chin but shut him up long enough for me to think. I didn't even know if the kid could walk by himself or what. I knew nothing about this kid except he belonged to Rose. I hoped she'd call soon. Meanwhile, I would spend the night with the kid, mostly in transit, then call Denise. She'd know what to do, all right.

By the time I made it back to Frisco, around daybreak, I'd made it my New Year's resolution to plan my life out a little more carefully from now on.

The kid could barely walk. He wobbled around my hardwood floor as I dialed Denise's number. She was just waking up, and had the day off because of the holiday. In the background Sammy spoke baby gibberish to himself, or maybe to me, but I wasn't paying any attention. So far he hadn't said any recognizable, intelligible words, like "help" or "thanks," so I had no idea where he was coming from.

"Denise. Vic. Sorry to bother you, but I got a situation here."

"Vic?" She yawned. I heard her husband grumbling beside her in the bed. "What's up? Besides me now, I mean. This better be good. I'm hardly awake yet, and you woke my husband, not a good thing to do—"

"I know, I know, but I have . . . I'll just put this to you straight: I have a baby here, about one year old, and I don't know what to do with him."

"Wait, wait, whoa, whoa," she said. She was awake now. "Is that what I hear in the background? A baby? Vic, what haven't you been telling me?"

"It's not mine."

"You *kidnapped* it?"

"Who you talkin' to?" I heard her husband grumble.

"Nobody. A friend," Denise told him. Then she said to me, "Vic, are you in trouble? Because I like you, but I don't want to get arrested as an accomplice."

"All I need is advice. The kid belongs to a client. I'm just, uh, babysitting for a few days, maybe not that long, hopefully not that long, and I have no experience whatsoever with babies." I looked at my watch. The Caddy was due back an hour ago. "Actually, can you come over?"

"*No.* I have a life. Just feed him and change his diapers. What's the big deal? Where's the mother?"

Then the odor hit me. Sammy had wet and crapped his diapers big time, no telling how long ago. I'd just noticed it when she mentioned it. My nose was still stopped up with dried blood. "Yeah, diapers. What do I feed him, though?"

"Food. Soft food. I don't know."

"But you *own* one of these things!"

"They're not *things*, they're people. Just remember that and you'll do fine."

"Denise, please. I need a hand here. I know I owe you my life already, but I'm desperate."

"You know who you should call? I'll give you Stephanie's number."

"Who?"

"Stephanie. From the blood bank. Remember? And I can't remember her last name, so you're on your own. Call *her* to babysit for you. She does that part time anyway. She's good with kids."

"I don't know. I'd be imposing."

"What do you think you're doing right now?" she asked.

"I know, but . . . you *know* me."

"Do I ever."

"Talk to Flora lately?"

"Yes. She's still upset, so I didn't get into it. Just let it rest for a while. So what's the story on this kid? Whose is it?"

"I told you, a client. I . . . I can't tell you more right now."

"Are you in trouble? I don't want to get Stephanie in trouble by mixing her up in some shenanigans."

"No, no. I'll call her if I need to."

"She may have plans, though. People sometimes make plans without consulting you first. I know that's rude and selfish, but . . . "

"What's her number?"

Denise gave me the number for Stephanie's home in San Mateo, but I didn't call right away. I tried calling that daycare center in Sausalito where Mrs. Parsons worked, but it was closed for the holidays. Sammy kept screaming. I called Doc but he wasn't home, and The Drive-Inn was closed as well. I'd have to rough it for the rest of the day. I hated fucking holidays. Just an excuse for most people to be lazy while I had work to do.

I went down to a Chinese-owned grocery store that was actually open, probably because they sold a lot of liquor on a day like this, and bought some Gerber's baby food in assorted flavors, some ice cream, sodas, milk, fruit, potato chips, candy, any junk I could think of. I got all the way home before I realized I'd forgotten to buy more diapers, so I had to go back. One year old and not even toilet trained. Or was he? We had been on a long car trip, and whenever I stopped off to leak by the side of the road I hadn't even thought to ask Sammy if he had a full bladder. So he burst on his own, poor little bastard (so to speak).

I was building up some serious resentment toward this kid by the time evening fell. He wouldn't eat anything I bought him and he gave me a hell of a time with the diaper change. On the way to the car rental place in South San Francisco he peed all over himself *again*. It was very embarrassing. I had to take a cab all the way back to my place. I was a nervous wreck anyway, waiting for the cops to show up with a warrant. Finally Sammy fell asleep on my bed around ten or so that night, and I fell asleep on the floor of my office, next to the phone, waiting for Rose to call.

The next morning the phone rang and Sammy started screaming again. It hadn't been a nightmare after all. It was around 9 a.m. Stephanie from the blood bank.

"Hey, Vic. We've never officially met, but Denise says you're in a bind and you need a babysitter. This is Stephanie, by the way. She said you might be expecting my call, so she gave me your number—"

"How soon can you get here?"

She was over by eleven. She was pretty voluptuous and cute, around Monica's age, well into the danger zone, but I had no time to ask what her last name was or even discuss compensation. I was out the door and to the Rendezvous for a little peace and quiet. Well, there was a lot of noise, but it was *adult* noise, and it wasn't my responsibility. Jesus, I thought. No wonder Rose dumped this kid off. No, wait. Luke was keeping him from her. Or was he? This could have been another ploy. What if Rose never called me again? Big joke.

The Rendezvous usually played classic jazz and lounge music over the sound system, and as I sat there sipping my coffee, dreaming, Nat King Cole singing "Rambling Rose," the lyrics haunted and tormented me: *"Ramblin' Rose, Ramblin' Rose, Why I want you, Heaven knows . . . Though I love you, With a love true, Who can cling to . . . A RAMBLING ROSE . . ."*

"Stop torturing me!" I said out loud, turning a few heads. They were all in on it, I just knew. It was a conspiracy of epic proportions.

When I returned to my place, Stephanie had bathed and fed Sammy, and he was peacefully sleeping on my bed with the door closed. She was sitting in my office, reading a fashion magazine.

"Hi!" she said cheerfully.

"Hey there," I said, sitting in the chair next to my desk, where clients usually sat. "I can't thank you enough for this."

"That's okay," she said with a sweet smile. "Denise says you're a good guy, and that's enough for me. Good guys are hard to find these days. Gorgeous kid, too. Whose baby is it? Yours?"

"Mine? Oh, no. Belongs to a client."

"So you really are a detective after all."

I looked at her for a beat. "What did you think I was?"

She shrugged. "I don't know. I just heard so many things from people at the blood bank, and I've seen you donating pheresis so often I thought it was like your *job*." She giggled.

I smiled back. My face was so beat up even that hurt so I stopped. "You've seen me? So how come I've never seen you?"

She snapped her gum. "Too busy watching Flora, I guess."

"Or the movie."

"You like movies, eh?"

"Yeah."

"You . . . I don't mean to pry, but . . . how'd you get so messed up?"

"Huh? Oh. My face or my life?"

"Let's start with your face." She laughed.

"Occupational hazard," I said stiffly.

"Does it have something to do with the baby in there?"

"Sorta."

"How long do you have him?"

I shrugged. "I'm not sure."

"You have any other clothes for him? I washed the ones he had in the sink with some hand soap because they were so grungy, but he could use some new duds."

I shrugged again. "I'm not sure when my client will collect him. She's off somewhere, and I can't get in touch with her."

"That's weird."

I nodded. *Ow.*

"I could maybe get a few things from my sister in San Jose tomorrow," she said. "She has a kid about five or so, and she may have some old clothes he could borrow. What's his name?"

"Sammy. Hey, thanks a lot, but you don't have to—"

"It's okay. No big deal. But . . . how long do you need me today? I came on short notice, but I could come back tomorrow. My sister's coming up tonight to San Mateo, and I could call her and tell her to bring some stuff."

"Stephanie, you've been more than kind. You can go anytime, come anytime. About your pay—"

"Don't worry about that. I'm off tomorrow from the blood bank. I could come over for a little while and look after Sammy, if you want."

"You're a sweetheart. If you can bring some clothes, great, if not, he'll just have to do with what he has for now. His mother should be calling me any time, anyway."

"If she doesn't, she isn't a very good mother," Stephanie said, walking toward the door. I agreed and thanked her and kissed her on the cheek. She was wearing strong perfume, which I'd just noticed because of my busted nose. She had a very nice smile, and as Denise had mentioned, a great pair of knockers. Maybe some other time, I thought. When this is all over.

I peeked in on Sammy. He was still sound asleep. No Sinatra, no TV. I sat in my office thinking as the afternoon wore on and dusk fell and darkness filled the room. I waited and waited, but the phone didn't ring all night long.

As I sat there, I remembered a girl I once knew named Valerie. She was an interesting girl, very pretty and intelligent, a living Gil Elvgren pinup with a brain to boot, popular with men but devoted to me. She had looked up to me because I was an established writer, though she was too young and naïve to differentiate between getting printed on a regular basis and being truly successful. She never received letters from or wrote to her family about her experiences in New York, on the town with an up-and-coming hotshot, a sexy scribe, a romantic Runyon who took her to all the big parties and cultural centers and nightspots. At least, not to my knowledge. She told me she had cut herself off from her past completely. I envied her, because my mother was in an insane asylum and my father had been a crooked cop who bought it in a dark, dirty alley. I told her my old man had been a drug dealer with a badge, and she felt sorry for me. She was there for me when I needed her.

As I sat there all these years later, silently staring into the darkness, I thought about that girl, listening to Tom Waits' "Blue Valentines" inside my head, where Sammy couldn't hear it. She was like no other girl I'd ever known, before or since, and I wondered if I'd ever see her again. I missed her. Rose sounded a lot like her, reminded me of her, but she wasn't her, I had discovered after all my tribulations to find her. Rose had brought her to life, and then she had murdered her.

But now I had fallen in love with Rose.

12

Poison Passion

I KNEW I COULDN'T get away with it. Not the way my life worked. What had I been thinking? Oh, that's right. I *hadn't* been. My brain had a malignant *amour*.

Police Inspectors Sharp and Shoemaker, a man and a woman, respectively, both in their mid-forties and with cold eyes and brusque attitudes, showed up at my doorstep the next morning around 8:30, waking me out of a much-needed slumber and typical fog-enshrouded nightmares. They flashed their badges and invited themselves in. Fortunately Sammy was still asleep, or dead. Either way, I was still in trouble.

"Let's cut to the chase," Sharp said. He was tall, thin and had a mustache. Shoemaker was heavier and softer but seemed tougher. "We knew Captain Marcus, we know he liked you like a nephew and that he was tight with your old man on the Brooklyn force way back when." Shoemaker looked around the office while Sharp spoke. Both were dressed to the nines, which impressed me, considering how early it was. For all I knew their shift was just ending. My stomach churned as Shoemaker opened the bedroom door and went inside. Sharp continued, "You know why we're here. LAPD called us because of a report of a gunshot victim at a hospital in West L.A. The victim says you're the shooter. It's just a flesh wound, but that's not the biggest issue. You know what the issue is." I nodded, but said nothing, just standing there with my head bowed and arms folded like I was being scolded by the principal.

Shoemaker came out of the bedroom and nodded grimly at Sharp. Sharp nodded back. The old silent cop code routine. I knew it was baloney, but it made me uneasy just the same. "There's a variable, though," Sharp continued in my direction. "The victim's wife's pressing charges against *him*."

I looked up. "What?"

"She has a conflicting story. Says the guy beat her—she a huge head wound where *some*body clubbed her, she says he hits her all the time and he has a sheet as a woman abuser a mile long, so that checks—but she says the intruder was a woman around twenty-eight years of age, black hair, a looker, named Rose Thorne."

My eyes gave me away.

"You *know* her?" Sharp pressed.

"Nope," I lied anyway. "I don't know a Rose Thorne."

He pulled out a notepad and looked at it quickly. "Says that she assumes the surname of 'Myers' as well."

I felt like I was being kicked in the head all over again. I shook my head again. "Sorry, can't help you."

"The woman says Rose Thorne or Myers hired you to abduct the child from their home, but you didn't actually shoot the victim. She says Rose was the shooter and you drove an unidentified vehicle, which makes you no less than an accomplice if this goes any further."

"If?" I said, badly shaken but maintaining an iota of poise.

"Well . . . we'd like to extend you some courtesy in the memory of Captain Marcus, whom we owe our jobs, basically. He told us about you before he died, said we should give you as many breaks as possible, because your old man was a . . . let's just say the captain felt sorry for you. So we want to honor that request out of respect for his memory, but we have to do some follow-up on this, turn in some kind of paperwork. All we need is your cooperation."

"Which means what, exactly?" I asked.

"Give us Rose Myers," Sharp said.

"I told you I don't know her."

"Then why do you have her child?"

"I . . . I . . ."

"It's obvious you're trying to protect her," Shoemaker broke in. "We ran a check on her and she's clean. We think someone is lying, probably the woman down there, who seems to have a vendetta against her husband and maybe Rose, too. We figure he was screwing this Rose, the other broad found out, they got into argument, and the woman shot him."

"April?"

Sharp smiled. "So you're on a first name basis with them. Jig's up, Valentine. Just tell us where we can find Rose, and we'll take it from there."

"What if I told you . . . *I* shot him?"

"*Did* you?" asked Shoemaker.

"I won't say till I have a lawyer present. I'm just being hypothetical."

"So you'd lie to protect Rose Myers," Sharp said. "Interesting."

"I don't know where she is. That's the truth. Actually, I was hired by her husband to find her, and she wound up calling me. She didn't ask me to retrieve her kid, I volunteered because . . . she's an old friend."

They were both staring at me now in a way that made me very uncomfortable. "Is that kid yours?" Sharp asked me directly.

"Yes," I said without even blinking. "It's . . . it's a long story. Rose and I were having an affair, her husband doesn't know this and no, I won't give you his name, but . . . it's just a coincidence, okay?"

"Hard to believe," Shoemaker said. "Think of a better one."

"That's the truth," I lied. "That kid belongs to Rose and me. I went down to get him back from Luke Brandon, who was holding him from us."

"So you shot him?" Shoemaker asked. "They still haven't found the weapon. They just know it was .38 caliber, standard cop issue. Anybody can get one, though. You have a license for one, in fact, so it could be you after all."

"It was," I said with a swallow. I didn't want Rose implicated in this. I had to come clean and face the music. It was my fault. I'd hung myself.

Sharp laughed lightly. "This is a tall order, champ. I mean overlooking this for the sake of old friends and promises. But . . . give us Rose anyway. Let her take the fall. She'll walk anyway, but we need a body for the LAPD."

I shook my head. "No way."

"Then you *want* to go down for it?" Sharp asked.

"For *what*? Kidnapping my own son? Anyway, he attacked me first. Look at my kisser. Where do you think I got all *this*, sparring with Mickey Rourke?"

"What was Brandon doing with him?" Shoemaker asked, checking out my bruises.

"He's . . . a friend of Rose. Or was."

"So he *was* screwing her," Sharp said. "Nice girl, this Rose."

"She is, actually," I said bitterly. "Look . . . can't you just drop this?"

They laughed at me. "This isn't a jaywalking beef," Shoemaker said. "This is major league. We could bring you up on charges of assault with a deadly weapon, abduction, a whole dirty laundry list. But we'd rather not in deference to the captain's memory. It's up to you."

I thought for a moment. "Let me talk to Rose first, explain the situation. She had no part in this."

"You'll just warn her and she'll skip town," Sharp said. "No can do."

"She won't leave without the kid," I said.

"We're detaining the child," said Shoemaker. "We have to."

"Then Rose will never see me," I said shakily. "She won't see me without the kid. We had a bargain. It's a long story, but I can tell you—no baby, no Rose."

Just that moment Stephanie walked in, perky and polite, her makeup on and her smile bright. "Hey, what's going on?" she asked.

Sammy must have heard her, because he cried out at the sound of her voice. She ran in to calm him, leaving her purse on the desk. Shoemaker went over to it and pulled out her wallet.

"Who's that?" Sharp asked me.

"Stephanie, the babysitter," I said. "I have work to do."

Shoemaker wrote down Stephanie's name in a notepad. I kept hoping she'd ask for Stephanie's last name. Instead she walked over to Sharp and asked him, "What do you think?"

He was looking at me. "Two days," he said to me, holding up two fingers. "Then we're coming back and taking in whoever is here—you, the kid, anybody. Two days. And don't try leaving town, because we'll have a man posted."

Then they left like two dejected Fuller Brush salesmen. I took a deep breath and went into the bedroom.

"Who were they?" Stephanie asked me.

"Clients," I said.

"Sure is early for business," she said. "I thought I'd come right over. I have a sack of things in my car, and I figured Sammy would want some breakfast, so . . ."

I leaned over and kissed her on the forehead. "You're a peach."

"What's wrong?" she asked. "You look sick."

"I am," I said. "Very sick."

"Flu?" she asked, concerned.

"Something like that," I said. Then I went to my desk and sat down, resting my head in my arms while Stephanie made coffee and breakfast for all.

The day passed uneventfully. I didn't leave, and Stephanie stayed until four in the afternoon. We just talked about life in general. She was very sweet but young, full of blood bank gossip, especially about me. I had quite a rep over there, according to her, varying from lady killer to serial killer, depending on who you talked to. She thought Flora was crazy not to dump her boyfriend and go out with me, and I had to agree. That's what she would do, she told me, blushing. But Flora was a distant memory to me by now. I kept watching Stephanie play with Sammy, and as I did, I felt an odd attachment forming for this kid, as if he really was a product of Rose's and my loins. He seemed to settle down as the day wore on, like he was getting used to it here. He actually seemed relieved to be out of his previous environment. But I didn't want him getting too comfortable. He wasn't my kid, after all.

Just before Stephanie left, I gave her a signed blank check, telling her to fill in whatever amount she thought her services had been worth. I told her I'd call her the next day at the blood bank if I hadn't heard from the mother yet. But something told me I would hear from Rose that night, and I was right.

But first, Tommy called. He was back in town. My imagination was working overtime. Stephanie was almost out the door. I told her to wait.

"Remember me?" Tommy said in his usual winning way. "I'm comin' over, and you better have something for me."

"No!" I said too quickly.

"Why the fuck not?" He didn't seem drunk now. He was dangerously sober, in fact. "You hidin' somethin'?"

"No, of course not. Jesus, Tommy. The truth is . . . I have company." I motioned for Stephanie to come over to the phone. "You know the kind." I winked at Stephanie. She understood.

"Vic, darling," she sang loudly in a sing-song voice. "Any more champagne?" It was a corny line, but delivered with conviction, and anyway Tommy was no mental prodigy.

"Oh," he said with a guffaw. "I get ya. If *any*one I know needs to get laid, it's *you*, Valentine. Don't let me stand in the way of progress. So when can we talk? You find Rose yet or what?"

"Yeah. I mean no. I mean . . . I got a few leads, but nothing definite."

"Valentine, I'll be over to see you tomorrow about noon, whether you like it or not." He hung up. I'd deal with it then.

"Still need me to stay?" Stephanie asked flirtatiously.

I smiled at her, thought about it, briefly imagined her long, brown, curly hair swinging in my face as she ground down on my cock and I gripped her juicy ass while sucking on those enormous tits, then decided against it. I knew Rose would call that night. It was intuition. I didn't need the distraction, or Rose hearing female voices over the phone. This had worked out perfectly because Stephanie had thrown Tommy off as far as Rose was concerned. At least temporarily. There was a chance I'd need Stephanie's talents in the future, though.

"I'll call you when I need you," I said to Stephanie. I kissed her on the cheek again, but she responded by kissing me flush on the mouth, giving me an instant boner I struggled to suppress. She made me feel like James Bond.

Then she tore up the check I gave her. "I feel like I'm in a detective movie!" she exclaimed. "I'll just chalk it up to experience." I was glad, since the check would've bounced anyway.

I was surprised Sharp and Shoemaker had been willing to cut me slack in the face of a confession. Flesh wound or mortal, it was against the law to shoot people. I could plead self-defense. It helped that the two cops had seen my battered countenance. And April was actually defending me. But I knew why. She resented Rose, and wanted her to suffer. Everyone involved was guilty of something, and with all this finger pointing a plea bargain could probably be reached, maybe even out of court. Captain Marcus's influence from beyond the grave was a welcome bonus I hadn't counted on.

That crack about him helping Sharp and Shoemaker to get their jobs was bogus. The captain was crooked as hell, just like my old man, and there were kickbacks aplenty, enough for any palm the captain wanted to grease. "Profits" from drug busts, union scandals, and even some gangbanger bribes were thrown into a kind of trust fund, of which I was a beneficiary. Marcus was paying people off six feet under, and I was grateful to have him on my side, wherever he was. It was the earthbound conspiracies that worried me.

And just who the hell was Rose *Thorne*, anyway?

That was the first thing on my mind when Rose called me just after midnight. We were finally in sync, after all. Karma. Fate. Coincidence. Whatever, we were happening now. "It's about time," I said. "Miss Rose Thorne."

She paused, then said, "I'm sorry, I've been busy."

"Oh, *you've* been busy? Not half as busy as me, I bet. Vic Valentine—Mercenary, Baby Sitter, Actor, you name the tune, I dance to it."

"You have Sammy?" she said simply in an even tone. I thought perhaps she was stoned because she was so cool, but that's just how it is.

"Yep, sure do, and a whole lotta grief."

"I'll just take Sammy, if that's all right with you. I have my own grief to deal with."

"Nuh-uh, it's a package deal, sweetheart. We need to talk in a big way. We have Sammy, but we also have some wrinkles to iron out."

"*We* have Sammy?"

"He's here, isn't he?"

"I'll be right over—"

"I wouldn't do that, if I were you. There's an unmarked police car cruising the neighborhood, or maybe parked with some dough-nuts and coffee across the street, waiting for you to show up."

"What?" She wasn't too cool now. "Why? What's going on?"

"I'll come to you. No one can follow me, I'm an ace."

"An *ass?*"

"You heard me, no time for games. And is it Myers or Thorne? Be straight for once."

A pause. "Thorne for a while, but I was born Myers. You can check on it, if you like. Thorne was going to be my pen name, since I wanted to disassociate myself from my family and my father's name and heritage. Okay with you?"

"Dandy. I just want to know who I'm dealing with, and that we're on the same wavelength."

"You sound funny," Rose said. "What's wrong?"

"It's the middle of the night, I'm tired, beat up, a suspect on charges of kidnapping and assault, and I'm hopelessly in love with a psycho. Other than that, I can't imagine why I sound funny to you."

She was silent for a few moments. "Vic, this is getting out of hand," she said gently. "I appreciate what you said you did—"

"Oh, I did it, all right."

"—and I'm sorry for any trouble it's gotten you into, but . . ."

"But what?"

Another pause. "Do you know the Cliff House?"

"I'll meet you in ten minutes. I live in the Richmond."

"I live in Pacifica, it'll take me a little longer. It's very cold out, though. Maybe we should wait."

"We both have cars, right? I'll bundle Sammy up. And it'll be easier to spot a tail at night, fewer cars and people to hide behind. Say forty minutes?"

"Make it an hour. I can't wait to see Sammy!" *Now* she was excited.

"How about me?" I said dryly.

"I won't really know how I feel about that till I see you," she said patly. Sometimes her honesty was brutal. Either that, or invisible.

"Right on the cliff then?"

"I'll park by the restaurant. Not the coffee shop, the—"

"Yeah, yeah, right on the water, near the house. An hour."

"Okay. Thanks, Vic. See you."

I hung up with a mixture of emotions. I felt like a blender trying to liquefy a handful of rocks.

As I bundled Sammy up in my bedspread—he was wearing new threads courtesy of Stephanie's sister—he was strangely silent and calm. He kept staring at me like he was going to cry. Then right when we were leaving, just as we were going out the door, he said his first intelligible word to me: "Da-da." It sounded like "daddy," anyway.

I made the unmarked cop car right away, a Buick Skylark, largely because the idiot assigned to me dropped his coffee when I waved to him. I took a roundabout cruise of the neighborhood before gliding down Geary Boulevard to the Cliff House. They only assign amateurs and rookies to guys like me, anyway. The guy would lie and say I never left the office in order to save face. Whatever. Wasn't my problem.

I turned on the modern rock station as I drove through the crisp, only slightly misty but rather windy night. I was hoping for a blast from the past, a New Wave oldie from my golden years in New York with Valerie. Instead I got Chris Issak singing "Heart-Shaped World." Even *more* appropriate. Fate was steering the wheel after all, I thought, as well as supplying the soundtrack. I flipped around the dial and found "In the Air Tonight," by Phil Collins. That clinched it.

When I arrived at the rendezvous point, I shut off the engine and sat at the designated spot with Sammy in tow for fifteen minutes before I saw a black jeep pull up a few yards from me. That seemed like a pretty butch vehicle for an angel like Rose, but then maybe I was projecting my own outmoded tastes. No one got out for a few minutes at least. We just sat there. Then I saw the jeep door open. I opened the Corvair's door. I saw a shapely shadow climb slowly out of the jeep, slam the door, and walk toward me, her long, wavy hair whipped by the marine breeze, her Gil Elvgren pinup figure, a tasteful slice of cheesecake, moving with painfully familiar grace and poise. Class. Like my mother always had. Like Valerie had. Like Rose . . .

I had Sammy in my arms as I walked toward her. We stopped a few feet apart and stared at each other. It was very cold but neither of us shivered. Our faces were flush from body heat, from warm memories, from old passions resurfacing in a rush. She was crying. So was I. Sammy cried "Ma-ma!" I handed him over to her. Our hands and arms touched as I did so. We looked into each others' eyes at close range for the first time in six years. It was Rose's face and hair but I saw Valerie in those eyes. She was different somehow. I couldn't pin it down. Overcome with emotion, I reached over and kissed her cheek as she cradled Sammy. I tasted tears. At first I couldn't tell if they were mine or hers. They were both. We were mingling bodily fluids, just like old times. Except now we had a baby between us—literally—and it wasn't mine.

"Life is strange," I said.

She choked back a sob. "No shit, Sherlock," she whispered, smiling.

We were warm, but Sammy was cold. We went into my Corvair since it was cozier than the jeep and I turned on the heater. She sat in the passenger seat, I sat in the driver's seat for once, Sammy in the middle. We just looked at each other through moist eyes for a long, long time it seemed, exchanging feelings and thoughts but had no words to communicate them sufficiently. That would have been clumsy, anyway. It seemed like hours passed before I broke the silence. I had to. The sun would be up soon, and daylight would illuminate our collective sins. While under the cloak of night I wanted to break the emotional impasse so we could work together in solving our problems, which seemed overwhelming but far away, like an approaching army. I touched her face as I spoke. Sammy had fallen asleep, so she concentrated solely on me.

"I love you," I whispered. "But . . . I don't even know where to begin." I could hear the seals on the rocks below, and a gull passed overhead, squawking ominously like Poe's raven. I wanted to shoot it. "I've waited a long time to see you again, and I'd given up hope I ever would . . ."

"Vic . . ." She took my hand from her face, kissed it once tenderly, then gave it back to me. "I told you, I'm a different person than the one you knew."

"I know," I said. "Valerie's dead. Buried. It's you I'm talking to now."

"But you don't even know me," she whispered.

"Better than you think," I said feebly. "And I want to know more. Everything."

"What about?" A tear trickled down her face, and I wiped it away softly, quickly, then drew my hand back again to my side.

"You," I said. "Jesus, you're beautiful. You look so much like my mother when she was young, except for the hair now. Why black?"

She smiled and shrugged. "Why not? I liked how it looked. It suited my mood."

"Black?"

"Um-hm. I . . . have a darkness inside of me . . . not all of me, but . . . I can't help it sometimes." She looked away at the sea, the waves crashing against the rocks, and I felt a chill. "Your mother . . . she went crazy, didn't she?"

"Hey," I said, gingerly touching her shoulder so she'd face me again. "That's not what I meant. She was . . . she wanted to be an artist, like you. She had dreams she gave up on, or that gave up on her. She wanted to play jazz piano, I ever tell you that?"

She nodded. "So do I."

"Still the jazz buff. We always had that in common. Except I was more into swing and West Coast and you were more into bebop and Dixieland."

"I go to the Monterey Festival every year, and New Orleans for Mardi Gras."

"My mother only played piano in church, and she wasn't even religious."

"That *does* sound like me. See, Vic? You're looking for your mother, someone to save you from a similar fate. You're trying to save me. But . . ."

She actually made sense to me. I was terrified, but fascinated. "But what?"

"It's too late." Her tone wasn't bitter, or even remorseful. Just eerily matter-of-fact. "This will be me until the day I die. And . . . I love you, Vic. I always did, even when I left, but . . ."

I could barely look in her eyes now. "Go on."

"I love another man, too. My heart belongs to him."

I swallowed pain. "Tommy?"

She nodded. "I have to go back to him. Soon."

"But not tonight," I whispered, and I reached over and kissed her on the lips, careful not to wake up Sammy. At first she flinched and wouldn't reciprocate, but I broke her down finally, and we locked in a passionate embrace, kissing, caressing flesh I had once known so intimately, but now had to rediscover, re-establish trust with all over again. When I touched her breast she moaned and stopped me, pointing to Sammy.

"My place," she said, starting to scoop Sammy up in her arms.

I stopped her gently. "Collateral," I said smiling, my hand on Sammy's shoulder.

She looked at me, smiled, then nodded in accord. She shut the door, walked to her jeep, started it up. My heart raced as she revved the engine and started driving down the Pacific Coast Highway. I turned on the jazz station as I followed her. Gerry Mulligan was doing his dirge-like version of "My Funny Valentine." I let it play as I stayed right on Rose's bumper all the way down Highway One, over the winding road paved through steep seaside cliffs, the waves foamy and dramatic beneath us, the moon and fog alternating control over the night, which was rapidly becoming morning. Not another soul in sight.

"Key Largo" by Sarah Vaughan was playing on my car radio as we pulled up in front of her little bungalow close to the shore, a few blocks off the highway and a short walk from downtown Pacifica, which was provincial and charming but somehow sad and desolate. Pacifica was famous as the foggiest city in the area next to Half Moon Bay further south. The residents were isolated except for the connecting highway. It was an artists' colony like Benicia up north, but not as chic. I had figured Rose was in Benicia or here. Maybe our souls were connected after all.

We parked close to each other, then she led Sammy and me inside. It was a small dwelling with one large room and an adjacent bathroom and kitchen. It was full of her paintings in various stages of completion, books, plants, a small television, a humble stereo system, some casual furniture, and a bed with rumpled sheets. She offered me tea, and since she had no coffee I accepted.

While I sipped my tea, she made a makeshift bed for Sammy on the floor beside the bed after playing a song on CD called "Sweet Lullaby," a mix of modern ambient music and singing pygmies recorded in Central Africa. She hummed along with it as she stroked Sammy's head and face with a maternal tenderness I'd never seen in her before. "This song always reminds me of him," she explained in a whisper. "It's so soothing."

My mother used to sing me to sleep, I remembered as I continued to watch.

"That tune will always remind me of you now," I said softly.

"I'm glad," she said, continuing to hum until Sammy fell asleep. Then she shut off the CD and came over to me. She gently touched the bruises on my face. "Luke?" she said. I nodded. "Just your face?" I shook my head. "All over?" I nodded. She carefully removed my shirt, gingerly touched my purple ribs, and I winced.

"Bastard," she whispered, her eyes full of tears. She began kissing my bruises, on my torso, then my face, then my torso again. I massaged her shoulders as she did so. I took off her blouse, and she was wearing a black lacy bra, which I unhooked from the front. Her breasts were as supple but firm as ever. I touched her hard, pink nipples. She moaned with pleasure, kissed me deeply, then unzipped my pants, kissed her way down, and took me in her mouth. I let her give me delirious head until I almost came, then I stopped her, kissed her with the taste of me still in her mouth, pulled her up, laid her on the bed, finished taking off my pants, removed her tight jeans and black silk panties, and made love to her until dawn and after, oblivious to everything beyond the perimeter of her bed, even Tommy, who would be waiting for me at my office at noon, when I was asleep in Rose's secret bungalow, entwined with her naked Vargas Girl body, the baby Tommy despised beside us, as if he were our own.

13

Double Deader

I WOKE UP AROUND one in the afternoon after the best sleep I'd had in ages. Rose and Sammy were gone, though, and I momentarily panicked, but I got myself together, threw on my clothes, and walked outside to find them.

I didn't have to go far. The fog was thick but I could see them down by the shore, sitting on the seawall separating the beach from a pathway for pedestrians and bicycles. It was chilly and I felt it. I was shivering when I reached them.

Rose smiled when she saw me, but her face looked pale, which I attributed to the cold. Sammy stared at me silently, sitting on the barrier as his mother held him. I kissed Rose on the cheek because she wouldn't give me her lips. I was scared now.

"Good morning," I said anyway, acting nonchalant.

"Hi," she said. "Actually, it's afternoon."

"How long have you been up?"

"Oh, a while. I'm surprised you didn't wake up. I gave Sammy a bath and got him dressed and went out for a walk, then I came back and made a few calls, then—"

"You did?" I said. "To whom?"

"Well, Luke, for one."

"You talked to Luke? He tell you he sicced the cops on me?"

"Yes, I'm sorry, Vic. He's dropping charges, though. April just wants us out of their lives. He's going to marry her, after all. He's not getting any younger, and he doesn't care about Sammy, especially now that he knows I'll never go back to him. He has nothing I want now." She held Sammy close to her with an intensity that made me jealous, but also touched me. I didn't think she loved even Tommy as much, because Sammy would always be her son, would forever belong to her, could never leave her; I was beginning to understand, a little.

"I was wondering why you and Tommy just couldn't adopt," I said, "but I realize you wanted someone that was part of you, that you couldn't lose except through . . . natural causes."

She nodded.

Finally I said, "You seem . . . distant today. Thinking of us?"

Again she nodded. "Yes. Vic . . . I care about you, I really do, and you're a wonderful lover, like always, but . . ."

"You love Tommy."

She didn't say anything.

I changed the subject, or reverted it anyway. "So Luke is off my case now?"

"I think so. He knows that he can't have April *and* me, and frankly the fight is out of him. He's no spring chicken anymore. He doesn't have time for futile battles."

"Who does?" I said.

"April only involved my name to force Luke to forget the whole thing. She didn't want Sammy around anyway. April was only taking care of him for Luke, but she was relieved when you showed up. At first she thought you were a hit man"—she laughed—"but when she realized you just wanted to take Sammy back, she made up the story she did. But now she told the police she was lying, that she shot her husband and tossed the gun in the ocean. They're writing it up as a domestic squabble. Luke won't press charges against her because for one thing she's lying, and also he has a record for assault and battery already, especially on women."

"Even you?" I asked.

"Even me," she said.

"Did Tommy ever hit you?"

She sighed. "When he had reason to. I gave him plenty."

"Rose, why go back to someone like that?"

"I love him."

"You love me too, you said."

"Yes, but . . . we had our time already. Last night was just . . . a relapse."

"You make me sound like a disease."

"No, just you personify a part of me that's . . . gone. I was visiting it again. But now . . ."

"You want me to tell Tommy I found you?"

She smiled. "You found me or I found you?"

I shrugged, feeling hopelessly inept. Time for a career change, definitely. "Whatever," I said. "He's probably pacing out front of my office now, wondering where the hell I am. If he only knew . . ."

She grabbed my arm. "No, he mustn't know. Please, Vic. Don't get vindictive and—"

"Hey, I'm not like that. I would never hurt you, Rose. Not like . . ."

"I hurt you?"

I looked away from her at the gray sky and silver sea, and said nothing. She touched my face, and I tried not to cry.

"I'm sorry," she whispered.

Sammy pointed at me and laughed.

The fog seemed to thicken as we stood there, and we started walking back toward the bungalow.

"Why did you tell Luke he was the father?" I asked her.

"Because I needed his help. It was selfish, I know, and bad, but I told you. I have a darkness inside of me sometimes. I don't know why or where it comes from. It's just *there*."

"And Simon Brewster? He's convinced he's Sammy's dad."

"I told him that to make him feel better about us being apart, like he'd always be with me because of Sammy, in a way."

"Father figures?" I asked, smiling wanly.

She looked at me sharply at first, then softened. "I suppose. You have a mother thing, I have a father thing. It's all so Freudian, isn't it?"

"I guess that's the polite term for it. I prefer the phrase 'fucked up' myself. But you'll tell Sammy Tommy is his dad?"

"I don't know. If Tommy wants him to think that, then fine. We'll see."

We walked in silence for a while, then stopped in front of the bungalow. "You know. I told the cops he was *my* kid," I said to her.

She smiled and kissed me lightly on the lips. "Want some lunch? It's the least I can offer you."

"All right. Might as well get a meal for my services."

"That's not *all* you got."

For some reason that remark made me cringe.

We went inside. I was quiet as Rose prepared lentil stew for us. I didn't know what to say or do. The phone rang and Rose picked it up as she continued cooking.

"Hello?" I heard her say. "Yes . . . Yes . . . Yes . . . No . . . yes, he's here . . . yes, *here* . . . he'll be leaving soon . . . no, no, I can't today . . . it doesn't matter what I *said*, this is what I'm saying *now* . . . next week would be better . . . none of your business! Goodbye!" She was stirring the lentils savagely after she hung up, obviously upset by the call.

After waiting politely and in vain for her to explain, I said, "Who were you telling I was here?"

"Actually, I was referring to Sammy," she said without looking at me.

"Okay. But who was it?"

"Bobby."

I felt a jolt. "Bobby Bundy?"

"Yes. Oh, that's right, you met."

I stood up and walked over to her. "You know damn well we met. What's going on?"

She looked at me now, hard as a stone. The wall that had come crashing down the night before was being rebuilt in a hurry, and there was nothing I could do to stop it.

"Nothing," she said in a spooky tone, echoing my own thoughts. Then she started dishing out the stew. When she handed me mine I just set it back on the kitchen counter, but she ignored me in favor of Sammy, whom she set on her lap as she sat down at the kitchen table, alternating feeding herself and the kid from the same bowl. I just watched.

"Aren't you going to eat anything?" she asked, peeking over the wall.

I decided to try drilling holes in it. It had worked the previous night in a different way. "Always come out smelling like a rose, don't you?" I said.

Her eyes went back to Sammy, who was watching both of us intently as he slurped, dribbled, and swallowed. Just like Rose had done with me not long before. I suddenly felt like I was being spit out. "Maybe you should go," she said.

"You didn't answer my question."

"What question?"

"Should I tell Tommy where you are?"

She thought for a few moments, eating and feeding. "No, please don't," she finally said, a softness in her voice now.

I kept the edge in mine just to be safe. "He's my client. He paid me to find you. I've found you. It's my duty to—"

"Fuck me?" The hardness made a quick comeback.

"You should be careful or Sammy's next words will have four letters."

"They will," she said. "Starting with 'love.'"

"Good, because that's what's going on here right now."

"I don't feel love from you. Only bitterness and resentment. That's why I think you should go before Sammy gets upset."

"Tommy's waiting for an answer."

"I'll give it to him myself when the time is right. You can tell him I said so. Just not where I am. I'm not ready."

"What are you waiting for? He's losing it. You know what the poor guy's been through on account of you? His career is in the toilet, he's in AA, he's—"

"That's not my fault," she snapped. "He's a grown man. We're each free to make our own choices, independent of each other. Tommy only has himself to blame for the shape he's in, and I'll thank you kindly not to lay any more fucking guilt trips on me."

"Your conscience is on a permanent vacation, though," I said.

She'd ignored that crack, but it was too late. She'd already lost her cool. I was breaking through the wall, but no longer liking what I found on the other side. I still loved what I no longer liked, however. That was my problem.

I continued my penetration of her psyche, via her kid. "Sammy, can you say 'fuck'?"

"*Get out!*" she yelled. "*I mean it!*"

"'Fuck' is not the same as 'love,'" I continued, addressing both of them, "but sometimes they both have four letters, and involve two people on intimate terms—"

"Get *out!*" She stood up, setting Sammy on the chair.

"—but one lasts much, much longer than the other. Take my word for it, Sammy boy. 'Fuck' is much easier than 'love,' and healthier for you, too."

Sammy was staring at me, wide-eyed. Then he suddenly lit up. "Fug!" he said, laughing and clapping. "Fug! Fug! *Fug!*"

"God*damn* it!" Rose hollered. "You leave right *now*, Vic! I mean it! I appreciate what you've done but now you're spoiling . . . *everything*. Let's just remember last night and not—"

"Casablanca?"

"Fuck off." She waved her hand with disgust.

"Yes," I said, heading for the door. "We'll always have Paris. Or Pacifica, as the case may be." I walked out and slammed the door behind me. At least I'd made a classy, dignified exit, even though I was oatmeal on the inside.

As I walked toward the Corvair, I looked around at the fog-enshrouded beach and neighborhood. It's all going to sink one day, I thought, and then what difference will any of this make? It was all an illusion, a sick charade, a bad dream in God's head that went on and on. Maybe He was in a coma. Nothing lasted. Computers were rapidly outmoding people. Virtual reality would replace actual experience. Man was creating machines that obliterate him, render him obsolete. What the hell, it was nature, not science. Progress. Natural selection. Emotions would be artificially created, so sex would become an historical anecdote as well. That would cure AIDS all right—total, worldwide abstinence. Then people would become automatons, get bored, kill each other, and die out to make room for the next species. Or earthquakes and tornadoes and exploding star systems would wipe out all life, period. Just a matter of time until God woke up and smelled the coffee, then the dream would finally, mercifully end.

While meditating on these pleasant notions I heard Rose calling my name, just as I was revving up the Corvair. I turned off the engine. She was running toward me, crying. I got out, walked toward her, and she jumped into my arms, sobbing. We just held each other for a long time. She kissed me. I kissed her back. We were pals again.

"Please don't tell Tommy," she said. "Not yet. I need time to think."

"About?"

"Us," she said. "Come back tonight. Okay? I . . . I don't want to be alone, not after last night."

I kissed her again, and wondered if I was dreaming all this, but then decided it didn't matter. Even if it was all temporal malarkey, there was no reason I couldn't have a little fun once in a while. I told her I'd be back, then left, driving back up the 1 to 280 and then 101 and across the Bay Bridge to 80 and into Berkeley. I still had a score to settle with Bobby Bundy, and I wanted to make sure I got there before God woke up.

It was drizzling slightly as I drove up University Avenue to Shattuck, went up to Dwight Way, turned left and then drove up to College Avenue and right to the Bundy house. I knocked politely on the door. A pretty Japanese-American girl, petite and feminine even while dressed in a blue Cal sweatshirt and baggy pants, answered the door.

"Bobby home?" I said with a smile.

"Yes. Whom may I say is calling?"

Bobby sure had her trained. What was with all these yellow-feverish bastards? He was not only a punk, but a sexist punk. I couldn't wait to see my old pal. "Tell Bobby it's an old friend," I said. She walked away, leaving the door ajar, so I went inside and followed her. I tried remembering her name as she knocked on the door to the bedroom and entered. Lisa. I was right behind her. Bobby was lying in bed wearing a Catwoman T-shirt and jockey shorts, munching on Doritos as he stared at a TV with a VCR hookup. He was watching Ray Dennis Steckler's *The Incredibly Strange Creatures Who Stopped Living and Became Mixed-Up Zombies*, which sounded like the cast of my life these days. Lisa hadn't realized I'd been behind her all this time. Call me The Shadow, clouding men's minds so they cannot see me. Well, sometimes.

Bobby saw me, all right. Lisa noticed his expression, and turned and gasped, "I wanted you to wait outside!"

"You can go now, Lisa," I said, taking off my shades and staring Bobby down, *Miami Vice* style. "Me and Bobby need to be alone for a few minutes."

Bobby fumbled for his glasses. "Go on, Lis," he said. "This guy is nobody." He put on his glasses and glared at me. Lisa gave me one last look of disapproval and walked out.

"You need a job, Bobby," I said.

"That's none of your business," he whined.

"And a new script writer. How is it you can watch TV without glasses but you need them to see me?"

"Is this a house call? Are you my optometrist all of a sudden?"

"Yeah, matter of fact. I came here to make 'em black 'n' blue. I think that's why you put on your glasses, you phony pseudo-intellectual cowardly big-mouthed lying sack of *shit.*" I went to grab him by the arm, but he scampered off the bed like a lizard.

"Don't touch me, man. You're crazy!"

"Frank Sinatra sent me," I said. "Says you're a rat fink who needs to be taught a lesson."

"So I lied a little, big deal," he whimpered as I closed in on him. I had him cornered, and he was cowering. It felt great.

"You dropped dimes on me to Luke, to Simon, and especially to Rose," I said, moving closer, insane with power. I wouldn't even need my gun this time. "I'll forgive you for Rose, though I *would* like to know what your little conversation with her today was all about."

"Nothing," he lied. "I wanted to know how Sammy was, and when I could come visit." His beady eyes were welling with tears. That made everything right. Almost.

"You knew I was there."

"So? Who cares?" Rose had lied to me after all. Oh well.

"Did Rose set me up?" I asked out of the blue.

"What are you talking about? Set you up for what?"

"Maybe you told Tommy I was a private eye now. Rose had you call him, suggest he hire me to find her. But you didn't tell him I used to know Rose. Rose knew who I was because of my ad in the paper, just as I had always hoped. But she didn't contact me directly.

She had you call Tommy up, suggest my services—no, something more adamant than that. Lie about me, say I was the best, which really isn't a lie in some circles, but you had no way of knowing that. So Tommy hires me to find Rose, but she calls instead now that she's sure I'm the Vic Valentine she knew in New York. But the game's just beginning, because her real objective isn't to see me. It's to use me, play with me, knowing all along I'd go down and get her precious little toddler back for her. Then she could reunite with Tommy and blow me off as a hired hand whose services had expired. No strings, all business-like, but at the same time she could get her rocks off toying with my heart, even sleeping with me, which is just a pastime for her, like, well, playing ball. Do I give you a solid rundown or what?"

Bobby was shaking, his eyes enlarged despite their beadiness. "You're one crazy sick paranoid motherfucker," he hissed.

"Oh, am I?" I was breathing in his face now. I had been thinking up this scenario on the way over, not sure whether I believed it myself. In a way, it made sense, except for a few loopholes. Every theory has those, though. "Maybe it was kismet after all," I said. "All part of the beautiful scheme, the grand design. Life, laughter, love. That's the secret, right? Sure. That's the ticket, all right. Sure."

I turned to walk away, leaving him a nervous wreck. I heard him sigh. I turned back around. I looked at him. Then I hit him once in the face. I heard his glasses crack, or maybe it was his nose. I didn't stick around long enough to find out. "That's for throwing that Venice welcoming party for me," I said as he slumped to the floor, hands cupping his face, blood gushing between his fingers. Lisa ran in and screamed. I brushed by her. "I'm a loan shark," I said in her ear. "He's way behind. Get a new boyfriend. He's a punk." I looked at him as she ran over to give him solace in his moment of truth. "No," I said. "Scratch that. He's a bum after all." Then I left.

I stopped by Trader Vic's in Emeryville for an original 1944 Mai Tai on the way out of the East Bay. Few people realize that Vic Bergeron invented the Mai Tai, at the old Hinky Dink's bar (which eventually became Trader Vic's) on San Pablo Avenue in Oakland—nowhere *near* Hawaii. That's why I always call Oakland "Home of the Mai Tai, not just the Drive-by." That poor city gets a bad rap in the Frisco-dominated media. Someone should start a campaign to have the Mai Tai declared the official cocktail of Oaktown, just for the positive press. Maybe I'd do it someday, if I got bored enough. They'd have to name a cocktail after me first, though. But what ingredients would be in a "Vic Valentine," anyway? Something fresh and forbidden that would fuck you up good. Anyway, after a couple more exotic elixirs I drove straight back to Pacifica, arriving at Rose's bungalow around dusk.

She hugged me warmly as I stood in her doorway, but I remained rigid—except for my penis, which was flaccid with forlorn fatigue. "Plan on taking me out at the ballgame?" I said.

"What?" she said with wrinkled brow.

"Just a play on words I thought up on the way over," I said, going inside. "Means nothing. Just playing with myself. I do that a lot."

She let that pass. "Where have you been all afternoon? I tried calling you."

"How did you get my number, anyway?" I asked, sitting on the edge of the bed.

"From your business card. You gave one to Simon, remember?"

"And you had Simon check me out, make sure I was the real, the one and only Vic Valentine."

"Yes, I told you that. I'm just being honest with you. I had to be sure before, before . . ."

"Before what? Rose, how come you've never even asked me how I got into this racket? Last time you saw me I was an up-and-coming journalist in New York. Now I'm a down-and-out private dick in San Francisco. Not a natural transition, normally."

"All right, then," she said, sitting down beside me. Sammy was asleep farther up the bed. The Deep Forest CD with "Sweet Lullaby" was playing on her portable stereo system. It was difficult to remain hard, at least on the inside, but I had to, at least for a little while. "Tell me. I've been wondering, but there was so much else to deal with. It doesn't seem like such a stretch to me, knowing your retro personality."

I took a deep breath. "My father had a boyhood pal who moved here, hooked up with the SFPD, became captain. When I decided to move out west I was originally aiming for Portland or Seattle but settled for San Francisco since I had this connection. He took me under his wing and suggested this so-called profession after I couldn't break into local music or movie journalism. It beat waiting tables, and since I was a freelancer by nature, what the hell, I thought. I gave it a shot. At least I was my own boss. Or so I thought. I have no formal education to fall on. My options were always limited. So I set down roots here, and . . . full disclosure, in the back of my head, I thought maybe I might run into you by chance, because you had always said how much you loved it here as a little girl. I had no idea you had actually *lived* here, of course. I became a detective for one real reason: to find *you*. I tried tracking you down, actually, with the captain's help, but we were looking for a Valerie Myers, not a Rose Myers, or a Rose Thorne."

"Oh, Vic . . ." That's all she could say. For once, she was speechless.

I took out the white gown photo from my pocket and showed it to her. "I've been carrying this around with me ever since Tommy gave it to me so I could find you for *him*. Big joke. Now I'll *never* give him this picture back. I tore up all my pictures of you, or of Valerie, a year or so after moving here. I wanted to forget you, I really did. I *tried*. But . . ." I threw up my hands. Rose was crying now. She took the white gown photo from me and looked at it, then handed it back to me. "How did you know I knew who *you* were?" I asked her. "You never asked me that either."

"I assumed Tommy would show you pictures," she said. "I knew my hair color wouldn't fool you. I knew you'd find me eventually, and in a way, I *wanted* you to."

"Did you get Bobby or Simon or somebody to tell Tommy about me, so he'd hire me?"

"*No*," she said emphatically, with a grimace. "Of course not. That's ridiculous. Those guys *hate* Tommy. They'd never have anything to do with him behind my back."

"I said, did you *tell* them to."

"No! Why would I? How would I know about you?"

"Ad in the paper. I ran it in all the local rags, hoping you'd see it and contact me."

"Well, I didn't. If I had, I would have called you myself, wouldn't I?"

"I don't know," I sighed, lying back on the bed, careful not to disturb Sammy. "I just don't know anything anymore."

She stretched out beside me, and delicately stroked my forehead. The Deep Forest CD ended and there was silence. Obviously disturbed by this, Rose hopped up and put in a mixed tape she had made, apparently with me in mind, a compilation of classic jazz—Ella Fitzgerald, Sarah Vaughan, Billie Holiday, Dinah Washington, Count Basie, Duke Ellington, Billy Eckstine, Ben Webster, Johnny Hodges, Mel Torme, June Christy, even Bobby Darin singing "Beyond the Sea." But the one she really wanted to play for me was our mutual favorite, our former theme song—"Cry Me a River," by Julie London. It was also featured in one of our favorite late night cuddle flicks, *The Girl Can't Help It*, starring Jayne Mansfield. The irony of the lyrics at this time overwhelmed both of us. No wonder that had been our song. It was prophetic.

We listened to the tape for a while, looking into each others' eyes for the truth, but finding only twisted versions of it, rewritten, revised for our own personal benefit, to suit our own divergent agendas.

This was always the case, though. She still hadn't answered my questions, which boiled down to one—was this a karmic catharsis, or another calculated head-trip down memory lane? Her eyes only told me she loved me, at least for the moment, and mine returned the sentiment, in spades. For a while, none of the rest mattered. The fact was we were together, for however long or short a period of time.

Tommy. I'd clean forgotten all about him. I supposed he was no longer waiting for me at my place. And Sharp and Shoemaker wouldn't be looking me up if what Rose had told me was on the level. Case closed. They had more important things to worry about than a tangled love affair. I wished I had, too.

Rose stuck her tongue in my ear and wriggled it around, driving me crazy like it always did. She stroked my loins, and all common sense began draining out of me. So I stopped her.

"We need to talk first," I said. "You know—the *other* thing you do with your tongue."

"This is more fun." She giggled like a little girl.

"Did you set me up or not? I need to know."

She matured quickly. "Want some lentil stew? I kept it warm," she said in a monotone, rising from the bed and heading into the kitchen.

I followed her.

"I don't know why Tommy hired you," she said as she stirred the lentils and then dished out a bowl for me. I was starving so I took it and began to eat as she talked. "It's hard to believe. I couldn't believe it myself when Bobby told me a guy named Vic Valentine was poking around asking questions about me, saying I was a girl he once knew in New York. I knew right off it was you, but I had to be sure. I really wanted Simon to find out what you wanted with me, if in fact Tommy had hired you or you were using that as an excuse. I thought maybe you wanted to kill me or something. It was too strange to conceive that it was just coincidence, that we were in the same city after all that time, and of all the—"

"—of all the detective offices in all the towns in all the world, Tommy Dodge walks into mine." Couldn't resist.

"Grow up," she said, sitting at the kitchen table. I sat across from her with my bowl. "Life is not a movie," she added acidly.

"Rose, why Tommy? I just don't get it. *Or* Luke. *Or* Simon. And Bobby told me he never slept with you, but obviously you're friends. These are just as mysterious as Tommy hiring me."

"Why? You met Tommy. He's like a god."

"A *god?*"

"Well, a mortal one. He's gorgeous, athletic, great in bed . . . a hero to kids, and . . . a nice guy."

"A real genius, too. Rose, you have to have next to nothing in common with this guy, and don't tell me otherwise. All the rest of it is superficial, and you know it. I mean, what do you *talk* about with a guy like that?"

"Sports," she said patly, looking down. "I like sports. And he's very intelligent, in his own way."

"You could say the same thing about a chimpanzee."

"You're just jealous," she snapped.

"Yep."

She looked at me and then down again. "You shouldn't be," she said softly.

"I want you in my life, Rose. In some way. I'm terrified of losing you again. I'm afraid you'll vanish on me all over again, and . . ."

"Would you try to find me?" she said coyly.

"No," I said with a sigh. "I'm too worn out. I'm getting too old for this game. I want to settle down, and at least attempt a normal life. Some semblance of it, anyway. Maybe we can move to Seattle together!"

She laughed. "Too wet for me."

"I thought you liked rainy days, like me."

"Yes, but not *constantly*. See? I like change. We don't have *everything* in common, after all. But don't worry, you'll find the right girl someday."

"I already have. Long time ago."

"*No*, Vic. I belong to someone else."

"Tommy? Jesus."

"Neither. *Me*."

"Next you'll say you're still trying to find yourself."

"In a way. *Everyone* is a detective, in that respect."

"Is that why you've been sleeping around so much?"

"You sound like my father now."

"I thought you liked that."

She glared at me. "Let's make a deal, okay? I won't be your mommy and you won't be my daddy, all right?"

"All right. But that doesn't mean we couldn't take care of each other *now*, as adults."

"I'm someone else's mommy, anyway. I'm not alone now, and never will be again."

"I wouldn't mind being Sammy's dad, if I had you too."

She laughed. "You? Come on, Vic. You're not cut out for family life."

"And you are?"

She stood up, her arms folded defensively. "This is getting nowhere. I really care for you, and I'd like to have some sort of friendship with you, but I just don't see how, given your intensity."

I stood up too and took her in my arms and held her. She was tense at first, but I kissed her smooth neck until she relented and kissed me back. "Let's just do the other tongue thing," I whispered. "Otherwise we'll just get into trouble. We think and talk too much."

She nodded and smothered me with her full luscious lips and we became passionately entwined, removing each other's clothes with urgency. But as I began to make love to her there on the kitchen floor as Sammy slept obliviously in the other room, the low-volume jazz music providing a romantic mood, I kept getting mental flashes of all the other men who had shared this type of moment with her. I pictured the looks of pleasure on her face as they held the same beautiful body I was holding, stared deeply into the same emerald pools that were her eyes, kissed the same tender ivory flesh, shared the same moments of discovery and intimacy and ecstasy. I tried to ignore these jealous fantasies, but the more I touched and smelled and consumed her, the less special I felt. Just as we were almost nude and ready to consummate our mutual lust, I stopped.

"You're right," I whispered. "This won't work anymore." I started putting my pants back on as she just watched, sadly and silently and stoically.

"I'm not thinking of anyone else when I'm with you," she said as a tear trickled down her lovely face.

"I am, though. I'm thinking of that brute Luke heaving and puffing, laughing even, and Simon falling in love with you, and all the others you've hinted at, even when you were with me . . . Rose, I'm sorry I'm not mature enough to handle it. And it isn't even the guys from the past . . . it's the ones from the *future* that bother me. You're so damn hell-bent on having your freedom and independence I don't think you could give yourself completely to any one man, even Tommy. Either you're fooling yourself or you're trying to fool me. If you really wanted Tommy all you'd have to do is go home. You were using Sammy as an excuse not to face Tommy, just like you're using Tommy as an excuse to run away from me. I think when you saw him back in New York in the ballpark you developed this adolescent crush on him just so you'd have a fantasy to believe in once you were alone again."

"Then how do you explain my running into him after that, and falling in love?" she said.

"Who knows? Maybe God is setting us all up. Maybe this whole planet is one big ball game, only we think it's chance when really it's rigged. You say you didn't put Tommy on to me. So how do you explain that? Rose, what's the point of finding you against all odds only to lose you all over again? Is God just sadistic? I don't want to believe this universe is run by some malevolent being. That's too scary, because that means there's no escape from this pain, even in death, like my brother thought. Like *I* think sometimes whenever I see a goddamn bridge anywhere. As hard as it is for me to deal with, I'd rather think *you* set me up. But not intentionally. I don't believe in your heart you'd intentionally hurt anyone. You *do* have a heart. I've seen it, at least when you're with Sammy. If there's anyone I'm truly jealous of, it's him, because I know you'll always be there for him, no matter what."

I got to my feet and finished dressing. Rose was just sitting on the floor in a daze, wearing nothing but her black silk panties and lacy bra, which was unhooked in the front so that her lovely breasts were exposed. But I felt nothing sexual for her at that moment. In a way, I felt sorry for her. I felt sorry for everybody, like Sammy, getting lugged around all over Creation with no one place to consider home or one person to rely on, unless Rose came through. I even felt sorry for the dead people on the jazz tape, who despite their passion and artistry would one day be completely forgotten, absorbed by cold, mechanical history, reduced to a computer chip in a library somewhere, which was more than could be said for me.

"You're right," Rose said, wiping her moist cheeks. "We think and talk too much. When you do, you realize . . . how futile everything is after all."

I bent down and kissed her forehead. "No matter what, in spite of God and the Universe and Tommy Dodge and your darkness . . . I love you, Rose."

She jumped up into my arms and we embraced as if for the last time.

As we held each other, I remembered that postcard she had sent to Tommy from The City, wherein she called their relationship "the stuff dreams are made of." That's what ours was, too. Her favorite quote was from a poem by some Latin dude named Octavio Paz: "To love is to battle." For a moment it all made sense. Maybe life was a movie after all, and when we died we just walked off the set and returned to reality. Maybe we were taking the illusion too seriously. But what happened to people you played a scene with and never saw again before the final fadeout? Would you see them outside of the film set, ever, somewhere in the eternal realm? I thought of this as I held Rose, my eyes closed, a torrent of emotions and memories enveloping us. We were making a memory now, one I would cherish and that would make me sad in the wee small hours of many a morning to come, lying awake and alone in my room, dreaming of her.

Half naked and tear-streaked, she led me to the door and kissed me lightly on the lips as I opened it.

That was when all Hell broke loose.

Tommy was standing there with a baseball bat, aptly enough. He took one look at Rose and then hit me across the collarbone. I felt something, either the bone or the bat, or both, crack as I went down. At the time I was too numb to understand everything that was happening, suddenly and quickly but in slow motion. I remember he kept slugging me with the bat and I kept feeling and hearing my own body parts break and bleed as Rose screamed and screamed, and then Sammy woke up and screamed and screamed, and then finally I saw Tommy's pain-wrenched face one last time as the bat came down on my head and everything faded to black.

14

The Wrong Goodbye

I WOKE UP IN the hospital almost two weeks later. I'd been in a coma, had numerous broken bones and abrasions, and for a while they thought I would buy the farm. But I pulled through, postponed the sale even though I'd made a solid down payment I probably wouldn't get back. I don't remember the clinical terms for everything that was wrong with me. Suffice to say I was fucked up real good.

While I was out of it, my court date for the DUI came and went, and I'd been ordered to pay a fine by mail, though they wouldn't suspend my driver's license thanks to my cop connections, but this was on top of medical costs, which were in the stratosphere somewhere, and naturally I was completely uninsured. Doc brought my mail by, along with some of my cheesecake magazines and pulp novels from home, but I wasn't really in the mood for them. Sharp and Shoemaker stopped by as well, telling me Luke Brandon had abandoned his story of me being the shooter. LAPD didn't know or really care anymore who had shot him since he wasn't pressing charges anyway. I was off the hook, but did I want to press charges against Tommy Dodge? No, I shook my head painfully. Let him go. He'd suffered enough, poor bastard. I told the cops this even though secretly I fantasized about shooting him in the kneecaps when I got out. But I would've had to have gone far to do it. He had already moved back to Pennsylvania, quit baseball altogether. He had finally found Rose—in the arms of the guy he paid to find her. For some reason I didn't feel lousy about this, though in my state I would have been stupid to give in to guilt; I'd paid the price for my indiscretions, such as they were.

But where the hell was Rose?

No one knew, but Sharp and Shoemaker were disappointed, since she sounded really interesting and they wanted to meet her. All they did know, through Tommy Dodge, was that she had moved out of her Pacifica bungalow, possibly to Miami Beach to live with her parents for a while. Tommy was finished with her, the cops told me. My job was done. I had effectively pulled the plug on Tommy's life support system by trysting with his true love, who also just happened to be *my* true love. I considered it a mercy killing, something I would've appreciated myself at the time.

I was laid up for another two weeks wallowing in self-pity as fractures healed and so on, watching the tube, especially *The Honeymooners*, the most reliable tonic for depression I know. I also tried to do some reading to take my mind off things, Dashiell Hammett and Mickey Spillane and Charles Willeford and Jim Thompson and David Goodis and Charles Bukowski, *real* literary tough guys, but mostly I just sat staring into space, books on my lap, thinking of Rose.

It was the first week of February, right before I was scheduled to be released, though I was still bandaged and beat up, like Kharis, the love-struck mummy, when Doc made his usual visit with my mail, all bills I had no way of paying. But this time, he also brought something a little extra special: a letter, postmarked New Orleans. I knew right away who it was from. I tore into it like a thirsty man lost in the desert plunging into a pool of water, even though he knows it's only a mirage. It was practically a goddamn novella.

Dear Vic,

By now you've woken up. I know, because I called your hospital from my French Quarter hideaway to make sure. Your bills are taken care of. Tommy gave me a lot of money because he felt bad about everything, even practically killing you. He's afraid I'll hold it against him so he paid me off. He's in Pennsylvania now in early retirement. He says he might get into coaching Little League. That would be good for him. When Sammy is old enough maybe Tommy can coach him. But enough of them. On to you. And me. Us. You realize that since I am here I'm not there by your side, except in spirit. I'll stay through Mardi Gras with my friend here and then move on, to Miami for a while so my parents can get to know Sammy, and then Europe maybe, where I have some friends and even some relatives. So I'll be on the move a lot. You were right. I use excuses to run away from people. But you made me realize why—I AM AFRAID. Not of commitment, but of ennui, and ultimately of pain. Even when two people love each other as we do there will be grief, from separation, from untimely loss, from lack of communication. Tommy and I stayed together for so long because we have an open relationship, quaint as that now sounds, though invariably jealousy and possessiveness came in from both sides and ruined it. I'll never do that again.

I give myself to many men in order to avoid one-on-one intimacy, because I don't like being vulnerable and I don't like hurting people. Pain just seems like the natural outcome of romantic love. But with Sammy our bond is mutual and unbreakable. We can never alienate each other forever. I will always be his mother and he will always be my son. I hope I don't try to mold him into something he isn't, a better version of my father or Tommy or even you, all of whom have traits and qualities I would love for Sammy to possess.

As for our reunion, and what it meant . . . I don't know. You can believe what you want and you will anyway, so I won't bother to defend or rationalize my position. I do believe in karma and destiny, and for me that offers enough explanation. Obviously this was all meant to be.

Why? That's where I personally stop asking questions. We are not meant to know everything. All we are given are clues, for us to sort out and arrive at our own individual conclusions. For a detective this is a frustrating premise, since he is compelled to find the absolute truth and then nail someone for it, but to me life is not in black-and-white. Perhaps I watch old movies because they are. Life would be so much simpler if it was like an old movie. But we are in color, Vic—blinding, radiant Technicolor, with all the complexity that implies. Stop trying to find your young mother and save her. Please. Just save yourself first, and then maybe your mother will see the light as well. You can only lead her or anyone out of the darkness if you know the way to go.

Anyway, enough stream-of-conscious rambling. I'm sitting in Café du Monde as I write this, on Decatur Street, right on the river. Try to make it here someday, and remember I sat here thinking of you, and that wherever I am in the world, I'll be thinking of you there as well. DO NOT TRY TO FIND ME AGAIN. If we're meant to see each other again, we will. If nothing else, the recent past proves that.

Enclosed is a tape I made of "Sweet Lullaby" and a few other songs to commemorate our special night together. You told me once you'd always think of me when you heard it. Well, here it is. Think of me, Vic.

Love, Rose

P.S. Bobby blew the whistle on you to Tommy because you beat him up and humiliated him, and because he was jealous of you and me. Please leave him alone. I'm only telling you this because you'll figure it out anyway and take it out on him. Let it go, Vic. It's all over. I'll see you in our dreams.

I fell in love with her all over again.

"I met her," Doc told me as I gave him the letter to read. The tape and letter had been sent in one package. "She was here when they first checked you in," he told me as he scanned the letter.

"She called 911 and an ambulance brought you here, and since you have no immediate family anyone knew of, they got a hold of me."

"How'd they know were we friends?"

"Rose knew, somehow," he said. "She even said it was nice to meet me. I guess she'd been keeping tabs on you or something. Doesn't make no difference now. She was a nice lady, really gorgeous like you said, but you'll forgive me if I say I won't miss her. I was glad to see her go, which she did soon as she knew I'd be here for you when you woke up."

"Maybe she did set all this up," I murmured.

"What's that, my man?"

"Nothin'. Just finish the letter."

He did. "I would've told you sooner I met her, but I wanted your head to be clear first. You've been kinda spacey lately. Couple of times I came by you hardly recognized me. Either that, or you were just ignoring me 'cause of our tiff about Monica."

"What tiff?"

"I guess it was just me, then." He handed me back the letter, which I held like it was the Declaration of Independence. In a way, it was. "She sounds about like she looks: smart but slippery."

"Slippery? You mean like slimy?"

"No . . . elusive. She's right. If you're meant to see her again, you will. If not, you won't. Just let her go, and live your life as if you *won't* see her again. Chances are, this is a closed book."

"Think so?"

"C'mon, Vic. Look at you. I've never seen anyone so fucked up over a broad. Literally. You got the life beaten out of you chasing her tail around. What's *wrong* with you?"

I nodded, and something hurt when I did. "Yeah, let it go. She's gone. My mother . . ."

"Your mother? What about her?"

"Nothin'. Where'd you say yours was from again?"

"Arkansas. She met Bill Clinton once."

"That's right. It's all coming back to me now."

"Your brain too much like pulp to remember who your best friend in the world is?"

I grinned.

He held my hand for a minute, then pulled it away. "Okay, 'nuff of that homo shit. Here. I got somethin' for you." He reached down into a brown shopping bag and pulled out two items: A huge dart board shaped like a heart, candy apple red with little cupid darts to go with it, and the new official Bettie Page calendar. I looked them over as Doc flashed his gap-toothed grin.

"Thanks, Doc. Where'd you get this dart board?"

"Made it. You inspired me. Get the symbolism?"

"You're deep. Real deep. I dig it, though. And the calendar's great, though it looks like the year started without me. I never really noticed, but Monica looks a little like Bettie, the eyes and thighs. Hey, how *is* Monica, anyway? Where is she?"

"She's okay. She wanted to come see you but I told her you weren't ready yet."

"Tell her I'd like to see her as soon as I get out."

"She's a good kid, Vic. Be kind to her."

"You still doin' her?"

"Naw, you know me. I don't like long-term things. There ain't no love lost, though. We're still friends."

"Why don't you ever talk about your love life?"

"Ain't nothin' to talk about, my man. And I want to keep it that way. I get plenty of satisfaction just listenin'. And no way I could entertain myself the way *you* entertain me. You get enough action for *both* of us."

We laughed. But inside I was miserable, aching for Rose's touch.

When I finally made it home I relaxed and tossed darts at my heart board, which I hung over my wall safe. I jerked off to the Bettie calendar, but thought of Rose when I climaxed. I was beating off so much I even did it in my wet dreams rather than actually getting laid. Back to the same old lifestyle, if you want to call this a life, and you consider that style. I was feeling sorry for myself, but in an odd way, I felt triumphant. I'd weathered the worst and I was still here. There was a reason for that. I had work to do.

I also took small consolation in knowing Rose was thinking of me down in The Big Easy, and would be wherever she went. I knew I had made an indelible impression on her soul. Something told me I'd see her again, even if it was at that big wrap party in the sky. There are still dark moments of doubt and loneliness when I grapple with internal wounds that lasted long after my physical abrasions had healed, but everyone has those scars. *Everyone.*

Valentine's Day was fast approaching and I had no date, so I decided to ask Monica out as a warm-up. The worst day of the year was only a few days off, but maybe by then I could force myself to fall in love with her. So one day after her shift at The Drive-Inn I took her down to Rendezvous for a casual meal and coffee. They were playing classic love songs like "Since I Fell for You" by Lenny Welch, "Then You Can Tell Me Goodbye" by the Casinos, some Roy Orbison weepers, and Nat King Cole doing "Unforgettable," which meant "Ramblin' Rose" was coming up. I tried to ignore it. I used to love Nat King Cole. Now he just seemed like a mean guy. But I didn't want to be traumatized to the point where just the mention of the word "rose" would throw me into a fit of rage. Having Monica there helped. A little.

"Why haven't you ever been married?" she asked me, licking whipped cream from her lips, giving me nasty ideas.

"Haven't met the right one yet," I said. "Ramblin' Rose" came on, and my eyes watered, but I fought it.

"Have you ever been engaged?" Monica asked me.

"Once. Long time ago. Didn't work out."

"What happened? You seem like such an interesting guy. Was it over money?"

"Money? No. Not an issue there, though it has been since with other women. No, this girl just wanted her freedom to explore all her options, and I . . . I wanted too much from her, wanted her all to myself. You can't do that, try to own people, bend them to your will, force them to make you happy."

"I know what you mean. Guys try to possess me all the time, but I'm not ready for that."

"No? Well, you're young anyway. Just be honest with them. Try not to hurt anybody. There's too much pain in this world already. Once you open up to someone, you have a responsibility to respect their feelings."

"You sound like a counselor. Maybe you should try that some day."

"Maybe. I gotta change *some*thing in my life, that's for sure."

"Ramblin' Rose" finally ended. I made it, even though the lyrics echoed in my head, drowning out the world around me, including Monica.

"Who will love you, With a love true, When your ramblin' days are gone . . ."

I walked her back to my place, but we didn't fool around. I explained to her I'd just been in the hospital and sex was the last thing on my mind, which was a lie, but she bought it anyway. So we just sat and talked for a little while. I appreciated her feminine companionship, but in a way she made me miss Rose all the more, because she wasn't Rose. I felt like I would never fully recover. All that seeing Rose and rekindling the flame had accomplished was re-opening ancient wounds. I felt like I was bleeding all over Monica and anyone close to me. There was no way I'd fall in love with her by Valentine's Day. I was doomed to another lonely one.

"Doc told me about your parents," I said to her as we sat on my bed, watching Dean Martin in *The Silencers* with the sound down. Monica seemed uncomfortable when I mentioned her parents, so I talked about mine. "My old man was a dirty cop," I explained.

"My mother went loony and had to be committed. My old man's dead, too. Got shot down in an alley one night while off duty, right near this bar in Brooklyn where he played pool all the time."

She stared wide-eyed with wonderment. "Wow. What happened?"

"What do *I* think? Drug deal gone sour maybe. Or he owed money to a bookie. He dealt and gambled all the time. Slept with hookers, too. All kinds of women, I heard, so maybe it was a pissed-off husband or boyfriend who took him out. It was messy enough, could've been a crime of passion. Anyway, my mother knew a lot of this but was so wrapped up in her own life she almost didn't care. Then she flipped out one day, hearing voices, seeing visions. Thought I was there when I wasn't, couldn't see me when I was. My Aunt Florence committed her when I was a teenager, after my brother had killed himself. That was when my mother started going downhill in a big way. *Swoosh*, just like that. I tried to help her but I couldn't. I was too young to understand what was happening. She was very intelligent. Talented, too. Played piano. And so pretty. What a waste . . . am I depressing you?"

"I came home from school one day and found my father had shot my mother and himself in the head," Monica said. "Since then nothing really depresses or affects me much."

I held her tight for a while, and kissed her like she was my sister. "I want to be your pal," I told her. "Really. Think of me as your best buddy. Okay?"

She nodded and sniffled. "Okay. Thanks. I need one."

After she left I lay in the dark listening to "Sweet Lullaby" by Deep Forest, picturing Rose and Sammy in that little Pacifica bungalow. I got up and drove down there, just to make sure she was gone. The place was empty, deserted like no one had ever lived there. The fog was swirling and thick, like it had sucked Sammy and Rose into its midst. I drove back to The City, briefly stopping by the Cliff House, half-hoping she'd be there, waiting for me in her jeep, Sammy laughing by her side.

But I knew she wouldn't be. She was gone now. I had to accept it. For whatever reason, she had re-entered my life, then disappeared again, leaving me nothing but more memories to torture myself with. And to cherish. At least this time I got a letter. All that just to get a goddamn letter. And it was much longer than the one she left Tommy. But then, I could actually read. No, that's cruel. Tommy was as much a victim of Rose's uncertainty as I was. The ultimate victim, of course, was Rose. She had to live with the pain of all those people, as well as her own. Oh well.

Valentine's Day.

I was in my office, trying to piece my life back together, wondering what could possibly happen next. I was sick of movies, of being a small-time PI with an uncertain future and an anemic bank account, of being alone so damn much. I needed to lose myself in my work. I tried a little creative writing but it was too depressing even for *me* to read. I just sat there, tossing darts at my heart board, listening to Frank Sinatra, waiting for something to happen, when the doorbell rang.

"It's open," I said, wondering who the hell it could be. It was around five in the afternoon, getting dark already. Almost over. The worst day of the year. At least it came and went early, so I could get it over with and move on. But who could this be now? A client? My office was closed, sorry. Sharp and Shoemaker back to harass me? Rose begging for a reconciliation? Luke or Tommy returning to kick my ass? Office closed. Bettie Page? Yeah, right. But no one would have surprised me at this point.

Or so I thought.

It was Flora.

"Come in, come in," I said, rising to greet her and practically tripping over myself in the process. "Jeez, what a surprise!"

She looked beautiful as always, but there was a sadness in her eyes that overwhelmed the crazy look. She'd been crying, obviously, though she had put on some makeup and her best face to see me. She was dressed in a tight, curve-hugging mint green dress with no flowers that contrasted nicely with her thick, dark red hair, and she was wearing nylons with high heels. God, she had a great set of gams. And the rest of her was pinup perfect. She was sexy and elegant even in her hour of need. And whom had she turned to? I took her long black coat from her and hung it up, and she took a seat in the client chair at my desk.

"I hope I'm not disturbing you," she said as she sniffed. "I know it's a holiday and all, but—"

"Not to me, it ain't," I said. "Just another day. What, uh, to what do I owe this unexpected pleasure? It's been a while, and last time I saw you . . . well, I guess I should apologize. I will, in fact. Flora, I am *so* sorry about what happened. I'd been under a lot of stress lately, and—"

"No, no. It's me who should apologize," she said, shifting seductively in the client chair, bending forward so that I could see her creamy cleavage and burgundy bra. Happy Valentine's Day, Vic, and here's some candy! But no flowers! Perfect. "I don't know what I was thinking," she went on. "Joey and I were having problems and I wanted to make him jealous, for one thing. And I wasn't sure about marrying him, not yet. I love him and all, but . . . do you mind if I smoke?"

"No, please." I did mind, since secondhand smoke makes me gag, but I let Flora slide. I sat down at my desk and folded my hands, which were shaking. I tried not to let her notice. After all, I was Vic Valentine, Private Eye. The Essence of Cool. At least until some smoking heartbreaker blew my cover.

"Everyone at the blood bank misses you," she said with a brilliant smile. I realized then how much she looked like Stella

Stevens, at least to me. "Denise, Stephanie . . . you're quite popular with the ladies, Vic."

I nodded like this was old news. "Are you here on their behalf, then?"

"Huh? Oh, no. No. I came here to apologize for putting you in that awkward situation. I was really flattered by that 'Date That Never Was' thing, even though . . ."

"Even though what?"

"Well, actually, Joey wasn't too happy about it. He was just being polite at the nightclub when he saw you, but he was really, really mad at me for accepting it from you. He knows about the flowers and cards, too."

"Really? How?"

"I told him. I *had* to."

I nodded. Dames. "You never really told me to stop, though. So I assumed you kind of liked the attention."

"I had mixed feelings. I still do. Joey knows that. I guess that's why I sent you mixed signals sometimes. I wasn't sure how to respond. On the one hand I was very flattered, but then again, you kind of scared me. I mean, all this attention, with no encouragement from me whatsoever."

"But no *dis*couragement, either," I pointed out politely.

"Mixed signals, like I said. I'm sorry if I misled you. It seems you inspire conflicting emotions with your approach. Anyone ever tell you that?"

"Hmm . . . not in so many words."

"That's what Denise says, anyway. We had a long talk about it. She's been trying to contact you but you haven't been returning her calls."

"I was . . . away for a while. I plan on calling her soon. Please tell her that, won't you?"

"Sure. What . . . ?"

"Happened to me?"

She blushed. What a doll. "You look all beat up. Are you okay?"

I shrugged. "Part of the job description. Getting the hell beat out of me on a regular basis."

"Well, that brings me to my point in being here," she said gently. "Stephanie told me you really *are* a private detective after all. Just like in the movies."

"Of course. What else? I told you that."

"I didn't believe you. Anyway, now I see it's true, so . . ."

"So you like me better now?"

She laughed. "I always liked you."

I beamed. "So what can I do for you, Flora?"

"It's Joey. He's . . . missing."

"Joey Link, your fiancé? Is missing?"

"Not anymore. I mean, he's still missing, but I called off the engagement. Just a week ago. Not permanently, understand. I need time to think, that's all, so I gave him the ring back. He flew off the handle and we fought, and he . . . I hate to tell you this, but he tore up 'The Date That Never Was.'"

My gut knotted. "But it's a *classic*! He could've at least *sold* it or something."

"He was pretty upset." She was really puffing away now. "Anyway, this morning I woke up in Alameda and . . . he's gone."

"You live together?"

"No, but we may as well. We're neighbors."

"So he wasn't at your place?"

"*His* place. His closet is empty, and a lot of personal things were missing. Even his saxophones were gone, both of them. That's when I knew . . ."

"You slept through this?"

"I heard him up and about, but I thought he was just going to rehearse with the band like always. I called some of the guys and they said he'd quit them weeks ago and hooked up with this new lounge-type band in The City, and he never even told me that, so I know he's been making plans without me, and . . ." Her eyes started to mist over. I was loving it.

"Maybe he just took a trip."

"No, I don't think so. See, he left a note. I'll read it to you." She took out a little sheet of white paper. "*Flora—Thanks for the memories. Fuck you, Joey.*"

"That's it?" I said.

"He liked Bob Hope a lot. There's a P.S.: "*You slut.*" She started to weep. I got up and went over to console her. There I was, holding Flora in my arms, completely vulnerable. She sobbed for a time, then dried up. "I didn't know what else to do," she whimpered. "So I came here."

"You did the right thing, Flora," I said. "By the way, what is your last name again?"

"Paige. With an 'i.'"

"Hmm. Flora Paige. Nice. Very nice." I sat back down in my chair and stretched, putting my hands behind my head as I looked at her.

"You think you can help me?" she asked. "I have no idea where he is. His family up in Mendocino is worried, too."

"Helping people like you is what I'm all about," I said. "But first, tell me about yourself, Flora. Where you come from, what your interests are, what you want out of life. And be perfectly honest, please. I need to know as much as possible about you before we begin."

"Really? Well, all right. You know I go to art school, right?"

"No, I didn't know that. Go on."

"Why do you need to know this kind of stuff?"

"Trust me."

She looked deeply into my eyes and said, "I do."

Just the words I'd been waiting to hear. I'll never change, and neither will Rose. We're trapped, tormented romantic souls imprisoned in imperfect bodies. Until our souls met again, I had work to do down here.

"Are you sure you're up to this now?" Flora asked me. "You look like you could use some rest. I could tell you the story of my life some other time. *Any* time."

"That's all right, Flora," I said. "Life stories I can handle. Save the heartbreak stuff for later, though, okay?"

"Why?"

I smiled as I looked at her and said, "Love stories are too violent for me."

The End of
LOVE STORIES ARE TOO VIOLENT FOR ME
But Vic Valentine will return in
FATE IS MY PIMP